Sympathy flo healing unguent upon those invisible hurts that had festered for so many years. Beyond the gray veils of her eyes he caught a momentary glimpse of an anguish that mirrored his own, a need that was all the more aching because he felt its throb within himself.

His hand rose slowly to smooth back a stray lock of hair from her forehead as he sought for an answer in her eyes. The curtains of her lashes parted, revealing puzzlement, pain and wonderment. Her fingers rose to touch his cheek, all the permission that he required as he bent down.

As their lips met, he clasped her to him as if he could somehow absorb her into himself. All at once, dream and reality melded into one, but this was no phantasm in his arms.

"Rita Boucher proves herself one of today's finest authors of Regency romance with *Lord of Illusions*, a compelling and imaginative tale of magic and healing love." —Mary Jo Putney

"A mesmerizing and powerful love story, this wonderful tale offers an outstanding reading experience." —*Romantic Times*

Lord
of
Illusions

Rita Boucher

A SIGNET BOOK

SIGNET
Published by the Penguin Group
Penguin Putnam Inc., 375 Hudson Street,
New York, New York 10014, U.S.A.
Penguin Books Ltd, 27 Wrights Lane,
London W8 5TZ, England
Penguin Books Australia Ltd,
Ringwood, Victoria, Australia
Penguin Books Canada Ltd, 10 Alcorn Avenue,
Toronto, Ontario, Canada M4V 3B2
Penguin Books (N.Z.) Ltd, 182-190 Wairau Road,
Auckland 10, New Zealand

Penguin Books Ltd, Registered Offices:
Harmondsworth, Middlesex, England

Published by Signet, an imprint of Dutton NAL,
a member of Penguin Putnam Inc.

First Printing, June, 1998
10 9 8 7 6 5 4 3 2 1

To my own Lord Byron
for supporting me through the mad,
the bad, and the dangerous times

Prologue

Spain, 1814

Surrounded by a bevy of subalterns, the Duke of Wellington scanned the valley below him. Like red sand through the bottleneck of an hourglass, the British troops sifted across the swift-running waters of the ford. The cacophony of an army on the march almost drowned out the rumble of distant thunder. Men shouted curses, wagon wheels groaned, horses whinnied, balking at the crossing. Nonetheless, the general heard that faint reverberation, had half been expecting it, dreading it. His eyebrows knotted as he looked toward a burgeoning line of darkness above the distant hills.

With an anxious snap, Wellington shut his telescope and turned to one of his officers. "Tell Picton to hurry them across. A cloudburst, and the river will become a veritable Red Sea."

"But, sir," his adjutant protested. "There is not a cloud for miles."

"Do as I say, Major, immediately, else we risk having our forces divided," Wellington demanded. "And though Whitehall may expect me to perform miracles, I am no Moses to be parting the waters."

As the officer sped off, the duke reluctantly turned his attention to another part of the promontory. His gaze swept past the knots of conversation and camaraderie, seeking the man who had predicted the coming storm and endured the laugher and jibes of his fellow officers for his pains. Wellington winced as he recalled how he had left England's chief mage twisting in the winds of their mockery.

As usual, Damien, Lord Wodesby, stood alone. His hair ruffled in the breeze as he stared off into the horizon, the shock of gray at his forehead like a streak of lightning amid the coal-black sweep of his Brutus. A night-shaded mastiff

loped to his side. Abruptly, faint zephyrs grew into a stormy
blast that sent the mage's cloak billowing majestically behind him. Wellington supressed a shiver as Wodesby turned,
his green-eyed scrutiny steely with rebuke. No words were
necessary. *I warned you,* that stare declared. *My sorcery told
true. Yet you chose to ignore my vision because you feared
ridicule. I begged you to defer the troop movement, pleaded
in front of them all.*

"It appears I was wrong," Wellington said, the unaccus-
tomed words scraping uncomfortably at his throat.

Damien, Lord Wodesby, nodded, accepting his comman-
der's admission as the closest kin to an apology that would
be offered. The mage closed his eyes momentarily, using his
power to gauge the winds, questing among the clouds. No
Gift of Foretelling was necessary to discern Wellington's
next question.

"How long?" the general asked softly.

"No more than an hour," Damien replied, adding the
equation of the elements and coming up with the sum of disaster. "Less, if the currents pick up. It will be a deluge."

"Not enough time," Wellington muttered, surveying the
milling host on the far side of the valley floor, his gut
clenching as he envisioned the river below swelled by rain,
sweeping through his army like a watery fist. Retreat now,
and the body of troops would be split in half, caught on in-
defensible ground between the French and the river. Continue . . . ? Scudding clouds were beginning to form into a
solid column. "Do you have any visions, Wodesby? Any
inkling of what is to become of us?" he demanded.

Damien shook his head. "None, Your Grace," he said, his
flat tones masking secret fears. For the past few days, it
seemed as if his powers as a seer had deserted him. Every
mage had his dry spells, to be sure, but what if there were no
visions because there was no future in store for Damien
Nostradamus Wilton? In the history of the Blood, there had
been but a handful of seers who could predict a destiny beyond their own span. Was the line of Wodesby, descended
from the Merlin of Camelot, destined to end on these sere
Spanish hills? Damien shrugged inwardly. What was fated

would be. Right now his sworn duty was to England, and he would do whatever was in his power to avert disaster.

Once again, the mage sent his thoughts chasing among the clouds, testing the elements that propelled the coming storm, trying to see if the tempest could somehow be turned aside. If he could work in tandem with nature, there was a greater chance of success. But his survey soon revealed that the natural forces arrayed against him were far too strong. The only available countervailing wind in the vicinity was little more than a puff by comparison to the approaching gale. Though it was scarcely enough to cause the rain to by-pass them, that zephyr could provide a means of delaying the inevitable. It would be extremely dangerous to trifle so with the elements, yet magic seemed the only choice . . .

"I will do what I can," Damien promised, unfastening his cloak and shrugging off the red coat of his uniform. "Keep the area around me clear, Your Grace, for I can ill afford distraction, and my immediate vicinity may soon prove to be a rather risky location. Please take Angel with you."

The mastiff howled uncannily.

"No nonsense, my friend," Damien said, dropping to his knees. "You know full well that you cannot help me here."

Wellington hesitated, watching as the dog licked Wodesby's cheek in a gesture that was oddly like a human farewell. The mage rose with fluid grace, rolling up his sleeves to reveal a thin band of hammered gold upon the rippling muscle of his forearm. "What do you intend, Wodesby?"

"To buy you time, sir," Damien said with a grimace, "to play with lightning, which is always iffy business even for the best of sorcerers. Should I chance to go to seek my final rest in the Light, would you make certain that Angel brings home my ring and this band from my arm along with my regrets?" He touched the inscribed talisman lightly, and the runes seemed to twist and shimmer, England's band, his father's in his lifetime. Damien had always hoped that his son might wear it someday, but now . . . "My mother will convey them to my heir. Poor Mama, she has been after me for years to do my duty to the family. I would hate to prove her right."

Never before had his magician seemed more young, nor more human than with that wry admission. There was no room for denials or false heartiness in Wodesby's stark gaze. Wellington had seen that look of resignation more often than he cared to remember. Beneath that cool hauteur was the fear of a man with unfinished business.

"This would not have been necessary had I heeded your warnings," Wellington said, gripping Wodesby's hand. It was like holding a block of ice. "I am sorry, Damien."

"You did what you had to, sir, as I do what I must," Damien said, touched despite himself. Although he had been working as Wellington's mage for nigh on to two years, this was the first time that the duke had addressed Damien by his given name. He returned the general's clasp firmly, trying to convey comfort, to keep his fingers from trembling with the knowledge that this might be his last corporeal contact.

No sooner was the summit cleared than the air began to shimmer strangely. Clouds gathered to hide the cliff and the sorcerer who stood upon it. Hats were torn off of unwary heads by sudden winds and lightning blazed through the skies, scenting the air with the threat of rain—an unfulfilled threat. For three hours the storm hung above the army like the sword of Damocles, but the rain did not fall, not until the final wagon had crossed the river.

When they brought down Wodesby's motionless form, the ford had become a raging torrent. Although there were many who credited luck rather than magic, even the most vociferous of the scoffers gawked at the sight of Damien, a rain-bedraggled ghost, his dark hair turned the silver of lightning, his staring emerald eyes tinged with an unearthly blue.

"They are all across, Wodesby, every last man," Wellington said.

Damien nodded weakly and let himself drift into darkness as Angel licked his rain-numbed hand.

Chapter 1

France, 1814

"*Kek-kek, kek-kek!*" With a complaining cry, the merlin shifted restlessly on its red velvet perch, chittering continuously as the ancient carriage clattered from rut to bone-shaking rut along the ill-kept roads.

Rowan, the Comtesse Du Le Fey, reached out to soothe her familiar's ruffled feathers. "Patience, Mignon," she said, stroking the mud-brown plumage gently. "Soon the comte's final bit of business will be done."

"Will we be much longer, Mama?" Giselle asked, echoing the bird's question. "I want to go back to Paris. Why do we have to go see my brother now? Etienne never came to visit us at all when the comte was alive."

"The comte," always "the comte." Rowan was irritated to realize that they both still addressed her late husband by his title, tinging their words with a tremolo of dread as if he was somehow watching them from Hades. Rowan stifled a sigh, looking into her daughter's eyes, that look of innocent inquiry a testament to eleven long years of effort. Somehow, Rowan had managed to shield the child from her father, from the intrigues and rivalries that were as much a part of the French branch of the Du Le Fey coven as magic itself. Although the child had feared the comte, she did not yet understand the full extent of his evil.

Hopefully, she never would know, since now, by the mercy of the fates, the old web spinner was dead. Yet Rowan could not rid herself of a growing foreboding, as if he were somehow reaching from the grave. *He is gone,* she reminded herself, *buried. You put coins on his eyes for Charon the boatman's fare. You took the talisman of France from his corpse.*

"We have to deliver your father's things, *ma petite,*" she

said, keeping her tones calm. High upon the hilltop, she could see the outline of the Chateau Du Le Fey, its imposing presence limned in the setting sun. Beset by images of long ago, twelve years vanished, and she was once more a helpless girl of thirteen, broken of heart and spirit, heavy with child. *"Home, Comtesse,"* the old comte's mocking words echoed across time. *"My home."*

"Etienne is now chief mage of France." Rowan squeezed her daughter's hand as much to be comforted as to comfort. At least some good had come from those years of unremitting hell, Rowan reminded herself. Whatever she had done, though she had sullied her magical Gift, defiled her very soul, it had been worth all to protect Giselle. "The comte's talismans belong to your brother now." She touched the black velvet box on the seat beside her as if to assure herself of its reality. Soon she and her daughter would be free.

"And are you still mistress of witches, Mama?" Giselle asked.

Rowan smiled ruefully, touching the thinly wrought chain of twining serpents at her throat—her badge of office, the last chain that bound her to France and the Du Le Fey coven. "I am afraid so, my dear, until your brother decides to take himself a wife." The carriage swayed abruptly, and the case slipped onto the floor, the catch springing open to disgorge the dull band of beaten gold and an inscribed emerald ring.

"Kee, kkkkek," Mignon cackled angrily.

"Is it a bad omen, Mama?" Giselle asked, translating the bird's pronouncement anxiously.

Rowan snatched the band and ring from the floor, quieting her familiar with an angry glare.

"Of course not, *ma petite*," she said, quelling a frisson of fear. "All will be well, I am sure."

From behind the curtained window, Etienne watched the creaking coach lumber to a halt. As his father's widow stepped into the pool of torchlight, he exhaled sharply. Twelve years . . . he had heard reports of the comtesse's beauty. Somehow those secondhand accounts had never managed to supplant his memories of the girl that she had been. Now, as he evaluated her with a calculating eye, Etienne could see that the full flower of her womanhood far surpassed the youthful promise of his father's budding child bride.

Mourning suited her; her black gown flowed about her like liquid night. The coal-black abundance of her hair was bound behind her in a net that shimmered with pearls, beaded moon drops against the gathered silken dark, framing his stepmother's piquant face. With her familiar perched easily on her shoulder, she seemed the essence of witchly grace. Beside her was a child, as fair as her mother was dark, a Du Le Fey countenance, much like his own. The sister he had never seen was as lovely a child as her mother had been. So much the better; it would make Giselle a more powerful pawn should he need to use her against Rowan.

"You see now what your father stole from you, Etienne?" Claude asked, downing the remnants of his brandy and wiping a hand across his fleshy mouth with a satisfied sigh. "The comte persuades the girl's father to break her betrothal to Wodesby, for you, Etienne, he tells me, for you. She was to be your woman, Etienne, yours!" He slammed his glass to the table. "Then your father takes her for his wife. Why do you think the comte bans you from the house these years past, eh? And now, by the Laws of the Blood, you may not have Rowan, since she was your father's woman."

No trace of Etienne's anger was visible as he turned to face his cousin. Mage though Claude was, it was sometimes difficult to believe that he shared the Du Le Fey heritage. The boor lacked all subtlety. Only a fool would bring up that history now; and the reminder that Rowan was beyond her stepson's reach was an unnecessary goad.

"I know the Law as well as you, Cousin. Still, she serves Du Le Fey. At present nothing matters beyond that," he said, a chill in his voice as his father's words echoed in his mind. *What matter is it, my son, if the infant is yours or mine? She serves the Du Le Fey . . . she serves the Du Le Fey.* He looked down absently at the writing quill in his hand, snapped in two beneath the pressure of his fingers as he began to comprehend the full measure of his father's perfidy.

Though Claude was a fool, even a lackwit could speak the

truth. It was obvious now why the elderly comte had risked all to break Rowan's betrothal to Wodesby's heir and then chosen to steal her for himself. His stepmother! This enchanting creature was Etienne's stepmother, when the comte had promised to make her Etienne's wife. A claw snagged at his trousers, bringing him abruptly back to the present with a sharp hiss.

"You are correct, Suzette," Etienne said, looking down at his feline familiar with a sardonic chuckle. "Have the comtesse shown directly to the library, and make certain that her companion is offered food *in the kitchens.* I do not wish to have that meddling bird interfering, is that clear? See that my sister is taken to the nursery and guarded carefully."

The black tabby meowed and padded away to do her master's bidding.

"What did your familiar say to make you laugh?" Claude asked, eyes glaring suspiciously above bloated cheeks. "I have an owl myself and little mastery of the tongue of cats."

Etienne shrugged. "Loosely translated, she reminded me that 'all witches are the same in the dark.' "

Claude guffawed. "Flesh or fur, a female still has claws, eh, Cousin?"

"Claws indeed. And on that note, I think that you had best hide yourself away," Etienne commanded. "From what I recall, my *belle-mère* cannot abide your presence. She has not yet forgotten that you were my father's companion on her betrothal journey."

The rotund mage reddened. "What has she told you, Etienne?" Claude sputtered.

"Nothing," Etienne said, his brow quirking with interest. "Is there anything that I ought to know?"

"I had better be gone," Claude said hurriedly. "Before she comes."

When Rowan was ushered in, the room was empty.

"Maman! It has been a long time."

Etienne rose from his chair to greet her. Other than a mild frost of silver among waves of blond hair, her stepson had changed little, and was still a youthful portrait of his father. That resemblance alone was more than enough to put her on guard.

"Maman?" she mocked, affecting the tinkling laugh she had perfected at court. "It must be long indeed, if you finally address me as your father once demanded."

For a brief instant the formal mask slipped. "He is dead, Comtesse, and you must admit, it was something of a shock to be required to call a slip of a girl, five years my junior, 'Mother.' "

He gave a Gallic shrug. "At least in death, I will honor his wishes."

"I, too, keep my word. The talismans of France's chief mage, Etienne," Rowan replied, setting the box on the table, noting that he made no move to take her hand in welcome. Obviously, he trusted her no more than she trusted him. If Etienne feared that she might read his thoughts with a fleeting touch, then it was clear that something was on his mind, something that he wished to conceal from her. She would play the game until he revealed his cards.

Cloaking her discomfort, Rowan seated herself, pretending to study her surroundings. All the furnishings were the same, except for one thing. The old comte's favorite portrait of King Louis had been replaced with a painting of Napoleon. Still, she could not entirely evade the stark hunger in Etienne's look, the undercurrents of long-ago events.

Many times she had wondered what might have been if the comte had not forced this marriage upon her, if she had been truly allowed to choose freely between the suitors for her hand. Her husband had taken far more than her innocence all those years ago.

Time folded upon itself as dark memories flooded her mind. How often had she sat in this very chair waiting for the ax of the Du Le Fey's displeasure to fall?

It was the Corsican's portrait that saved her. Napoleon's mocking stare made her aware that she could ill afford to be distracted by the shades of the past. Rowan removed her gloves slowly, reminding herself that the man before her was not her husband.

"Brandy?" Etienne asked, lifting the cut-glass decanter.

Rowan shook her head.

"A bite to eat? Your journey from Paris must have been—"

"Shall we dispense with the pleasantries, Comte?" Deliberately, she chose the formal mode of address, emphasizing the barriers of blood between them. "When your father died in Paris, I had hoped never to return to this pile of stones. It will not surprise you, I think, when I confess that my memories of this place are less than happy. Yet you insisted that I bring the talismans to you."

"Not even a bit of gossip, Comtesse?" he asked. "What do you hear of Marshall Ney these days?"

"Seeking the king's favor, the last I was told," Rowan said suspiciously. "You know the man has ever been the cur of the master with the meatiest bone. But I am not much at court since your father's death."

"I do not ask for hearsay, *belle-mère*," Etienne said with an annoyed wave of his hand. "I wish to know his present thoughts regarding Napoleon."

Rowan rose from her seat, molten fury burning in her silver eyes. "If you wish to know Ney's mood, then you may ask him, by the Merlin. Do you think that I abuse my Gift for mere amusement, Etienne? I will not read minds anymore, not for you or for any other."

"Even for the sake of France herself?" Etienne asked, toying with his glass.

"And when have the Du Le Fey ever concerned themselves with anything other than the advancement of the Du Le Fey interests?" Rowan asked, mockery in her voice. "Your father planned it well, did he not, with the family's paws planted firmly in each kennel. You, Bonaparte's hound, and your papa, Louis' dog. Well, this bitch is finished, do you hear? Never again will I be a voyeur of thoughts. Napoleon is rotting on Elba. *C'est finis!*" She turned to go.

"No, Rowan. It is not yet over." There was something in Etienne's tone that compelled her to face him once again. An odd cast in his eyes caused her breath to catch in her throat. "You have had a Foretelling," she whispered.

"I saw Napoleon, a ragtag army about him," the young comte's voice assumed the singsong cadence of the seer recollecting a vision. "On the road ahead was Ney, with soldiers, wearing the white cockade of the king. The emperor goes toward them, without fear, though his rabble would be helpless against an obviously superior force . . . Ney dismounts, . . . pulls out his sword, and presents it to Napoleon."

"Past, Etienne. Perhaps you see the past," Rowan said, a plea in her voice.

"Do you think that I do not know a vision from the echoes of a memory?" Etienne thundered, coming around the desk and seizing her shoulders in a bruising grasp. "Napoleon will come back, Rowan, he will return as I have seen, and he will have our help."

Rowan tore herself away as if burned, her eyes widening at the brief glimpse that her mind-reading power revealed, the depth of his passion, the emotions that seethed so close to the surface of his consciousness. Fear possessed her as she realized the extent of her danger. He believed, to the very depth of his soul, Etienne actually *believed* in Bonaparte.

Where his father had been content to parley with whomever held the reins of power, Etienne was willing to risk all for the Corsican's sake, to throw the Du Le Fey allegiance to the emperor's side, win or lose. "No," she said, her chin tilting high as she rose to confront him, "I will have no part of this madness."

He opened the box and slipped the gold band upon his arm, slipped the small emerald mage's circlet off his finger, and put the larger ring in its place. "As mage of France, I command you—"

For a moment he so reminded Rowan of his father that she nearly cowered before him, but then she recalled the chain at her neck.

"You have no right!" Rowan grasped at her own talisman and raised it high before her. "As mistress of witches of France, I refuse, by hearth, by home, and by Hecate. It is true your father kept me ignorant of a witch's craft, but this much I know."

"I remind you of your oath to the family!"

"I swore myself to seek the survival of the House of Du Le Fey. Your actions will put us all in peril," she said with a strange serenity, as the talisman grew warm in her palm. "Regardless of my feelings, I served your father faithfully; I owe *you* nothing. No more will I be a slave to a Du Le Fey, to any man."

Etienne tried to contain his anger. He had hoped to persuade her, but his renowned charm had somehow deserted him. The amulet of her office glowed golden with the force of her fury, serpents twisting in her hand. If she knew how to harness that power . . . the very thought made him shudder inwardly. But her lack of knowledge was like a two-edged blade, push her too far and that unbound magic might well go wild and destroy them both. It was time for a change in tactic.

"Surely, you cannot leave before I make the acquaintance of my charming little sister. How old is she now? Almost eleven years, I believe." Etienne was pleased as the amulet suddenly slipped from her fingers to rest upon her bosom. He knew for certain that he had found the lever to move her. "She is quite attractive, even more perhaps than you were the first time that I saw you. Of course, she still has that aura of childish innocence."

Rowan's face had paled. Etienne tsked softly as he seated himself in a chair behind the great mahogany table. "My, my, eleven and with no handfast. How could my father have been so remiss? But I am certain I can find a suitable candidate for her." He paused significantly. "Cousin Claude, for instance."

"I will not allow it!" Rowan advanced, her eyes glinting steel. "Claude is nigh on to fifty!" Rowan shook her head in disbelief at his indifferent expression. "You would not, Etienne; Giselle is your sister."

"The years between her and Claude are less than the disparity between you and my *cher* Papa," Etienne said, his smile chill. "And look how happy *you* were . . ."

"No . . . you do not know what Claude is," she whispered, her eyes widening, "I will not—"

"—allow it?" Etienne cut her off with a mirthless laugh. "I am head of the family, Maman, by France's law."

"A witch may marry where she wills," Rowan quoted weakly.

"As you did?" Etienne asked, sarcasm in every word. "A child's resolution is easily swayed, especially if she is kept from her dear mother, *n'est-ce pas*? Giselle will stay with me, I think, Comtesse."

Rowan blanched, and he could almost see the struggle for composure in those vivid gray eyes. Almost . . . the old man had taught her well, for otherwise, her expression did not betray her. In his bitterness Etienne could not resist taunting. "Perhaps I am wrong to think only of Claude. Shall I open the field? Will every ancient mage on the Continent come a'wooing her, old stallions seeking the young filly?" But she was not as strong as he thought; Rowan wavered, swayed, then sank to her knees.

"Do you wish me to beg?" she asked, her voice hoarse with unshed tears. "Did you inherit this from your father, Etienne, this need to humiliate, to flay every shred of pride from those in your power? If it is groveling that you desire, I will grovel as your papa taught me. Do not do this to your sister."

Never before had he so thoroughly hated his father, or himself. Etienne bent to touch her on the shoulder. "Get up, Rowan," he commanded, keeping the pity from his voice. This was none of her doing, but as Claude had convinced him, she was the only tool who might provide the means of achieving Napoleon's freedom. "Do not force me to do this, Comtesse," he said roughly. "All you need do is this one small task."

"This one small task . . . and the next time?" Rowan swallowed, as she saw the future stretching out before her. "Do you know what happens every time that I walk into the depth of another's thoughts unbidden? I pay the price with my soul, Etienne, a piece of my self. Is that your aim then, to spend me bit by bit, until I am a shell or until my mind is so weak that I lose myself utterly?"

"One last task, and then you and Giselle are free."

"Free," she whispered, her eyes dull with pain. "And what is the price for this freedom you promise?"

"Information," Etienne declared, unable to meet her stark gaze. "It will be very simple really. There is a man, an Englishman who holds the key to Napoleon's prison. Unfortunately, he is incorruptible and would sooner give his life than see Bonaparte at large again."

"You wish me to pick his mind . . ." she stated mechanically, "so that the monster can roam loose once more."

Etienne could not even bring himself to rebuke her for her disrespect to the greatest man that had ever lived. He merely nodded.

"I will not accept an oath without a specific end," Rowan said. "Name a date."

"Samhain," he said, trying to extend the boundary into winter. He had seen violets blooming in his Vision.

"Midsummer," she countered adamantly.

"Done!" Etienne agreed.

"And you will swear to me, by the band of your magehood, by the Merlin that you will renounce all right of kin and coven to me and mine for this information that you crave?"

She was choosing her words carefully, allowing him no room to renege once she had fulfilled her part of the bargain. Reluctantly, Etienne clasped his armband with his right hand.

"Swear it," she commanded hoarsely, rising to face him. "Say the words, you filthy swine, or by the Merlin, I will see you in Hades. Even if it means I must forfeit my place in the Light because of it, I will take your life, Comte. I do not know much of spells, but this I can do." Once again, the amulet was in her hands, electric with a magical force that reflected her wild rage. "State the bargain aloud, swear to it by all you hold sacred or I will see you dead before sunrise, though it means I die with you, accursed as a killer of kin."

"By the badge of my magehood, by the Merlin himself, father of us all; if you fulfill your word, I renounce all right of kin and coven, Blood and bond, over you and your daughter," he declared, but in the face of her opaque stare, he could barely keep his voice steady. What would it have been to have the love of this woman, a love so great that she would give her life to protect a child's happiness? Once more, Etienne damned the selfish old man who had fathered him.

"So be it!" she intoned.

Hades help him if she ever discovered the full depth of the well of power within her.

"As mistress of witches, I record and seal your oath. And if there be bloodshed, upon your head shall it be, Etienne of the Du Le Fey, upon your head and upon your soul. May I bid my daughter farewell?"

Etienne shook his head. "I will send a man to Paris with your instructions."

"I had thought you better than your father," Rowan said, her eyes silver with fury. "Now I know different. Bastard!"

His expression was stony as she turned and left the hall. It was only when he heard the clatter of the carriage wheels in the courtyard that he sat down, his head in his hands, trying to convince himself that no cost was too great for France's salvation, even Rowan's undying hatred.

"She will do it! Although I do not see why you made that foolish promise." Claude crowed in glee, rubbing his hands together as he emerged from his hiding place.

"If I had made no promises, I have little doubt that she would have used her talisman and brought this chateau down upon our heads. She has the power, Claude, even though my father made certain that she would not have the knowledge to use it," Etienne said coldly.

"A lucky thing for us! Shall I go to greet my little cousin, Etienne?" his cousin asked. "An excellent idea that; I will charm her into a match, *n'est-ce pas?*"

"I will honor my oath, Claude, as Rowan will honor hers," Etienne told him, not bothering to eliminate the disgust from his voice. "She would kill for her daughter. You would do well to keep that in mind."

"Of course," Claude murmured, looking away to hide a secret smile. "Of course."

Dense fog obscured all vision, fingers of mist touched Damien with an icy chill as he tried to find his way . . . Lost but not alone . . . Sibilant voices called to him mockingly, "Lord Wodesby . . . Lord Wodesby . . ." The sounds of a woman weeping drew him to the center of the miasma. She was on her knees, her face buried in her hands. Slowly, her head lifted, but even before he could see her face he knew her, the Dark Lady . . . skin made of moonlight, eyes like mirrors, reflecting the innermost reaches of his soul. Hair flowed behind her like a river of black silk, framing a face that seemed made of Chinese porcelain. Her utter despair touched him, her loneliness echoed within him as she reached out a hand, but as soon as he grasped her, she dissolved into wisps, blending with the fog itself until all he could see were those sad gray eyes, watching him . . . pleading for something that he could not understand.

Damien woke trying to hold on to the shreds of his dream. Something in those images was important. But in the haze of sluggish bewilderment, details began to slip away. Moreover, it was nigh on impossible to focus upon a dream when reality was proving to be something of a nightmare. As the mage took a slow inventory of his senses, the daze of incoherence only increased.

Blood pounded in his head; not surprising since he was suspended by his feet, every tiny movement causing him to sway. Though his eyes were open, he could not see; a hood blinded him, muffling sound. His hands were tightly bound behind him. From the cold feel that spanned around his wrists, down his back and to his ankles, it was obvious that he had been chained from end to end. Above the waist, he wore only the gold talisman of England; they had not dared touch Albion's band. But his shirt was gone, by Hades, along with everything concealed within its seams and folds.

As awareness returned, Damien attempted to swallow, but his mouth felt like sand. Drugs, he guessed from the metallic taste on his tongue; come to think of it, the soup had tasted rather odd. The sound of laughter below him confirmed his guess.

"Try to get yourself out of *that,* Wodesby, if you can!" a voice, garbled but familiar echoed from the walls. From another room Angel bayed mournfully, his howl conveying regret and anger that they dared treat the chief mage of England so. Damien could almost see the mastiff's forlorn expression. Clearly, there could be no help from his canine companion this time. The solid oak door slammed shut, and metal married metal with the turn of a key. He was entirely on his own.

Carefully, Damien tested his bonds, cursing as a gentle flex of his wrists caused a knot to tighten. Obviously, his opponent must have taken a fiendish delight in this bit of work, for no Christmas goose had ever been trussed so tight or with such fine attention to detail. He began the first words of an incantation, then stopped as the cold recollection hit him. Spells were of no use, and time was running out.

Sweat poured from his body, coating his bare chest with a slippery sheen that made controlled movement all the more difficult. Wincing in pain from the ropes, he doubled himself over, bringing his wrists to his ankles. Off came the hood, but sight was of little aid in the pitch-dark room. Muscle by muscle, he shifted, contorted, bending in ways that were nigh on impossible, manipulating with fingers and toes until his teeth pulled the lock pick from its concealment around his ankle.

At least, the fact that he had been unconscious when bound had served to his advantage. The complete relaxation of senselessness had afforded him far more leeway than his adversary could have suspected. Though the bonds were tight, there was room to wiggle, and that was all he required. Ropes fell to the floor with a dull plop; no more than ten feet to the ground he judged by the echo. The locked chains at his ankles and wrists were more difficult. Several times the thin wire of his picklock nearly slipped from his sweating palms. But soon the forged links clanked against stone. Damien winced as his bare feet made contact with the unyielding floor.

Using his pick once more, Damien worked the door with gentle skill. Resisting the temptation to rush, he explored the lock's recesses like a newfound lover, teasing with the thin metal until the latch released with a groaned click. Softly, he slipped up the stairs, moving with determined swiftness to confront his tormentor. Molding himself against the doorway, he waited for the right moment as light and laughter sifted into the hall.

"How long has it been?" The question floated anxiously among the company, ending in a pitch of feminine anxiety.

"The potion should have worn off, I should think. He is doubtless thrashing about in a frenzy by now. There were more than a few tricks in those knots that I tied, I daresay," a deep bass opined with more than a hint of laughter. "It should take him hours to free himself, *if* he can."

Damien's fists clenched, and he was about to show his adversary the full extent of his error, but the mage was stopped short by another familiar voice. "You underestimate the lad, Adam. He will be free before the five-hour limit that you agreed upon. I'll lay you a monkey upon the likelihood that he'll be breathing down your neck before the watch calls midnight, Lord Brand."

"Never been averse to easy money, Uncle Lawrie," Adam said, "but it goes against the grain to cheat an old man who is so dear to me."

"By midnight," Lawrence Timmons repeated. "A monkey."

"And a bonus of ten pounds for every minute before," Adam agreed. "Done!"

Damien grinned as Lord Brand sealed the wager with that costly flourish. With a cautioning finger on his lips, the mage stepped silently into the drawing room, noting with glee that his brother-in-law's back was to the door. Damien's mother, the former Lady Wodesby, sat between her new husband, Lawrence Timmons and her daughter, Miranda, Lady Brand. To their credit, none of the three betrayed his presence by so much as an eye blink. His stepfather smiled broadly as he raised a glass of sherry in a toast.

"To 'easy money,' " Lawrence said, watching with delight as Damien slipped silently behind Adam and nicked the watch from his vest pocket with all the skill of a first-class flash gent.

Adam rose with a start, a broad grin spreading over his face. "I must be a far better teacher than I thought."

"Easy money, indeed," Damien agreed, snapping open the watch lid. "If your timepiece is accurate, Brand, it lacks a full quarter to the hour. Five hundred pounds as the base wager, and one hundred fifty more for a total of six hundred fifty pounds. A neat profit, Lawrie, for your confidence in my abilities."

Miranda clapped. "Well-done, brother!" Although the advanced stage of her pregnancy made movement awkward, she rose in tribute. "I knew that you could do it!"

"Then, why did you do not dissuade your husband from his ill-advised wager against me?" Damien asked, moving to her side.

"As if I could move that mule of mine!" Miranda said with a delicate sniff. "You give my powers of persuasion far too much credit, Damien."

The fond glance directed toward her husband belied the trace of acid in her tone. No magic was needed to feel the warmth that flowed between them, both gentle and deep, like a current that came from the heart. It was hard for Damien to credit that he had once strongly opposed the match, pitted himself against this man who was now his brother-by-marriage.

Much as it galled Damien to admit it, though Brand lacked the blood of Merlin, he had certainly worked amazing sorcery upon Miranda. Never had his sister been so happy and confident. Moreover, during the trials of these past months, Adam had become one of the few Outsiders that Damien would name as friend.

"One would think, Adam, that you would have more faith in your skills as a tutor," Lawrence remarked. "After all, you have been Damien's teacher in the matters of escaping locks and bonds."

"Even the worst of teachers may succeed with an especially apt pupil," Damien replied, serving Adam a mocking bow.

"Unnecessary waste of energy, if you ask me," Lawrence's wife said. The former Lady Wodesby gave a derogatory snort. "I vow, I still cannot understand this lunacy. Why you even dress the part of the Outsider these days. Not even a ring upon your finger! Where is your mage's stone?"

Damien stiffened. "Have you forgotten, Mama, the Mage's Star has been missing since father's death? 'Tis the Heir's Star stone that I was wont to wear." The mage shrugged. "The band of England's chief mage stays on my arm only at your insistence, though we all know that it is little more than a sham these days. Why should I sport yet another reminder of what is lost to me."

"I did not mean to say—" Adrienne began agitatedly.

Lawrence sighed and took his wife's hand. "Now, now, Damien, there is no need to upset your mother. The Healers say that your loss of power may be only temporary."

"Or it may well be permanent," Damien said, coming to sit beside his mother, touching her shoulder lightly. "I have begun to face it, Mama, perhaps it is time that we all did. My Gifts may be gone forever; I may never see another glimpse of the future or fill a sky with rainbows."

"No," Adrienne whispered. "I cannot believe it. *Will not.*"

Miranda shook her head sadly, her fingers slipping into Adam's hand. "There are other magics, Damien," she said looking into her husband's eyes. "With all my heart I believe that your sorcery will return to you, but if the Fates choose differently, there are other ways of finding joy and meaning."

"I hope that I find them, little sister," Damien said, trying to keep the pain from his voice. "But until then, you must agree that it is best for me to learn to get on in this world without the aid of sorcery. That is why I have been traveling about and studying with your husband. I have learned a great deal these past months, things that would benefit me even if my powers do return."

Adrienne snorted in disbelief.

"Do you doubt it, Mama?" Damien asked, pulling one of Adam's locks from his pocket and sealing it with an audible click. "Try to charm this open, if you can."

"A trifle." Adrienne closed her eyes, coughed twice, then blinked. "There, 'tis open."

"I think not, Mama," Damien said, pulling visibly at the hasp. "Iron does not respond to magic, however . . ." A pick materialized in his hand as if plucked from the air. Within seconds the lock clicked apart.

"So you may now set yourself up as a cracksman," Adrienne said mockingly. "If you wish to do something truly of worth, Damien, there is still the matter of setting up a nursery . . ."

Miranda groaned. "Mama, now is not the time to discuss this."

"And just when will it *be* time?" Adrienne demanded, dismissing her daughter's protests with a petulant wave. "First you traipse across the Peninsula with the army, claiming that you are doing your duty to England. I did not complain, did I? Though an iron ball could have brought the Wodesby line to an end in a twinkling. Then you strain your powers to the point of breaking . . ."

"I take it you are complaining now," Damien asked, walking to the sideboard and pouring himself a glass of port.

"And rightly so!" The feather on Adrienne's turban fluttered with her indignation. "It is well past time for you to choose a bride, Damien."

"Mama, can we let this rest for now?" Miranda pleaded, watching as her brother's lips stiffened into an angry line. He brushed back his silver mane in a gesture that was a sure sign of rising annoyance.

"No, we cannot," Adrienne said, rising majestically from her chair, her ruby-red gown swirling around her as she moved to join Damien. "We have tiptoed about this subject for far too long." She took the glass from her son's hands and set it down, then took his palms and placed them upon her cheeks. "Look at me, boy, and tell me what you see."

"The most beautiful woman in the world," Damien said, the merest hint of a smile touching the corner of his mouth. "Not a day above thirty."

Adrienne shook her head. "It is not flummery that I am seeking, my son, but honesty. I am an old woman and nigh on to threescore, though I would deny it if you cried it aloud in Mayfair. There may be a few years left me, I grant you, but my strength is waning." She touched Damien gently on his shoulder. "I want to see your children, to teach them to read their first runes and to sing their learning incantations."

Damien stared into her face, touched by the tears he could see threatening to spill, but before he could speak he saw a shimmer within the liquid glint of her jade eyes. "And soon you will have your first grandchild, Mama," he said, gesturing toward his sister. "And perhaps she might even be Gifted with magic, if the Blood runs strong."

"Ah, but you should crave these things for yourself, Damien," his mother said softly. "It is pleasing, indeed, that magic may flow to the next generation through my daughter, but that is not enough. I want you to find your life's partner, Damien. A mage is not meant to be alone . . ."

Damien groaned, closing his eyes against her tear-laden pleas. Was there any way to find the words, to make his mother understand the measure of his feelings? How could he marry among his people, not knowing that his powers would ever return? They had managed to keep his incapacity hidden thus far, but once word spread, he would be viewed as nothing more than a stallion with a broken gait, worthy only as a stud for his bloodlines. Far better that he had died on that hilltop in Spain, than to survive broken, worthless, pitied by any witch unfortunate enough to be chosen as his bride.

A rough lick at his knuckles caused his eyes to blink open. Angel growled softly. Luckily, the comprehension of animal speech was not a magical skill. "I fear that we will have to leave this discussion for another time, Mama, unless you wish to make the Duke of Wellington a party to our family problems. Apparently, he is at your door, Adam."

"Have His Grace shown up at once, Angel, if you please," Miranda requested.

The mastiff barked a short affirmative and ran to do her bidding.

"I wonder what brings Wellington at this hour?" Miranda asked, looking at her husband in concern. "I had thought that he was in France, Adam."

"He was due back for Prinny's victory celebration," Adam said, his expression anxious, as he squeezed his wife's hand reassuringly, "but not for quite a while yet, according to his last letter."

"Ah, Lord Brand, I had not expected that you might have company at this hour. Adrienne, I vow, you look younger every time I see you," Wellington said, taking up her hand as he was ushered into the room. "You are a lucky man, Lawrence." Wellington looked at them apologetically. "I hope that you will all forgive the intrusion, but the matter is an urgent one."

"We thought as much, Your Grace," Damien said, rising from his chair and stepping into Wellington's view. "Especially knowing that tonight is Wednesday and you would as lief be dancing with Lady Jersey and sipping orgeat at Almack's."

"Wodesby, I should have known that you were somewhere about when I saw that hellhound of yours," Wellington said, as he raised his eyebrow to survey his former aide-de-camp. "Has Brummell started a style for bare chests in my absence?"

Damien reddened. He had quite forgotten his state of *deshabille*.

Adam laughed. "You should know by now, Your Grace, that our Damien sets his own fashions. I half suspect it was my brother-by-marriage's taste for unrelieved black that inspired Brummell's imitation. And with the heat that we have had these days past, I confess myself almost tempted to follow Damien's au naturel mode. But you have not come at this hour to discuss the latest styles in Mayfair, nor the London weather in June, I trust."

Wellington shook his head, his eyes losing the sparkle of amusement. "Unfortunately not, Adam, much as I would wish that it were nothing more than a social call that brought me here."

"Actually, Your Grace, I was about to escort Mama and Lawrence back to Portman Square," Damien said, setting down his empty glass. "If Adam would be so kind as to tell me where he hid the rest of my clothing."

The duke's eyebrow quirked again. "I shall not ask why your clothes have been hidden, for I have learned at my peril never to question a Wodesby."

"I have always thought you the wisest of men, Arthur," Lawrence said, taking his wife's hand and patting it gently. "We might all profit by emulating your wisdom."

"I am his mother, and it is a mother's right to question her children when she sees them stray," Adrienne warned, her lips tightening in disapproval. "I am not yet finished with you, my son."

"I know, Mama." Damien sighed. "You have always viewed me as a work in progress. Perhaps we should ride out with the coachman, Lawrie, for I fear my ears are about to be blistered. Newly wed as you are, you may not have seen this aspect of my dear mother's character."

"In fact, Adrienne," Wellington interposed, "if you could spare your son, I would appreciate his opinion on a rather pressing matter."

Damien's mother made a moue of annoyance. "Wellington has come to your rescue for now, my dear."

"Take advantage of the respite, m'boy," Lawrence said, tucking his wife's arm securely into his and steering her toward the door. "For if I know your mama, it will be a brief reprieve at best."

"You see, Arthur, they are all arrayed against me," Adrienne called over her shoulder. "Was there ever a general so besieged?"

"Madame, if I were called to wager upon the winner, I would place my stake on you." Wellington said gallantly. "I shall return your son to Wodesby House myself."

"I shall escort you both to the door," Miranda offered. "Neither the staff nor I will disturb you, gentlemen, so I will bid you all a good night."

"Pleasant dreams, my love." Adam's lips brushed her cheek gently.

"Excellent woman," Wellington remarked as the door closed behind her.

"The best," Adam agreed, pride shining in his eyes as he motioned the duke toward a seat.

"You will get no dispute of that from me," Damien said, picking up the decanter to pour himself another brandy. "Can I offer you some of Brand's admirable French stock? Newly acquired since the peace, of course."

"Of course," Wellington agreed, with a rueful smile, taking the filled glass from Damien's hand. "I vow, I miss you and even that hound of yours, Wodesby. Your cousin Lucas is a good lad, mind you, but I would far prefer the aid of the chief mage himself to any apprentice. That is why I wished you to stay. Is there any change? England could use the advantage of a seer in the upcoming negotiations."

Damien compelled himself to smile. "I fear, sir, that I am

still on forced holiday. Currently, I am as ordinary as Brand here." He nodded toward his brother-in-law.

Wellington knew better than to offer his pity. "I would scarcely characterize Adam as ordinary," the duke said, seating himself and pausing to sip his drink. "And I think that we might use your insights in our negotiations with or without your sorcery, Damien. Think about it."

Damien looked up in surprise. "I shall."

"Excellent," Wellington said, turning to Adam. "And now I will speak of the matter that brings me here tonight. Although you are not a mage, Brand, I know that your bundle of tricks is rather formidable. In fact, it is that unusual proficiency that brings me here tonight. According to the Royal Society of Illusionists, you are the best master of illusion in England."

Damien choked on his brandy.

"There, there, old man, we cannot all be the best, you know," Adam said, pounding his brother-in-law on the back with a bit more force than necessary.

"Is he all right?" Wellington asked, concerned.

"Other than a nose put somewhat out of joint, he is quite fine." Adam laughed. "You see, Your Grace, mages and witches are taught the skills of sleight of hand from the cradle. Much as I hate to admit it, in the arena of illusion, Damien's abilities are equal to mine, if not superior, with or without his magical powers."

"No offense meant, Damien," Wellington said, turning to Adam. "However, I suddenly find myself in need of a more commonplace kind of false magic. An illusionist to bait a trap." Wellington explained, his expression pained. "I hate to be the bearer of bad news, Adam, but your friend, Sir Hector Southwood has betrayed us."

Chapter 2

There was a tang of salt in the air, a seaborne breeze that drifted lazily inland. Rowan swept off her broadbrimmed hat, savoring the momentary relief of that cool touch. The leafy arbor afforded little respite from the afternoon sun, and even the hum of the bees seemed especially lazy. Mignon's perch stood empty in the shade; the little hawk had gone to seek food and relief. "Lucy, can you name the continents for me?" Rowan forced herself to ask.

"The continents . . . are . . . hot, torrid, and beastly," the ten-year-old moaned.

Her brother, Davy, stifled a giggle. "Those aren't continents, Lucy. You know that!"

"Well, they might as well be, since I can think of nothing else but how hot it feels," Lucy retorted, closing her book with a snap and looking up toward Rowan woefully. "My head is turning to library paste, Mrs. Penham. Please, please may we go for a walk by the shore path now? You said that we might when we are done with our lessons."

Rowan regarded the child's deep brown eyes, like a little puppy begging for a table scrap, so like her own Giselle . . . Rowan shook her head. She could ill afford such sympathetic thoughts, not when her daughter's life hung in the balance. "We are not yet done with the lesson," she said.

As it was, in these past few weeks, it had become increasingly difficult to maintain her distance from the members of the Southwood family. Their warmth was seductive, like a love philter that they were inviting her to share. If they knew who she really was . . . what she was . . . her mission, they would surely hate her. But that knowledge was scant protection against the guilt that had begun to gnaw her.

"Penny!"

When Davy tugged at her skirt, the corner of her mouth quirked into an inkling of a smile. From the answering light in his eyes, he knew that she was lost.

"Come, Penny," he pleaded, turning the full power of his six-year-old charm upon her. "It's cool near the cliffs."

"Very well," she agreed, salvaging her authority with a weak promise. "We will finish the lesson later. Perhaps you will recite for your father. He will be quite pleased at the knowledge of geography that you have gained." Particularly Elba. Somehow, she would manage to maneuver herself close to Sir Hector Southwood. The lightest of touches, on the shoulder, on the fingertip, and his thoughts would be open to her.

She was fortunate indeed that, for all his brilliance, her employer was an uncomplicated soul, artless and ingenuous, with all his thoughts as clear as a mountain spring. The discussion of Elba would naturally bring Napoleon to Sir Hector's mind, especially when a case of dispatches had arrived just this morning. The baronet was one of the prime keepers of England's cage, the Corsican the sole beast in his menagerie.

"Please, Penny." Davy tugged at her hand with all the urgency of a child trying to keep a fickle adult from a change of mind. "Can we wade in the water? We will be ever so careful."

His touch came so suddenly that there was no time for Rowan to shield her mind from the whirligig of the little boy's thoughts. Ponies and puppies, cakes and kites all tumbled together in a welter of feelings. Quickly, she brought down the barriers, but it was already too late. Through the link of those grubby fingers, Davy had touched a part of her that she had long forgotten. An indefinable sweetness lingered in her, the taste of simple innocence. This boy was beginning to love her, to share with childish generosity the affection that adults hoarded like misers.

Pain welled within her, cutting through all her carefully crafted justifications. She was using him, using them all.

"Yes, let's go to the shore." Lucy took hold of Rowan's other arm. "Papa never allows us to go alone, because of the tides, but Mama would take us there all the time when it was hot. Do you remember, Davy?"

"Yes, I remember," Davy added, his lip drooping wistfully.

There was no need for Rowan to walk through minds to know what they were feeling. Although Lady Southwood had been dead for over a year, her absence was still a gaping wound that had hardly begun to heal.

Infiltrating the household had been a simple task. So grateful was Sir Hector for a qualified tutor willing to take his wild children in hand that there had almost been no need for Rowan's forged references. Indeed, he had not even bothered to question her unusual choice of a merlin as a pet. No subterfuge had been required for the comfort of her familiar's company and Mignon's aid in Etienne's plans.

"I must admit that I find the idea of cool water tempting indeed," Rowan said, deliberately changing the direction of her thoughts, focusing on Giselle. Soon, soon, it would be midsummer, and then she and her daughter would be free. Free . . . the chain of Rowan's office hung beneath her fichu like an anchor, tethering her to the Du Le Fey.

Though the talisman was as light as thistledown, its weight seemed suddenly unbearable. As the cliffs came into view, she longed to pull it from her neck, to toss the ancient links far into the sea and watch that weighty gold sink beneath the waves. In the distance she heard Mignon's cry. The merlin soared above them, wheeling in the wind, drawing her attention back to the road.

"Look, Mrs. Penham, someone is coming," Lucy said, pointing to the crest of the hill ahead.

Rowan shaded her eyes with her hand. A cloud of dust had appeared on the horizon. Squinting into the sun, she discerned a colorful painted wagon half hidden by the churning haze.

"Gypsies!" Davy clapped his hands in glee. "The gypsies have come back."

"It *is* the gypsies," Lucy confirmed, her expression alive with excitement. "I didn't know that they would be coming this year. Papa said they might not."

"Your father expects the Romany?" Rowan asked, puzzlement in her voice. In all of her experience, she had never met an Outsider who viewed the traveling people with anything other than distaste, if not outright antipathy.

"He lets them camp on our land, though all the neighbors complain about it." Lucy looked at her sheepishly. "They are wonderful musicians. Every summer they would play at Mama's midsummer ball. She loved their music so. I thought that they might not come anymore, but Papa said that they were welcome even though we are not having an entertainment."

"And they know magic!" Davy added. "Real magic, Papa says. Last year, Dominick taught Papa how to make a chicken disappear."

"At least, he tried to," Lucy said, her tone making it plain that the Gypsy had not quite succeeded.

Rowan suppressed a smile. Sir Hector was obsessed with magic. His library held a clutter of automatons and devices for illusions. Unfortunately, the baronet was the most incompetent illusionist that she had ever seen. It was one of Fate's strange whimsies that had brought a witch without spells to the household of a magician whose tricks always failed.

As the wagon drew closer, Rowan warily surveyed the two men behind the team. The man at the reins was a Gypsy, but his companion clearly was not, though he was dressed in the colorful style that the Romany favored. His complexion, though dark, lacked the swarthy tones of the traveling people. Oddly shaded hair cut a bit longer than the fashion framed his face, its quicksilver waves ruffling in the light breeze from the water. Though his face was young, there was a sad wisdom in his eyes that somehow made that color seem fitting and right. His was a patrician's countenance with high-boned cheeks framing deep-set eyes. Only the bronze sun-warmed tones of his skin belied his aristocratic demeanor.

Gray-shaded brows accented jade eyes as he gazed at her, appraised her, and turned his attention to the children. Maddeningly, Rowan felt herself flushing. Even from the first flowering of girlhood, no man had ever dismissed her so easily. She knew that she ought to feel complimented on the skill of her disguise, but perversely she wanted him to notice her.

"See, Penny! I told you, it is Mr. Dominick!" Davy jumped up and down like a monkey. "This is Mrs. Penham, our governess, Mr. Dominick. She's ever so nice. Will you pull a guinea from my ear?"

The Gypsy laughed as he jumped from the seat. "A guinea, eh? You think me a rich man, Master Davy?" He tousled the boy's head and pulled a silver coin from behind his lobe. "Now, if it is gold you are wanting, ask that man on the box." He pressed the silver into the child's palm and pointed to Damien.

"Is he rich?" Davy asked, slipping the coin into his pocket.

"He is the world's greatest magician, little one," Dominick said, avoiding the first question.

His companion rose on cue. Shirtsleeves billowed as he jumped lightly from the seat. He was far taller than Rowan had realized, towering above her by at least half a head. Sweat molded his shirt to his torso, limning the muscular lines of his chest. Sweeping his straw hat off his head, he bowed deeply. "Oberon the Magnificent, at your service," he said.

As he came up, two bouquets of paper flowers had appeared in his hand. Lucy gasped as he presented the first to her. Rowan took the offering, her fingers inadvertently brushing his and a strange sensation flowed through her. It was wholly unlike anything that she had ever known, no surface thoughts, but an aura of potency, masculinity. Had her stepson Etienne sent some unknown to keep watch over her? Instinctively, her eyes went to Oberon's hands. With a tan so deep, it would have been all but impossible to wholly conceal the traces of a mage's ring. But there was no sign of a talisman upon him. It would seem that the man was no sorcerer. Rowan relaxed, even as she felt a strange sense of disappointment.

"And what about me?" Davy questioned plaintively.

"Now, Davy," Rowan scolded him with more waspishness than he deserved. Was she a green girl to be affected like this by a handsome face and the face of an Outsider at that? "It is greedy that you are."

The guinea nearly went fumbling from Damien's fingers. Deep and husky, Mrs. Penham's contralto sent a tremor down his spine. Her words had the flavor of the Welsh valleys, touched with another foreign music that he could not quite place. That fluid melodious cadence was wholly at odds with her appearance. As he waved his hands gracefully through the air, he made another covert inspection.

The quintessential governess, he concluded. Spectacles covered eyes that seemed a watery gray. Her dark hair was scraped back so severely beneath the cover of her hat that not a softening wisp dared to escape. Mrs. Penham's shapeless round gown was only feminine by nature of its category of dress, not by virtue of any enhancement to her figure. A pity that the voice of a nightingale was so totally wasted on this crow of a woman.

"The lad requested gold, madame," Damien said. "And he shall have it. But coins cannot grow behind ears that are not carefully scrubbed, Master Davy. That is why Dominick could only make silver appear. Shall we see if you have done better behind the other ear?"

Davy nodded, though his expression was doubtful.

"Hmmm!" Damien examined Davy's ear gravely. "This may take a little bit of a spell . . . Lavoisier, Macadam, Newton . . . There!" A guinea gleamed in Damien's hand. "Now, you ought to take better care with your washing, youngling," he said, as he pressed the gold into the boy's palm, "else I may only find pennies when next we meet."

"Lavoisier and Newton are names to conjure with, Mr. Oberon, for science is a form of sorcery these days." The woman's eyebrow raised above the rims of her spectacles. "But Macadam?"

"His roads, madame, are as near to magic as a mortal may achieve, for they make even this monstrous equipage into a passable chariot," Damien explained, adding wit to the credit of voice on Mrs. Penham's side of the ledger. Not every female could have caught that bit of whimsy. Moreover, she had been watching his pass, her attention on the guinea not on his flurry of misdirecting motion. Hastily, he revised his initial estimation. There was definitely more to this woman than was visible to the casual glance.

Green eyes flashed with humor and curiosity, coaxing Rowan into a half smile. She had barely seen him palm the coin, but then what woman would choose to look at this man's hands when she could gaze into those arresting eyes? His long fingers were quick and skillful, certainly as nimble as many of the erstwhile "magicians" that she had watched in Louis' court.

"Can you pull a guinea from behind Lucy's ear?" Davy asked, tugging at Oberon's sleeve. "Hers are clean, I bet."

With a quick wave of his hands, Damien obliged. Lucy clapped with glee as her coin materialized in his hand.

"And what about Mrs. Penham?" Lucy asked, as she wrapped her guinea in her handkerchief.

Oberon the Magnificent looked at Rowan questioningly.

"It would take a real magician to wring more than a tuppence from me, sir, despite any claims to cleanliness I may have," Rowan proclaimed, denying a perverse impulse to allow him to work his tricks upon her. "I am, after all, a governess. At that rate, Mr. Oberon, it is hardly worth your while."

"Let me be the judge of that, Mrs. Penham," he said.

Before she could speak, he reached out his hand and gently touched the tip of her nose. Once again, she felt that odd sensation, a shock that touched her very core. He turned up his palm, and there was a golden guinea.

"For you, Mrs. Penham," he said. "It would seem that you underestimate your worth, for I assure you that I have rarely found a guinea at the tip of a nose less than ducal in rank. Will you take it?" He held out the coin to her.

She shook her head in protest. "Really, sir, it would be most improper to accept it."

"Nonsense," he said, "you are the source of the gold, after all. I'm sure that Mr. Penham would not be offended."

"My husband is dead and beyond offense," Rowan said, coolly, trying to ignore the magician's close proximity and the extraordinary effect that it had on her. She wanted to feel that touch once more, to try and understand this unusual feeling. Never before had she encountered this uncanny reaction upon contact with either Outsider or mage. "Nonetheless, I could not—"

"Please take it, Mrs. Penham," Lucy begged. "He did get it from you. If you cannot keep yours, Davy and I have to give ours back, too."

"Speak for yourself, Lucy," Davy said with a pout. He looked at Rowan with a plea in his eyes.

"Very well," Rowan agreed reluctantly. "If your papa agrees, we will keep them. I fear that this may prove a frightfully expensive encounter for you, Mr. Oberon."

"Simply, 'Oberon,' Mrs. Penham," he said, with a bow.

"I suspect, sir, that there is naught that is simple about you," Rowan remarked, the corners of her eyes crinkling as she tried to plumb the secrets in those verdant depths. Like the facets of a jewel, they were, filled with a myriad of complexities.

"Indeed, I am a most mysterious man, with the wisdom of the ancients at my fingertips," the magician said, a brow curving sardonically as if he were mocking himself. "As for the coins, perhaps this might ease matters with your employer."

An envelope appeared in his hand as if from nowhere. This time Rowan gasped along with the children. He was by far the best Outsider illusionist she had seen.

"It is a letter of introduction. I am certain that once Sir Hector reads it, he will not look askance at my little gifts. Please inform him that I shall call upon him as soon as we are settled in our camp. Until next we meet." He bowed and jumped back up on the wagon board with lithe grace.

Rowan and the children moved back from the road as the caravan's wheels whipped up clouds of dust. The little ones waved and watched until the last of the wagons disappeared around the bend.

Lucy sighed. "Isn't he wonderful?"

No need to ask who she meant. Rowan gave herself a mental shake. The "wisdom of the ancients" indeed!

Damien blinked, shaking his head to clear his muddled thoughts. He shifted uneasily on the hard wagon seat.

"There is a problem, Lord Damien?" Dominick asked, but there was no answer from the mage. The Gypsy kept watch with an anxious eye until Damien's expression came back to normal. "A Vision?" he asked hopefully.

"No." Damien's brow wrinkled as he tried to analyze this odd sensation, not a Vision certainly. The signs of an impending foretelling were invariable and not at all like this. Although he had touched the woman for but a fleeting second, his fingers still held the memory of her skin. Her scent lingered in his nostrils; delicate, haunting; a fragrance that brought to mind hot summer nights and moonlight . . . Damien shook his head. "No Visions, my friend, merely daydreams."

"But dreams and prophecy, are they not as one?" Dominick asked, hope patent in his voice.

"The two are twined together, but not quite the same," Damien said, trying to keep frustration from seeping into his words. Was there to be no escape from the hopes and fears of his friends? Was his own apprehension insufficient? As each sun set without the return of his magic, he could feel the growing weight of disappointment and despair. He had believed that he might be free of the burden of his family's concern. However, it would seem that he had merely exchanged a nervous mother for a brooding Gypsy nanny.

"I suspect that I may be feeling the results of that wine we shared last night before the fire." Damien shrugged. "And this heat is enough to make any man hallucinate." He took a flask from beneath the seat and took a long swallow of tepid water before passing it on.

The Gypsy grunted and took a draught. "Still, I do not understand why you do this thing, Lord Damien." He lifted his hand to encompass the gaudily painted wagon with a gesture. "You, the lord of all mages to play at fooling the eye."

Damien sighed, pulling off his straw hat and wiping his forehead with a damp sleeve. "No more 'Lord Damien,' if you please, Dominick. I am now 'Oberon the Magnificent,' and believe me when I say that this situation pleases me no more than it pleases you. There are many things that I would rather be doing than bathing in my own sweat while every rut in this goat path they call a road batters at my behind."

"But you say it was Lord Brand that the Duke of Wellington wanted," Dominick pointed out. "So why is it *you* with me here instead of Adam? Lord Brand could have done the job just as well and your mother . . ."

"My mother, if you recall, finally acknowledged that Miranda would prefer Adam's presence to mine when their child comes," Damien reminded him. "This tangle may take weeks to unravel, and I had nothing better to do with my time. It made sense for me to go in Adam's stead." *And at last, I am doing something useful again,* he added to himself, *doing something more than wait unceasingly for a flicker of magic.*

The Gypsy shook his head mournfully. "Still, I cannot believe that Lord Southwood is a traitor. Every year he makes us welcome, gives us a place by his stream to camp. His woman, when she lived, she loved our music. When last we came, and she was so sick, she would ask us to come and play beneath her window to chase away sadness from her dying heart. Could it be that the woman's death changes him?"

"It is always a blow to lose someone that you love," Damien recalled quietly, remembering those days soon after his father's death, the feelings of guilt, of betrayal. "Yet, whatever the reason, it would seem that Sir Hector has chosen to turn his coat. But if it is any comfort, you are not the only one to doubt Southwood's guilt, my friend."

Damien set his hat forward upon his head, shading his eyes from the glare as the heat rose from the ground in visible undulating waves. "Adam could not credit it either. When it was discovered that information about Napoleon's confinement had been falling into the hands of the Bonapartists, the duke began to have false information whispered to Sir Hector, praying that those shammed echoes would not come back to Whitehall. But a few days later, the counterfeit communication came back from our agents in France. There is no question that Southwood is our man."

"Then, why does your duke not arrest him?" Dominick took his hand off the brake as the wagon reached a level stretch. "That would be most simple, it seems to me."

"It would be. But Wellington suspects that Sir Hector is part of a larger conspiracy, and the duke would see them all hang," Damien explained. "It could take weeks to sort this all out, and I could not deprive my sister of her husband's company at this critical juncture."

Once more, Damien felt a twinge deep within him as he marveled at the depth of love between his sister and Lord Brand. In Damien's leading string days, he had been pledged to ally himself sight unseen with a Peregrine girl. Since that betrothal had ended in disaster, his hand had remained unpromised, but he had few illusions about marriage. Damien had always known that his alliance would be more a matter of bloodlines than a joining of hearts. Why then did he feel this unwarranted envy? "In any case, Wellington was persuaded that my talent, meager though it may be, will suffice to gain me access to the Southwood home. So I have painted my wagon and filled my purse with guineas so that I may make them disappear."

"Aye," Dominick agreed, his face turning glum as his mind returned to the business at hand. "Make a coin vanish, and Sir Hector will dog you till you show him how it is done. Teach him, and he will claim you as his friend."

From the expression on the Gypsy's face, Damien knew what had been left unspoken. *Become his friend, so that you may betray him.*

The doors to the terrace of Southwood Manor stood open to the forlorn hope of an evening breeze. Rowan stood by Sir Hector's side as the children began to recite for their father and his guests. Winifred, Lady Stanhope, uttered a gusty sigh. As Sir Hector's nearest neighbor, the lady had taken it upon herself to become the widower's adviser on all things maternal. Her wrinkled face wore the look of a martyr at the sound of the lions entering the coliseum. However, her eighteen-year-old daughter, Diana, seemed to be almost eager to listen, a smile lighting her homely face as Davy unrolled the map of Elba that he had made.

"Notice the excellent drawing here, Sir Hector," Rowan commented, touching his shoulder lightly, ostensibly to direct his attention to a particularly fine aspect of his son's rendering. Just as she had hoped, the details of the morning's dispatches had slipped to the surface of the baronet's mind. It took but a few seconds to commit the pages to her own well-trained memory. Still, try as she might, she could not suppress other unwanted details that sifted from his thoughts to hers. *How pretty Diana is when she smiles. A pity that the child laughs so infrequently. The little ones love her so. If only . . .* There was a fragment of longing, quickly and ruthlessly buried. *Hector, remember your age, you randy old goat,* he told himself. *She is barely out of the schoolroom.*

Rowan broke the contact hastily, regarding the plain girl with new eyes. Diana was watching Sir Hector from beneath modestly lowered lashes. Even without a touch, Rowan knew the secret stirrings in the young woman's heart from that surreptitious gaze.

"You have done wonders with the children, Mrs. Penham," Diana said, her tones earnest. "They were like little lost lambs, before."

"More like wildcats," Sir Hector said regarding his children with fond honesty.

"Their manners are still less than pleasing," Lady Stanhope added, her disparaging look leaving no doubt upon whose shoulders the blame ought to be placed.

Rowan contemplated a vision of Lady Stanhope's nose further elongated by a wart.

"Indeed not, Mama," Diana said. "Did you not see Lucy's delightful curtsy? I could not have done better at her age. And Davy is quite the little gentleman these days. Mrs. Penham has done a splendid job, especially in so short a time." She colored beneath her mother's glower of disapproval, but she did not lower her eyes.

"Did you not mention that Lucy had written a piece on Italy?" Sir Hector asked smoothly.

As Lucy began her recitation, Rowan looked at Lady Stanhope's daughter in thoughtful surprise. No one, Outsider or of the Blood born, had ever come to Rowan's protection before. And though Diana's claws were but kitten size, Rowan still felt a surge of gratitude for that effort at defense. A favor done was a favor owed, and a means of repayment was close at hand.

Those fripperies that Diana's mama preferred did the young woman absolutely no good, Rowan observed. But beneath the layers of ruching, she suspected that there was a fine young figure. With properly styled hair and a bit of color to augment what nature had given, the girl might be almost pretty. As Lucy finished her piece on Italy, Lady Stanhope launched on a monologue regarding her daughter's upcoming season.

". . . As the daughter of a viscount and the granddaughter of a duke, Diana may set her sights as high as she chooses. When one takes her dowry into account, I suspect that my Diana will be wed before next summer, Sir Hector," she concluded, ignoring her daughter's flushing face. "Of course, she shall attend all the local entertainments until we go up to London in the spring, but there is nothing like a bit of Town Bronze, do you not think?"

"Nothing less than an earl, I would imagine, for little Diana," Sir Hector agreed heartily.

Diana winced visibly at the use of the word "little." *Shakespeare's Puck had the right of it,* Rowan thought, intercepting Diana's look of misery and hopeless longing. *What fools these mortals be.* Rowan looked at the girl and concentrated, before twirling a surreptitious finger three times widdershins, the counterclockwise motion reinforcing a suggestion of good taste toward Lady Stanhope.

A small spell of persuasion it was, one of the few that the comte had taught her, since it was useful, though, unlikely to change deep-seated inclinations. Rowan could only hope that Lady Stanhope's love of the elaborate was not too profound.

Yet despite the fact that the charm might not prove adequate, Rowan felt a curious sense of joy, the true bliss of a charm cast unselfishly, without gain or thought for personal indulgence. It had been so long, time beyond memory since she had acted entirely on someone else's behalf.

But, Rowan reminded herself, it was neither her mission to sort out Sir Hector's life, nor her task to clear the path of true love. She glanced outside, her stomach clenching as she realized that the sun was nearly ending its journey toward the horizon. There would be no opportunity to send Mignon across the Channel with what she had learned before darkness fell.

"Is it not past time for the governess to be getting the children to bed?" Lady Stanhope asked pointedly, fixing a Medusa-like stare upon Rowan, her disapproval apparent.

"Oh, no, not yet," Sir Hector said, pulling a packet of cards from his pocket. "The evening's entertainment is not yet over."

The children groaned in unison. "Oh, Papa, not again," Lucy said.

"Is this the same one as last time?" Davy asked as his father fanned out the deck of pasteboards in his hand.

"Now, now, my dears," the baronet assured them. "I have

been practicing. If you would please take a card, Mrs. Penham."

Rowan complied, picking the card that he was so obviously trying to force her to choose.

"Now, look at it carefully, and show it to everyone in a manner that I cannot see it," he commanded. "Then return it to the deck, and I shall bring it to the top. Remember that card, if you please."

Once again she obeyed. With a look of intent concentration, Sir Hector shuffled, missed the cut, and inadvertently sent the king of hearts to the middle of the pack. From past experience, she knew that failure would require her employer to try the trick over and over again until he achieved success. They all might be trapped in the library for hours on end. With a small shake of her head and twirl of her fingers, Rowan sent a suggestion of another shuffle that would send the card back to the top again.

"And now . . ." Sir Hector eyed the deck uneasily. "I shall ask you to blow on the deck three times, Diana."

Obediently, Diana puffed gently on the pack. Only Rowan noted the almost imperceptible tremble of Sir Hector's hand as her breath touched his fingers.

"Behold!" Sir Hector whisked off the top card, and held it aloft with the air of a man half expecting to make a fool of himself.

The children clapped gleefully. "Oh, well-done, Papa," Lucy exclaimed. "The king of hearts, the exact card that Mrs. Penham took."

"You are the bestest magician, Papa," Davy said proudly. "Almost as good as Oberon the Magnificent."

"By Jove, so I am," Sir Hector agreed with a relieved grin, putting down the cards and picking up a piece of writing paper from his desk. "Though, from what I have read in the letter that I received from the Royal Society of Illusionists, your Mr. Oberon is something of an expert."

"I cannot like it, Sir Hector," Lady Stanhope sniffed. "A charlatan and those Gypsies both. I vow, we shall soon start to hear of silver and jewelry disappearing as well as poultry and livestock."

"There has not been a single incident of theft in all the

years that these people have been using my grounds, Lady Stanhope," Sir Hector said stiffly. "As for this Oberon fellow, my friend, Lord Brand, informs me that he is of excellent character."

"Then, may we keep our guineas that Mr. Oberon gave us, Papa, please?" Davy asked.

"Ah, so now I know why I am being treated to such flummery," Sir Hector chucked his son under the chin. " 'The bestest magician,' indeed! Yes, Davy, you may keep your guineas. From what the secretary of our society tells me, your Mr. Oberon can well afford a few marigolds. It seems that he is quite warm in the pocket himself, and of a rather exalted family."

"Indeed?" Lady Stanhope leaned forward in her seat, like a hound who has caught the scent. "And just *who* is he?"

"Brand does not take me into his confidence," Sir Hector told her, "It would seem that this 'Oberon' business is merely a blind for the sake of the young man's family. One understands that they are less than thrilled to have him traveling about the country entertaining fair day crowds."

"I should say!" Lady Stanhope exclaimed in agreement.

"But why not?" Davy asked. "He is a very good magician."

"So Lord Brand informs me," Sir Hector agreed. "Brand claims that the lad is almost his equal, and Adam is one of England's finest illusionists."

"It is one thing, Davy, to entertain one's peers as your dear Papa has done this evening," Lady Stanhope pronounced sonorously, giving the governess a look that excluded her from the realm of "peers." "However, it is quite another matter for a gentleman to pass the hat in the marketplace. Do you understand, my boy?"

Davy shook his sandy head.

His father sighed. "Then, that makes two of us, laddie, for there are few things that I would rather do than ride about in a painted wagon and learn illusions from the masters."

Rowan intercepted the glance of accord between father and son. Although she had walked through the innermost thoughts of men, she had never seen such complete understanding. Sir Hector put a hand on Lucy's shoulder, making the family circle complete. Even without touching them, she could feel the warmth and comfort that they gave each other. Rowan looked at Diana and knew that she too felt and envied them this simplest of all magics.

Longing shafted through her, to touch her own Giselle, to see her again. At first light she would send Mignon across to France. Sir Hector would not be harmed by what she was doing, she assured herself. No one would ever guess the source of information gathered from the mind itself, sent on the wings of a hawk.

"But then, we cannot always do as we would wish, and sometimes I doubt that all our dreams would give us happiness were they to come true," Sir Hector continued.

Only Rowan saw the longing in his wistful smile.

"Still, I am rather glad that Brand has sent this fellow our way. Perhaps he can teach me to perfect my disappearing chicken trick," the baronet concluded.

"Papa's valet Burriss still talks of those two beaver hats that were ruined when Papa put the chickens in them," Lucy confided to Rowan. "And Cook got tired of making fowl every single night."

"Every night?" Rowan asked.

"The chickens died, you see," Lucy explained simply.

"Perhaps you might make puddings disappear this time?" Davy suggested.

"And I'm sure you will help me, then, if the trick fails, my Davy?" Sir Hector asked merrily, plucking the child up and setting him on his shoulders. He whisked Lucy into his arms, and she clung around his neck.

"Lucy and I both, sir," Davy promised stoutly. "We will help you."

"If you will excuse me for a moment or two, Lady Stanhope, Diana, while I bid my darlings a good night?" Sir Hector asked as he carried them through the door and started to climb the stairs. "Ah, I ask you, Mrs. Penham, was ever a man so blessed with wonderful children?"

"No, milord, I have never seen anyone so blessed," Rowan replied honestly as she followed him up to the nursery, wondering why her eyes had suddenly begun to sting.

Chapter 3

Night was falling as Damien set his ax down by the growing woodpile. "Enough?" he asked Dominick.

"For now," Dominick said with a smile. "You do not have to chop wood for us, Lord Damien."

"I will not live like a prince among you," Damien said stubbornly.

"You have split wood enough for ten fires," Dominick remarked. "Come, drink." He dipped a tin cup into the nearby stream.

Gratefully, Damien drank deep of the cool, sweet water, then bent to wash his face and hands. "A fine camp," he said, taking in the features of the surrounding glade as the two of them walked side by side toward the fire. The smells of cooking food tantalized his nose. "Water in abundance, shade, good pasture. I would say that this almost rivals the place our family has set aside for your people at the Wode on the Thames."

"Aye, Sir Hector is good to us," Dominick said, regret tinging his voice.

"He is very good man," Tante Reina rose from her place beside the pot, swinging a cunningly wrought-iron pivot to move the bubbling mixture from above the flames. She took a packet from her pocket and threw it among the logs. As the fire licked at the bundle, a pungent citrus odor rose into the air chasing the insects from the vicinity.

Although she said nothing more as she ladled portions of fragrant stew into the bowls, her wizened face spoke volumes of disapproval. With an infinitesimal nod of her head, she sent her nephew Dominick toward the wagon. Damien frowned as she directed him toward a fallen log occupied by laughing, talking members of the tribe. However, as the two of them approached, the other diners quickly abandoned their seats.

Damien stared into the heart of the flames, started to murmur the spell that would shield them from the fire's heat, then stopping midway, his chant trailing off into an embarrassed whisper.

"Is difficult, no?" the old Gypsy woman said at last.

"I begin to understand those poor souls who lost pieces of themselves on the battlefields. Sometimes, I feel as if I am walking about with a part of me sliced away," Damien agreed, relaxing slightly.

"But soon, soon, you will be whole again," Tante Reina said, her skirts billowing as she sat down beside him and took his hand.

"More wishful thinking," Damien said, setting the bowl that he had gotten for Angel down on the ground as the dog trotted to his side. "I may have lost my Gift, but I am not yet an Outsider, Tante Reina. Merlin's Blood prevents you from seeing my future in my palm." Abruptly, he changed the subject. "Wellington wants me to return with him to Vienna, with or without my powers."

"So again you will be leaving the lady, your mother, to bear your burdens?" Tante Reina's brow knitted into a frown.

Angel growled deep in his throat.

"Let the boy speak for himself," the old woman demanded.

Damien gave a moan of frustration. "I have a chance to do something that will be of help to England. As for Mama, I have already told her that I will seek a wife among the covens. I suspect that there might be more than one witch willing to wed so that she might be England's mistress of witches."

"A seeker after power, you would put in your mother's place?" Tante Reina asked. "Do you hold yourself so cheap, Lord Damien?"

Damien shrugged. "You speak as if I have so many choices." He pulled a blade of grass from the ground beside him, weaving it between his fingers, avoiding her eyes. "How many women of the Blood are there in all of England,

Tante, that are of age to be a wife to a mage. Forty-five? Sixty, perhaps, in all the seven branches of the covens, and not a few of those are marriage-bonded from the cradle with betrothals that will not be broken as mine was."

Bitterness rasped in his laughter, and he stared into the flames blindly. "Do you think that I have not seen them at the Beltane festivals, when we gather, watching me, assessing me like mares in heat? Even before, I never fooled myself with the supposition that it is merely myself that they desire. Those golden links that Mama now wears called to them like a siren's song. If I were as ugly as a demon and as old as Methuselah himself, it would not have mattered to them, not so long as they can wear those chains."

Tante Reina shook her head sadly. "Your birth, I remember, when your father read the stars for you. War, he saw in your days, great destruction, but a woman, he saw for you, also a great love. He knew the weight of responsibility in time would be yours. His heart was glad that you would be happy in love."

"Even a stargazer of Papa's powers could err, Tante Reina," Damien said softly. "He was reading for one of the Blood, for his closest kin. No wonder, then, that his interpretation of the stars was wrong and that he chose my bride so badly."

"You believe still this error was his alone?" Tante Reina asked, her lips tightening to a thin line.

Damien's fists clenched in his lap. "Obviously. Lord Peregrine's girl could not wait to inherit the place of mistress of witches. At the time, my father seemed hale enough for another score of years. No doubt, if she had known that Papa would be murdered within the week, she might have chosen me over a man old enough to be her own father. Still, she had what she wanted and what her father had plotted for all along, the mistress's golden links. What did it matter whether she ruled in France or England?"

"Think well before you judge," Tante Reina warned with a toothless frown. "A story, Lord Damien, will I tell you, about a young witch pledged to a mage. Even before his birth is this match made, two great families who would join in power. Twice ten years older than she, he was. This mage was wise, understanding the ways of women. Is his hand that rocks her cradle, is his face she sees when she first smiles, is his finger that she holds when she goes from crawl to walk. Gifts he brings her as she grows. He becomes to her a teacher. A dear friend, he is, before she even thinks of him as lover and husband. She is happy in her pledge to wed one she cares for so deeply."

Tante Reina paused, and her rheumy eyes regarded Damien with a look that told him this was no mere tale, but a truth.

"To London she goes to learn the ways of Outsiders, as was custom in her family. A man, she meets, an Outsider, and with first look, she knows that the other half of her heart beats in his breast. Still, to have desire of her soul, she must betray her Blood, but more so, her betrothed, her beloved friend. The honor, the power, they mean nothing to her, but to cause her dearest Peter pain—"

"My father?" Damien whispered, recalling something that his mother had mentioned when his sister, Miranda, had chosen to give her heart to an Outsider. But Damien had discounted those words about choices between duty and love, because they had been said in the heat of anger.

Tante Reina nodded. "Aye, it was Lord Peter your mother chose, not for the links of gold that came with his hand, but because of chains that your father forged for her heart from her first days, the bonds of friendship, Lord Damien. Lord Peter tried to teach you, but heedless you were."

Damien closed his eyes, recalling the many times that his father had urged him to travel to Wales, to visit with Lord Peregrine and make the acquaintance of the girl who was pledged to be his wife. Rowan . . . Rowan of the Peregrine coven; Gifted, rumor had it, with the ability to touch minds. A name that still had the power to rouse regrets . . . and rage at the ultimate cost of that young woman's fickle choice. "What does it matter now, Tante Reina?" he asked. "The past cannot be changed."

"This is true, yes!" she hissed, as she rose. "But you always place the fault elsewhere, all are to blame but you. Think upon that, you should, before you judge the child who refused a man whose face she knew not, who never wooed

her with word or gift. Take upon your self, a share of that
blame, else all the pain, your father's death, is worth nothing. Nothing!"

"I do not deny my part in Papa's death," Damien said
softly. "Not a day goes by without thinking of it. If I had
only gone with him to Wales."

She shook her head mournfully and hobbled toward her
wagon. Damien rose and dusted himself off, his hunger suddenly gone. He had to get away somewhere, anywhere.

"No, Angel," he ordered, as his hound whimpered a soft
question. "There is no reason for you to come with me. I just
have the need to walk for a bit."

The mastiff growled.

"Yes, I will take care," Damien agreed, trying to contain
his irritation. "By the Merlin, I may lack magic, but I will
not be put back in leading strings!" He strode off into the
forest, glancing behind him occasionally to make sure that
Angel was not following. As he reached the edge of the
copse, the night chants of the crickets were swallowed by
the sounds of waves surging against the cliff side, pounding
as relentlessly as his troubled thoughts.

All his life, he had believed that his parents had allied
themselves in a perfect union. Had it all been a sham, then?
A farce for the sake of appearances? Deep within, Damien
acknowledged the truth that had been apparent for months
now.

Since her marriage to Lawrence Timmons, his mother had
changed. It was as if a vital part of her had always been
walled away, hidden and forgotten. But Lawrie had broken
through to that secret garden within her, and made his
mother blossom as never before. Damien cast back to his
earliest memories, but he could not recall a time when he
had seen her this happy, this much at peace with herself.

Tante Reina's words wove through his mind in a plaintive
leitmotiv of blame. *Think upon that, you should, before you
judge the child who refused a man whose face she knew not,
who never wooed her with word or gift.*

Rowan pulled back the curtains, and made sure that all the
windows were open wide to any passing breeze. Lucy

stirred restlessly, and Rowan touched her brow, smoothing away a stray lock of hair.

"Thank you, Mama," the girl whispered with a soft sigh.

Rowan's throat tightened, her shoulders slumped in pain as she felt the web of lies tightening around her. For all that she told herself no harm would be done, midsummer was fast approaching. Once her mission was completed, she would be gone, leaving these little ones bereft once more, wounding them deeply. Much as she had tried to keep her distance, Lucy and Davy had grown to care for her. And what of Giselle? Who was tucking her into her bed at night? Was she alone, frightened as Rowan herself had been so long ago?

Slowly, she walked toward her own room at the far end of the nursery and threw the dormer window open wide. As she stared into the night, Mignon fluttered to the windowsill, cooing in sympathy.

"No, my friend, I doubt I could sleep right now, for all my exhaustion, but you do need your rest," she said, stroking her soft feathered crown before taking her up on her arm.

"Tttic!" Mignon protested as Rowan gently placed a hood over the merlin's head and set her on the perch.

"Now, hush, little one," Rowan commanded quietly but firmly. "You have spent nearly the entire day in the air, and you have a long flight ahead of you in the morning. Sleep you must, or else you might come to harm fighting the sea winds in the crossing. As for myself, perhaps a walk in the garden will put me in a better frame of mind."

The raptor shifted uneasily upon her perch, her noises softening to a chittering grumble.

"I *will* be careful," she assured him. "Never fear." But there was no answer from her familiar. From the even movements of her feathered chest it was clear that the bird had drifted off.

Rowan slipped quietly through the silent house, letting herself out through the gardens. Though the new moon provided little light to guide her, stars beyond counting salted the cloudless sky, but Rowan did not even know the names of the constellations. If her mother had lived . . . if the betrothal to Wodesby had not been broken . . . if . . . if . . . if.

Ruthlessly, Rowan suppressed thoughts of what might have been.

There was no changing the past. Lady Peregrine had died and Rowan now knew why her father had kept her deliberately ignorant, refused to nurture her Mindwalking Gift. Lord Peregrine had feared her, dreaded that one day she might truly see the jealousy and cowardice that gnawed at the core of him.

Without the force of her mother's support, the betrothal pledge to the usurping Wodesbys was worthless. Rowan's father had thought himself clever as Croesus to sell her to Du Le Fey for a purse full of gold and promises. As for the girl that Rowan had been, to at last feel wanted, to be wooed . . . how the comte had laughed at her naïveté even as he stripped her of the last of those childish dreams . . . mistress of witches!

The crash of waves roused her from her reverie. Rowan was surprised to find that she had wandered well beyond the gardens. Following the sound to the cliff's edge. Rowan stared across the narrow strip of ocean as if her eyes could span the miles. *Giselle!* her heart cried. *Giselle!* But she could not speak to her daughter across the void, she did not know how, yet another part of her witch's birthright that had been denied her. The empty beach below beckoned enticingly, recalling the hours that she and Giselle had spent playing on the shores below the Chateau Du Le Fey.

The woodland ended abruptly at the base of a path that led to the edge of a rocky outcrop. Damien halted instinctively, his eyes focusing in the dim light until he located the source of movement in the darkness. The woman stood at the head of the cliff path, a shadow against the shimmer of ocean.

Damien watched as her fingers reached to the nape of her neck, plucking at the pins that held her hair in place. His breath caught in his throat as the mass of darkness fell, tumbling down her back in a sensuous cascade. She shook her silky mane, lifting it in her hands, offering it to the breezes before letting it loose once more. Suddenly, in an eye blink, she was gone.

The Dark Lady of his dreams? For a moment he wondered if she had been an illusion born of fatigue, but as he neared the edge of the outcropping, he saw the rough semblance of a stair. Dominick had mentioned that there was a path to the beach, steps hewn into the side of the rock. Who was she? And who or what was she seeking down by the shore? If she could rely upon the stone stair, then he would too.

As Damien made his way down to the beach, he began to regret his hasty decision. The rocky path might have been well enough by day, but by night it was treacherous. Luckily, the echoing of the waves masked the sound of his scrabbling progress. He drew a breath of relief when he finally reached the pebbled beach. An outcrop of rock sheltered the small cove from the turbulent Channel and hid the winding path from the stretch of strand.

Thoughtfully, Damien evaluated the possibilities. A skillful seaman could easily maneuver a yacht into this hidden haven without difficulty. Perhaps he had inadvertently stumbled upon the solution to the conundrum that had so baffled Wellington and his friends at Whitehall. How had Sir Hector managed to convey his information almost as fast as the dispatches were delivered? A swift ship could easily deliver the details of Napoleon's confinement to Calais before morning.

Damien moved slowly, slipping from shadow to shadow until the shore came into sight. In his passage he almost tripped over a bundle heaped behind the rock. A pair of shoes and stockings were jumbled together, obviously hastily discarded; a gleam of glass shone from one shoe. He studied the pair of spectacles, a vague inkling taking shape.

Rowan imagined Giselle running through the waves, squealing with pleasure as the water surged toward her toes. Her daughter played beside her in her mind's eye, briefly filling the overwhelming emptiness. As Rowan let the water surge around her, she made promises to her phantom child of a place without fear, a home filled with love. Soon they would both be free. Once the Du Le Fey yoke was broken, Rowan vowed, she would learn all the knowledge that had been kept from her. She would not allow her Giselle to be powerless before mage or man.

"Never!" Rowan cried, raising her fist up into the air, letting the wind snatch her words and carry them across to France if it could. "Never!" A ridiculous gesture to be sure, but as she shouted at the surf, Rowan felt a curious freedom. It was a pledge to the future. For the first time in her life, she was looking forward with anticipation, not backward with regret. Joy surged; she wanted to run, to dance, to laugh out loud.

The object of his search stood barefoot on the beach. Her hand stretched upward as if she was defying the sky itself. As Damien watched from behind the rock, she chased after the retreating tide. Then, as the waves rushed toward the beach once again, she hurriedly backed away. Salt spray swirled as water dashed itself against the rocks, bejeweling her with glittering droplets. The ebony mantle of her hair streamed to her waist, fanning out behind her like a silken banner as she flew forward to flirt with the tide once more.

Once again, she retreated, and her laughter floated above the sound of the surging water, teasing Damien's memory, lapping at the edges of his consciousness with its almost familiar tune. He picked up the spectacles once more, staring through the glass in the wan light as the pieces of the puzzle came together. As he had suspected, the lenses had no vision correction whatsoever. This wild and gamesome creature was the Southwood's governess.

His mouth made a silent O of wonder as she skipped along the shore, cavorting like a *selkie* at play. She hitched up her dampened skirts to her knees, letting the sea foam around her. She was the embodiment of the old tales, a maiden from the waters sent to tempt the unwary with her siren ways. Once more, the rippling sound of her childlike delight mingled with the sounds of the surf.

As Damien watched her taunting Neptune, he felt a growing longing that had nothing childish about it. Moist summer air surrounded him, oppressing him with a weighted heat. His mouth went suddenly dry, and his body taut. Damien looked toward the waves, tempted beyond measure to join her, to cool this sudden startling wild blaze of desire. Fire to water, earth to air . . . deep within him something stirred, an ember, barely discernible, but before he could identify that faint spark, he heard a scream.

Rowan cried out as she felt her feet going out from under her. Seaweed made the rock face slimy as she scrabbled for a grip. She rose to her knees when another surge of the waves sucked at her, knocking her breath from her with its force, pulling her prone. Choking, gasping for air she struggled against the swell, reaching for the bottom with fingers and toes, but the sloping shore had disappeared. She had been swept out beyond the shallow shelf, toward the mouth of the cove. Beyond was the open sea.

Fragments of spells, too obscure for recall, floated through her head, dim recollections of the incantations that her mother had sung to the child that she had once been. *Not enough, Mama, you should not have died before you taught me to take care of myself . . . take care . . . Giselle! . . . I cannot die! Not yet!*

Weakly, Rowan struck out toward the shore, but the weight of her voluminous skirts and petticoats pulled her downward, sapping her strength as she fought for her life and her daughter's. In desperation she reached for her talisman, tearing at the buttoned throat of her gown, but the golden chain was trapped, useless beneath the fabric. She was sinking . . . falling. Water tugged at her below and . . . above? A shadow loomed between her head and the surface. Grasping fingers touched her shoulders, relentlessly pulling her upward toward the wavering blur of the moon. Rowan gulped air into her burning lungs, blinking away water as she tried to see her savior, but her back was toward him.

"Try to relax if you can," a hoarse voice advised her, before another wave engulfed them both, nearly tearing them apart. But those strong hands held firm, tugging her toward him in the midst of the breakers, clasping her close to his chest. Rowan closed her eyes, let herself go limp, trusting herself to that secure grip, feeling his warmth in the threatening chill of the undertow. Powerful muscles strained taut against her as he struck for the shore, his strokes determined as the currents vied against them, pulling them toward the ocean's gaping maw. After moments that seemed to encompass eternity, her feet scraped against the bottom. She felt arms lifting her, cradling her like a child.

"Mrs. . . . P-Penham . . . Mrs. Pen-ham?" Damien said breathlessly, smoothed her hair back from her face, wiping away the water left by the dripping coil. She was as pale as the wan moonlight, and the cold, clammy feel of her skin was worrisome. Though he could feel the tickle of her breath against his cheek, those soft puffs of air were distressingly shallow.

There was no telling how much water she had swallowed. His fearborn surge of strength was fading quickly as he looked up at the stone stairway, trying to calculate if he could carry her. The narrow steps had been risky enough for a lone individual; they would be impossible with an inanimate burden. Once more, Damien looked down at the woman in his arms, and hoping against hope, he searched within himself for that promising ember, that spark that might have been a mote of returning magic. But there was nothing. He was still as powerless as any mortal.

Just then, a paroxysm of coughing racked her slender frame. He set her upright, holding her heaving shoulders as she rid herself of the seawater. Turning her around to face him, he folded her in his arms, holding her, sharing his warmth as she shivered like a leaf in autumn. At last the quivering subsided, and she looked up at him with bewildered silver eyes. Gradually, he saw her shock and befuddlement recede as recognition came; embarrassment quickly followed. Flags of color stained her cheeks.

"O-Oberon . . . Wh-what are you doing here?" she asked, the gray of her eyes deepening with apprehension as she made a feeble attempt to pull away.

"Couldn't sleep," Damien said, keeping his tone deliberately light. "It seemed a fine night to go seeking for mermaidens." Reluctantly, he released her, but when she began to sag, he reached out to steady her once more. "But it would seem, mermaiden, that you have not yet gotten back your land legs. If you would permit me?"

He eased her onto a nearby piece of driftwood and knelt beside her, taking her hands into his and chafing them gently. Although the fear had disappeared from her face, mistrust was still palpable in the tension of those long exquisite fingers. The warm winds played with her wet hair, whipping it out behind her in teasing tendrils. Clouds parted to reveal the moon, and Diana's light seemed to imbue her with a special glow. Like a spellbound mariner in a tale, Damien was drawn to her, nearly overwhelmed by a need to touch, to taste the fruit of her charms.

But that desire dissipated when he saw the look in her eyes, wide as a full moon, laden with horror. As she stared out toward the sea, she began to quiver; not in cold, he suspected, but in shock. Damien had seen the phenomenon before in the most stouthearted of men. In all likelihood, she had only just realized how close she had come to being swallowed by that vast dark deep. A strangled sound rose from her throat like a stifled sob, and her eyes began to glitter. Damien waited for the tears, but they did not come.

She could not cry. If she wept, the Du Le Fey would note that sign of weakness and exploit her vulnerability. She had to be strong . . . could not show fear . . . tears had to be stopped before . . . before . . . All at once, she was surrounded by quiet strength, Rowan turned into the shelter of welcoming arms, like a battered ship finding an unexpected haven.

"Hush." A tender whisper tickled at her ear. "No need to fear now. All will be well." His phrases contained no real magic, mere words, a meaningless incantation as old as Mother Eve; yet they penetrated to the wounds in the most secret recesses of Rowan's soul. No matter that he was an Outsider. No man either stranger or born of the Blood had ever held her thus. Even without violating the sanctity of his thoughts, she knew that his aim was comfort. Kindness spread like a balm.

Damien held her, crooning the same singsong promises of well-being that had helped his little sister over dozens of scraped knees and many more hurtful taunts. Somehow, he felt a need to console, to protect. He stroked her hair gently, letting the wet silky softness slip through his fingers, feeling the rapid beat of her heart against his chest. Looking down into her eyes, he could see her fighting against the tears, blinking them back, closing her lids against the rising tide until the first drop seeped through. With a guttural choke the dam broke, and she wept a flood on his shoulder, the warm salt of her sobs penetrating to his center, touching something deep within him, momentarily filling the void in his soul, beguiling him and at the same time bewildering. Once again, a strange quickening of the heart roused deep within him, a lightening of the soul like the first time that he had been kissed by the bliss of true magic. But before he could examine that curious stirring, it was gone. Mrs. Penham looked up at him uncertainly, unspoken questions on her tearstained face.

When her cup of weeping brimmed, Rowan looked up, half afraid to see loathing in Oberon's eyes. The old comte had abominated any show of emotion even as he had exploited it. Yet, though she had grown adept at reading the faces of men, Rowan found his expression indecipherable.

She knew that she should move away from him. The danger they had shared had forged a powerful bond between them, albeit temporary. Yet, she found it difficult to deny herself the comfort of that contact, for all that she knew it was an illusion. Rowan looked away toward the angry sea and felt the full measure of her loneliness. Who, other than Giselle and Mignon, would have mourned her? A moment of heedless playfulness had nearly cost her life, and with her death, the end of all her daughter's hope.

And his life, Rowan reminded herself, conscious of the gentle weight of his hands upon her shoulder, the solace that seemed to flow when his fingers twined with hers. This man had risked his life for her, yet he had asked no boon, made no demand. Even his touch was a gift, given freely. Simple human contact, the basic succor of a human caress was easily taken for granted, but she counted it a blessing beyond price. In the world of a Mindwalker, even the most casual embrace became a matter of great complexity. An Outsider mind was usually a babel of emotion, intrusive and disorderly, to be shielded against or . . . Rowan shuddered . . . to be penetrated at the risk of losing herself in the deepest thoughts of another, to hazard insanity or a soulless death. Yet his mind did not intrude . . . why?

She swept that question aside, accepting the simple solace of the moment. Rowan found herself wanting more than his light caress. Madness to be sure, but what would it be like to share an embrace that was not a test of trust, a nightmare of tangled minds, an old man's lust, a child's fear and loathing? What would it have been like to be one with a man whose touch she craved? A man like . . . Rowan shook her head at the foolish direction of her thoughts.

"I should have known that there was a storm coming on," she said, forcing herself to step back. Yet she could not bring herself to abandon his touch entirely. Her fingers remained bound with his.

Damien looked out toward the sea and saw that the waves had gotten wilder. Acting on reflex, Damien reached for magic, trying to touch the innate weather sense that was part of his Gift. But once again, it was like a tongue tip searching the aching empty socket of a tooth. Pain surged from that void, reminding him once more of what he had lost.

Still amid that throbbing flood, he felt a tenuous thread of warmth, the gentle pressure of fingers twined in his. The force of life . . . he had pulled this woman from the sea. Coincidence was not a part of a seer's credo, every happenstance was part of the Creator's mysterious designs. In these months past, he had often wondered if there was a purpose to his survival, a meaning. Perhaps this was part of that divine plan.

"I grew up near the sea," Rowan explained, trying once more to read Oberon's expression, but his face told her little. A strange heat seemed to radiate from his touch, like a flame racing through her blood. She wanted to move closer to that source of warmth, to throw herself back into his arms and seek that calming strength, but she could not. Would not.

With the force of hard-learned habit, Rowan cloaked herself in a semblance of composure, willing herself to speak calmly, trying to ignore the fire that was raging inside of her. "If you live close to the ocean, you learn to recognize that there are signs in the winds, in the surf, even in the way the moon looks."

"Are there?" he asked, his brow furrowing.

"Indeed there are," Rowan assured him, trying to gently untangle her hands from his. "Although you might not credit it, I spent most of my childhood by the sea. In fact, I am usually a strong swimmer."

"Are you?" he questioned softly, staring down into those luminous eyes, fighting the urge to taste those trembling lips, to gather her back into his embrace. What in Merlin's name was happening to him? he wondered, telling himself that it was nothing more than weariness, the elation that followed cheating the reaper of souls. Yet, in truth, he knew that beyond those facile rationales, there was something here that defied easy explanation.

Perhaps she felt it too, for she suddenly snatched her hand from his, and he felt oddly bereft. More than anything in the world, he wanted to seize that softness and hold it once again, to warm the creeping cold of despair that was once more chilling his soul. But Damien quelled the impulse, knowing full well it would frighten her.

Her eyes turned to molten silver as she stared toward the rocks at the whitecaps frothing hungrily toward the shore.

"There is no use wondering about might have beens, Mrs. Penham," Damien said.

Rowan looked up at him, startled that he had somehow discerned the bent of her mind. "To the contrary, sir. I have learned a great deal in my life from considering my foolish errors," she said, not bothering to conceal her bitterness.

Aching, she wanted to lean her head on those supple fingers, to feel the touch of someone who did not dread her, who did not wish to use her, but that would be folly. To seek succor in an illusion could only end in disaster. "Perhaps luck was with me this time, but Fortune has never really favored me much before."

To her surprise, he laughed, the deep booming sound mixing with the roar of the breakers. "It would seem that we have something in common, mermaiden; Fortune has never been particularly fond of me either."

"From the look of the sky, the storm that you spoke of may be on its way." His dark head nodded meaningfully toward the now rushing swells. "Since neither of us appears to be among that Lady Luck's select, I would suggest that we remove ourselves from here before that fickle dame regrets her moment of mercy. Or do you wish to remain and place your trust in the sea?"

"Never do I make the same mistake twice," Rowan said, saying it almost with the force of an oath.

"And I repeat mine eternally," he murmured, the wind carrying his words back to her as he took a few steps up the beach.

The tide of loneliness washed over her again as he turned away. She closed her eyes, trying to understand this odd bewilderment.

Her eyes flew open as she felt a change in the substance of the air before her. Oberon was kneeling at her feet. Her shoes and stockings appeared with a wave of his hand. Despite herself, she gasped. "I did not even hear you coming back," she said.

"I am a magician, if you recall," he said, placing her things on the driftwood beside her. "And if you wish to leave this seaside, mermaid, I would suggest that you do so appropriately shod. I suspect those sharp rocks could wreak havoc on your delicate fins." He flashed her an impudent grin. "I would offer to assist, but I know that such improper suggestions might bring your wrath upon me, and a mermaiden's anger is not a thing to be courted lightly."

"Even the most powerful sorcerer would hesitate to cross a sea nymph, Oberon," Rowan said, allowing herself to enter into the ephemeral fantasy. What could be the harm of it? "And you had best see to your own toes master mage, and turn your back till my fins are decently clad, if you would, else you will be turned to stone."

"Egad! Medusa toes?" He clasped his palm against his forehead. "I am doomed to adorn the beach as a stone statue, for I cannot help but gaze in adoration at those ten delightful digits."

Despite herself, Rowan began to giggle even as an ineffable sadness clutched at her heart. Her lip quirked slightly. "A fine mermaiden it is, who nearly drowns in her own element," she said, deliberately turning her eyes away from his bare chest. Though his head was silver, she could see whorls of black hair still slick with the sea at the open neck of his shirt. His trousers were plastered against him, outlining every sinew in excruciating detail with all the sensuous promise of a *selkie. And the danger,* she reminded herself of the old tales of magic folk. *To touch a selkie is to court death by pleasure.* "I feel and look like a piece of storm-tossed seaweed."

From her rueful look, Damien realized that she honestly believed that absurd statement. Like a night-born Venus, her hair fell about her in a dark shimmering wave. Soaked clothing clung to her like a second skin, revealing every curve of her body in vivid detail. "With all those layers of clothing, you might as well have tried to tread water with a bucket of bricks tied to your back," Damien remarked, trying to ignore the lightning stab of desire that seared through him, electrifying to the core.

Tonight she had almost begun to believe in a future. She would have to content herself with dreams for her daughter. Yet these few moments of rapport left her longing for something more. This man before her, his face earnest with concern touched a part of her that had once dared to dream. *'Tis all an illusion,* she reminded herself with a rueful smile. *An illusion woven by an Outsider.*

"And the Siren's smile. I am utterly undone, mermaiden, utterly undone," Damien said, realizing that he spoke the truth in jest. The sooner he could get her home the better. He forced himself to turn away from her, he went down the shore to retrieve his own hastily discarded shoes.

"I am sorry," Rowan said, fastening her shoes, "I am not usually such a watering pot. In fact, it has been nearly twelve years since the last time that I cried more than a tear or two."

"You must have been about thirteen," Damien said, trying to match her casual tone.

Rowan frowned. "How did you know my age?" she asked.

"A fair day skill, taught me by the Gypsies," he answered. "Have you never seen them guess your years for a ha'penny?"

"I have never been to a fair," Rowan admitted, recalling the sounds of raucous music and laughter whose echoes had penetrated even the chateau upon the hill. The Comte Du Le Fey had shunned the Gypsies, perhaps fearing a power beyond his own, but even he had not dared to deny his peasants fair day entirely.

"Five and twenty and never been to a fairing," he said softly. "That is almost as sad as never having cried for a twelve year. But you have wept, and I vow, you will have your day at the fair, mermaid."

"There is no need to make promises you cannot keep," Rowan said sadly, looking out at the sea once more as a shower of spray misted around them. All traces of humor quickly vanished from her expression as she contemplated the wild dance of the waves.

Without thought Damien put his hand onto her shoulder, giving it a comforting squeeze. This time he felt a curious sense of communion, a sharing that held more solace than seduction. " 'Tis hard to credit that it was so calm but a few moments ago," Damien said, speaking as much of himself as of the sea. "You will have a fairing, mermaiden," he said, holding her at arm's length before releasing her. "I have given you my word, and I always keep my promises, Mrs. Penham."

The use of her false name was like the breaking of the spell that had held reality at bay. Though she herself had wished for the end of these enchanted moments, she could not help but mourn.

"Now, shall we try the stair before the clouds hide all the light?" He offered her his hand.

Rowan hesitated, fearing to lose herself once more in the nexus of his rapport. *He saved your life,* she reminded herself. *Are you so poor a creature that you would deny the hand that saved you?* She slipped her palm into his and allowed him to lead her up the path.

During the tortuous climb, she found herself marveling that she had ever found her way down safely. Jagged rocks threatened to trip them. Salt spray made sheer surfaces slippery, reminding her that yet another foolish risk ought to be placed in her dish.

"Hold tight to me!" Damien called above the rising wind. Her fingers were cold, but he held fast, pulling her close before she slid. She gulped a tortured breath in the lee of his sheltering body, hiding her face in his shoulder. The distance to the top seemed interminable. Once he could have used the wind itself to help him . . . Damien ruthlessly dismissed the thought. Though his own existence was worth little to him, to waver now would be to waste the life that he had rescued from the sea. He would have to survive, not as a mage but an ordinary man.

"Come on, now, just a little ways to go." He spoke as much to himself as to her, concentrating upon the task of putting one foot before the other.

Step by step Oberon led Rowan upward, hauling her back from the edge of disaster, teetering with her at the brink as she added chit after chit to her mounting pile of debts. At last they stood side by side at the cliffhead, breathless. Her heart hammered in her throat as lightning illuminated the beach below. Rising tides had swallowed the strand entirely.

"It would seem that I owe you the debt of my life many times over, sir," Rowan said, her voice rough with emotion. "Due to my present circumstances, there is little I can do to show my gratitude. In fact, if my employer finds out about this night, I may well lose my position. But whatever happens, Oberon, even if I must leave here, I will supply you with the means to find me. And if there is anything that is within my power to do for you, you need but ask. Anything, sir, without reservation."

Anything, Damien smiled inwardly at her offer. What could an Outsider possibly offer as a life gift to a mage? Mrs. Penham spoke almost as if she were of the Blood, as if she were offering to discharge a life debt as one of the coven born. But no witch would have been as helpless as she had been. A simple incantation, and she could have been dry on the land in a twinkling.

Yet, even as his amusement tickled within, his imagination began to conjure a thousand different "anythings," the intimacies of his dreams. Damien felt a burgeoning craving, an anger at her heedless pledge. To promise anything? Was she a fool, then? He could demand payment in the most carnal of coin.

But as he looked down into her earnest face, the innocence in her eyes quelled his annoyance. She was an Outsider after all, he reminded himself and could not know how such vows could bind her. Damien shoved his hands into his pockets, trying to keep them off of her, to keep himself from showing her the consequences of making such pledges to a stranger on a stormy summer night. His fingers found the metal frame of her spectacles. Perhaps she still believed that her guise was intact? Better so, better that he remind himself who she was, that she was beyond his touch.

Damien pulled out the lenses and slipped them on her pert nose, mourning the change as the storm-tossed gray was transformed by the hazy mask of glass. Gently, unable to resist, he pressed a kiss upon her forehead.

"Shall I escort you home?" he asked.

Mrs. Penham shook her head, and once again, he could see the signs of returning wariness.

"A governess cannot be too careful of her reputation," she said.

"Have no fear for your position, for I promise that your employer will not know of what passed here tonight," he said quietly. "Go home, Mrs. Penham, and dream well."

Like a startled wild hart, she fled into the trees. Damien frowned and waited a few seconds before following.

Chapter 4

Rowan pulled the last of the nursery windows shut just as the clouds burst. The rattle of the rain upon the roof and panes was a fitting accompaniment to her anger as she castigated herself. How could she have been such a fool, to put herself and her mission at hazard by playing at a child's game? Mignon gave a caw of alarm, and Rowan rushed to her own room. A curtain whipped at her face as she reached for the latch and contested with the wind for control of the frame.

When it was closed at last, Rowan wiped her hands against her damp skirts and reached out to soothe her ruffled familiar. Wordlessly, she crooned until the small raptor's breathing was even and calm. However, her own feelings were more in tune with the chaos that reigned outside. She stood before the window, letting the elemental feelings race through her. The stiffening salt on her skirts wed her with the waves that tossed beyond the rise, the rain on her fingers tied her to the tempest above, the mud on her boots bound her to the earth below.

Thunder raged without, rumbling even as Rowan quaked within. Maelstroms whirled around her, through her. Lightning lashed through the sky, illuminating the lawn and the fringes of the forest beyond. Still, were it not for her heightened senses, Rowan would never have seen the shadow at the edge of the trees.

Oberon.

Even though he was nothing more than a dimmed darkness, she knew that he had followed her in her heedless headlong flight back to Southwood Manor. Heat rushed to her face. What a dolt he must think her! To run like a fox before the pack when the man who saved her life had done nothing more than make a gracious offer of escort. No wonder he had felt the need to see her safe to her door, albeit secretly.

Yet deep within her soul, where truth was the only mirror, she knew that her near encounter with death had little to do with her present panic. In these past years she had walked through the minds of many men. They had desired her, feared her, hated her. Though her husband had tried his utmost to chain that part of her spirit, to make her wholly his tool, he had failed. No man had ever truly touched the most sacred part of her self. Until now. Rarely did Rowan seek her center, for in that repository of a Mindwalker's self, there could be none of the falsehoods that are part and parcel of all flesh and blood. But she did not stare truth in the face, not yet.

Rowan's fingers went unconsciously to her brow, tracing where his lips had caressed her. No stranger was she to the lust that dwelt beneath the most civilized of veneers. She had endured more stolen kisses than she cared to count so that she might creep into the thoughts of those who assaulted her. For the sake of the Du Le Fey's goals, she had suffered the groping of lecherous hands, and with each repulsive contact she had seen the darkest imaginings of their minds.

Rowan strived to recall her perceptions of Oberon's thoughts. Yet, try as she might, she could summon no memories beyond the comfort of his touch, the sense that she was safe in his arms. In the frenzy of her fears, she ought to have been as vulnerable to the tumult of his thoughts as an unshielded child. The Outsider's feelings should have flowed easily into her mind, like water through a sieve. No one, not even a mage, could guard the contents of his heart so completely from a Mindwalker's touch . . . unless . . .

A mindwall? Only once in her life had Rowan encountered a mind that was completely closed, a wizened man who had lost his wife and three sons to the war. Usually, such rarities were the exclusive province of the old, the mental construct of a lifetime of pain. Great sorrow, unbearable suffering, could create a barrier that was nearly impenetrable even to a Mindwalker. Rowan found herself wondering what the Outsider who called himself Oberon could possibly have endured to make his heart into a citadel, his mind into an unassailable fortress.

Perplexed, Rowan drew back from the window, summoning the evening's cavalcade of emotions for review . . . panic . . . relief . . . gratitude . . . comfort . . . apprehension . . . longing . . . desire. . . . However, she realized in shock, these were not Oberon's sensibilities, but her own. For the first time in her life, she had experienced something other than loathing when a man had touched her. And in the worst of ironies, that man was a stranger, an Outsider.

The fleeting light faded from the skies, and the blur of Oberon's outline blended once again into the sudden dark. The Blood . . . it always turned back to that unwanted Gift, always more bane than bliss. Even if Oberon could see her true self, even if he were to know that she was not as ill-favored as she appeared, nothing could come of it.

Her wavering reflection stared back at her in the darkened window glass. Horrified, Rowan realized that her hair was hanging about her in dark waves, and her drenched dress was clinging in a way that was entirely too revealing. Had her disguise been rendered worthless? It was no matter. She was far beneath his touch, and even if he knew who she was, what she was . . .

"Voilà la sorcière comtesse," she whispered mockingly. "The Du Le Fey witch." Many was the time that Rowan had seen looks of admiration turned to abhorrence the moment that the name "Du Le Fey" was murmured. *"Sorcière . . . sorcière . . ."* hissed from ear to ear by those who would not take the risk of saying it aloud. Even in these modern times, the centuries of fear and hatred could not be overcome.

She gripped the sill, her fingers tight upon the painted wood. On the night that the Du Le Fey had ripped away the last fragile vestige of her childhood, she had thought that the pain and bestiality would destroy her, that the twisted malignancy of the comte's essence would ultimately consume her. An untutored girl could never have detected the destroyer that lurked beneath the handsome exterior, the charming manner. As soon as his power was complete, he had discarded the cloak of chimeras that he had woven.

Oberon is no different, she told herself. *You simply cannot see what lurks beneath the illusion, fool.* Yet she could not stop the tears from slipping down her cheeks. When the thunderbolts made their next jagged strikes, the shadowy presence was gone.

Damien's wagon listed slightly as he pulled himself up the steps. Angel whined in annoyance, her black head lifting in a canine gesture of frustration before falling wearily back upon the blankets.

"Quite right," Damien agreed as he peeled off his wet clothing. "I suppose that I don't even have the sense to come in out of the rain. Sorry if the smell of wet human disagrees with you, my friend. However, if you recall, it was you who insisted upon accompanying me on this little venture. I offered to leave you with Mama."

The mastiff whimpered, turning herself around pointedly before closing her eyes with a snort.

"Yes, I know how you feel about her familiar. You are not overly fond of Thorpe, but most dogs share that prejudice against cats, you know," Damien said, hanging his dripping shirt from a hook. Amid the odors of sea, rain, and sweat, a faint whiff of roses reached his nostrils. Her scent. Obviously, it was little more than imagination, since no perfume could possibly have withstood the saturation of rain and waves. Yet he knew with certainty that she would smell of June blossoms.

Dreams again? Or was that knowledge a reality gleaned from his encounter with her and the children upon the road? The lines between fantasy and actuality were blurring once more as Damien recollected those moments on the shore. Surely, his memories were false, as was that feeling of absolute rightness when he held her in his arms. But long training in the art of accurate recollection would not allow him to deny the power of the Outsider woman's touch, almost like standing at the cusp of some unknown force.

She had fled into the night like a frightened deer, running through the gathering storm with a wild grace that had astonished him. His blood pounded as he recalled the heady thrill of that pursuit. Though he had told himself that he only wanted to protect her, to shield her from harm, his savage heart had drummed a battle tattoo. Fortunate indeed that she was so fleet of foot, for his feelings as he watched her close the door behind her had been more akin to rage than gentlemanly relief. Somewhere between the cliff and the lawn of Southwood Manor, he had been transformed into a slavering brute, watching for her shadow in the nursery window. By Hecate, if the moon had been full, he would likely have howled into the light.

Damien mopped the wet hair from his eyes as he put his hand to the lantern about to speak the two-word spell that would produce a spark. But he stopped himself at the first syllable. His fingers trembled as he fumbled for the tinderbox. Again and again, he struck clumsily at the flint until he finally created the first fragments of a flame.

As he nursed the ember and lit his taper, Damien grinned at his achievement. He had been more helpless than a babe at first, suddenly aware of how much he had come to rely upon the simple charms that were almost as much a part of his nature as walking or breathing. Opening a casket in the corner, Damien selected a cheroot. Carefully, he cut the end before setting it alight, puffing in satisfaction until the fragrant smoke rose like incense; another task that he would previously have magicked. Yet now his growing mastery of the everyday ordinary skills of Outsiders brought its own small sense of satisfaction.

Abruptly, the drumming of rain above him ceased. Damien stepped from the confines of the wagon, watching the clouds slip away to reveal a now gibbous moon. Trees dripped the remnants of the rain, and a new washed smell filled the air with the scents of fecund earth.

Damien closed his eyes and banished all thought, trying to concentrate on the simple sensual pleasures of an excellent cigar and a moonlit night. But try as he might his mind kept wandering back to the feel of her hand in his, the wet silken texture of her hair as it rubbed against his cheek, the arpeggio of her voice as it matched itself to the rhythm of his heartbeat. He threw the remnants of the cigar down, mashing the glowing butt with an angry heel.

"Eh, Lord Damien, your smoke gives you no pleasure." Tante Reina sniffed the air appreciatively. "Next time, to me you give what is left. A waste to send such tobacco to the mud."

Damien whirled sheepishly to face the old Gypsy woman. "My apologies, Tante Reina. I am sorry."

"For wasting a cigar?"

Her look was searching, and it took no spell for him to discern that there was another question hiding behind the first. "For wasting the cigar," he said slowly, "and for wasting precious time. You are correct, I still have much to learn."

Her gap-toothed mouth broke into a grin. "There is time still, Lord Damien. You may yet find the answers you seek."

"If only I could puzzle out the questions." Damien ran a nervous hand through his hair.

The elderly Gypsy nodded, her eyes alight. "Ah, so that you have discovered, that you do not yet know what to ask. Is good. Is very good."

"I do not see how," Damien said, leaning back against the wagon wheel. "It seems that just a year ago, I was the most certain of men. My life was like a grimoire, with all the formulas and incantations set out for me to follow. All that was required of me was to do what was expected of me, as had my father and his father before him on back to the Merlin."

The Gypsy smiled. "Ah, so young you are; that will be cured soon enough."

"And now I find that reality is not what I thought it to be." Damien stared up into the clearing sky. "My own sister was desperately unhappy, and I did not see it. My parents lived a sham—"

"No!" Tante Reina said fiercely. "Is not true! Great was the love between Lord Peter and Lady Adrienne. But many faces does love have, boy, and can be found in many ways. In duty and friendship did your mother and father find joy. Now your mother, she finds it with the companion of her heart. Your sister also, she finds her love in the arms of an Outsider."

Once more, Damien felt desire growing in him, like a ravening hunger. "Passion," he said derisively, trying to deny the pulsing of his own heart. "Nothing extraordinary about that. What can an Outsider possibly offer to one of Merlin's kin beyond that passing desire?"

"Still, you have not found the right question, if you yet believe only in such stirrings of the blood. You think truly what your sister and mother found is simple craving? To see in others what they see not in themselves, to give always and ask nothing . . ." She shook her head, her lip drooping sadly. "But teach this to you, I cannot. Is you must learn yourself." She touched a work-worn hand to his cheek and scurried back toward her wagon.

All morning long Rowan had tried to interest the children in their lessons. However, at present, even the fascinating history of good Queen Bess could not fully engage her, for all that Rowan had spent half of her free afternoon immersed in Elizabeth's saga. The comte had deemed history and science, mathematics and literature unimportant to his childwife's education. Rowan knew only what she had taught herself, gleaning and devouring whatever she could. Little did her charges know that their teacher was barely ahead of them in their lessons.

As Davy read haltingly, Rowan moved to the window. Unfortunately, the storm had not cooled the atmosphere one whit, merely added more humidity to the stew. She could almost convince herself that last night had been a strange dream, born in the heat and the new summer moon. But her salt-stiff skirts testified in silent witness, the smell of the sea was still in her nostrils, and the memory of Oberon's touch lingered upon her fingertips and forehead.

Until nearly dawn she had listened to the incessant thrum of the rain and her thoughts. Dreams, when they came, gave her no respite, haunted as they were by a silver-haired Outsider with eyes of jade.

"Why didn't Queen Elizabeth get married, Penny?" Lucy asked.

"She did not wish to share her power," Rowan answered, her thoughts elsewhere. "Elizabeth was no fool to surrender herself to a man who would only wish to use her. Bess knew that she was better off without a man to rule her."

"An excellent explanation, Mrs. Penham, albeit unexpected in the schoolroom," a familiar voice opined.

Rowan whirled, half convinced she had conjured him

from her thoughts. However, this was not the wave-tossed *selkie* that had plucked her from the sea, but the epitome of a gentleman. Fawn-colored breeches molded tightly to his form from the tops of his shining Hessians to his waist. The sound of his words was almost as disturbing as his touch, but in a different way. Deep in timbre, his voice flowed through her like a gentle stream, cool, clear, and for a brief instant, the confusion and fear that had been her constant companions disappeared. Once again, Rowan tried to fathom this mysterious sensation.

"Oberon!" the children shrieked in unison. "You have come to visit!"

Rowan's time in Louis' court had given her more than a passing acquaintance with the tailoring of Weston so favored by Englishmen. One could almost believe that the tailor was something of a sorcerer himself, for no one else could show a man's shoulders to such advantage, highlighting muscle and sinew. Her cheeks flamed; luckily Lucy and Davy were too enchanted with his presence to notice.

"Actually, I am playing footman this afternoon," Damien said. "Your Papa has asked that you come down to the library."

"I shall put the books away, children. You go down to your father," Rowan said, turning away quickly in the hope that he had not noticed her reaction.

"You are to come as well, Mrs. Penham," Oberon added, as the children seized the chance for a respite and scampered down the stairs.

Rowan stiffened, the history book slipping from her hand. Had she been naive to trust Oberon's discretion? What possible reason could Sir Hector have to require her immediate presence at this hour? Unless . . . ? Exhaustion easily inundated Rowan's native caution and flowed into anger, spilling out in words. "I believed you," she said softly, picking the book up once more and setting it on the shelf. "But I suppose it was far too good a story to keep to yourself, was it not? After all, what glory is there in saving a life if no one knows of it?"

His eyes narrowed, but she ignored the danger in that hard green gaze. "Did it make an amusing tale, Oberon? Foolish governess frolics upon the shore and sinks like a stone. Brave, handsome gentleman races to her rescue and saves her from her own folly. Of course no one will believe that she went out in the middle of the night because she could not bear the heat, the loneliness . . ."

"You think that I betrayed my word, Mrs. Penham?" he asked, stepping closer.

"What am I to assume?" she asked wearily. "I have yet to meet a man who could resist self-aggrandizement."

"Perhaps you have been associating with the wrong type of men," he said, his tones deceptively mild.

She piled the rest of the books and went to the shelf. "Bullies and braggarts, the lot of you," she said heedlessly. "I am certain that others will be glad to embellish the narrative, transforming it into a tryst."

"Will they?" Damien said, putting his hands upon her shoulders and forcing her to turn around and face him. "And what face will they put upon that, I wonder? Desperate spinster, seeking to seduce an absolute stranger? Or am I to play the villain's part in this tragedy? I have always fancied the role of rake."

Damien dragged her to him. "But then, if I am truly the rogue you think me, I would have done this last night." He brought his lips down angrily upon hers. How dare she doubt him? Question a mage's word? When he crossed the boundary between punishment and pleasure, Damien could not say. Perhaps it was when her fists ceased to pound ineffectually against his chest, or when she melted into him with a soft sigh? But somewhere within that span of seconds, those distinctions blurred into a glorious haze of sheer sensuality. Damien found himself questing deeper, seeking something beyond the lips that met his so sweetly, beyond the body that fit so well in his arms, searching for something within her that seemed to call out to him.

Rowan moaned, her fists unfolding, her arms creeping around his neck holding him tightly, knowing that if she let him go, she would surely fall. Her legs seemed too weak to support her, and the world was spinning. As she had suspected, his thoughts were sealed tight against her. Even so, the strength of his indignation penetrated those mindwalls, but that anger was somehow shifted, transformed into a blaze of sensation.

Rowan found herself adrift in an unexplored country where a touch did not bring terror and confusion, a place where she reveled in the taste of him, the feel of his fingers, the crisp scent of soap and clean linen that was uniquely male. But beyond her own perceptions was a glimpse of something that was oddly familiar. At the brink she hesitated, tempted beyond measure to let herself go, to seek the chink in his armor, but the fear of what she might find stopped her.

The elusive spark that Damien had felt the night before flared for a moment, strangely like the touch of magic, but unlike any sorcery he had ever known before. Was it in him? In her? Before Damien could explore further, that inexplicable glow was gone, and the void within him yawned even wider than before, devoid of light.

Damien fought his way past that inner darkness, opening his eyes to the woman who trembled in his arms. Her eyes were smoky with alarm, and he was startled to realize that he had given her more than ample cause for that fear. What was he becoming? He had never before touched a partner who was less than willing. Had all his convictions vanished with his Gifts?

"Mrs. Penham! Oberon!" Davy's insistent voice drifted up from below.

"I shall tell them that you will be down shortly," Damien said, in growing shame and confusion. "Your secret is safe, believe that, Mrs. Penham."

There was a plea in his eyes, as if her response was somehow important to him. "Yes, I believe you," Rowan whispered, surprised to find that she truly gave credence to his claim.

Damien paused uncertainly at the stair, knowing that he ought to ask forgiveness, but he could not find the words. Now that attention had been drawn to their absence, he risked compromising her by staying. From her state of disarray and bemused look, it would not require extraordinary perception to guess what had happened here. "Join us as quickly as you are able. I—I—I had better go."

As the door closed behind him, Rowan's fingers went unconsciously to her lips. She leaned against the wall, forcing herself to breathe deeply, willing her heart to slow from its rapid race. Painstakingly, she reassembled the shards of her dignity, even as she smoothed the fabric of her bodice to conceal the evidence of his caresses.

Quickly, Rowan ran into her room, grateful that Mignon had already departed for France. Her familiar was too meddlesome by half and not easily deceived. The physical contact required for stealing secrets from the depths of minds had often left Rowan fighting amorous men who wanted far more than a mere kiss. Unfortunately, Mignon had seen the aftermath of far too many of those assignations to be put off by tales that she might fabricate.

That hard-won experience guided Rowan's fingers as she smoothed her hair, rearranged her fichu, and splashed water on her burning cheeks. For her kiss-stung mouth there were no rapid remedies. However, a quick glance in the mirror showed that otherwise she was once again all prunes and prisms, the prim and proper governess.

While the face in the glass was the very picture of calm, Rowan's mind was in a tumult. As she descended the stair, she could not help but think of another more precarious staircase, the strength of his hands, a gentle coaxing voice. How could she have forgotten? She was indebted to Oberon for her very existence. In her world kindness had always masked an ulterior motive, and an altruistic deed had been as likely as Lucifer tendering his apologies to the Light.

Rowan halted at the library door, listening, judging. The excited cadences of the children's voices was entirely at odds with the dismal scene of exposure and denunciation that she had constructed in her mind.

Sir Hector's jovial greeting confirmed that Rowan had been a fool. Lady Stanhope sat in her usual chair, wearing her customary frown of incipient indignation. Diana sat beside her mother, gazing surreptitiously at Sir Hector with the adoration of a spaniel pup.

"I am sorry for the delay, Sir Hector . . ." Rowan began.

The baronet waved her apologies aside. "No need, Mrs. Penham. Oberon has already explained. 'Tis I who should be scolded for disrupting the children's studies, but I just could not wait." He smiled with a delight that was almost boyish. "Why do you not explain it, Oberon?"

"If you wish," Damien said, looking at her directly for the first time. His breath caught in his throat as he gauged the measure of the change in her mien. Once more, she was the essence of the unassuming servant. Her countenance held no vestige of feeling; the blush was smothered. Even her words were calm and measured without so much as a trace of heat. *What hellfires had forged this woman into steel?* he wondered. *And what suffering had tempered her?* "The children and I have a proposal to make to you."

"A proposal?" Rowan asked, her chin rising slightly in a gesture of challenge. "Of what kind?"

"I am so sorry, Mrs. Penham," Sir Hector said as he rose from behind his desk. "I really ought to have consulted with you before letting the cat out of the bag, especially knowing how you feel about maintaining a strict schedule for the children."

"Oh, please, Mrs. Penham," Davy said, coming to Rowan's side. "It will be ever so much fun, and if you let us, we will be extra specially good. We promise. Say 'yes.' "

" 'Yes' to what?" Rowan asked, looking around her in puzzlement.

"I cannot fathom why you persuaded Mr. Oberon to waste his time, Sir Hector," Lady Stanhope interjected with a disparaging sniff. "As if little boys would need lessons in making things disappear! And as for the propriety of teaching females to produce handkerchiefs from the air, I would not allow it were I you, sir. Many a match has been made due to a lady's felicitous need for a clean bit of cloth, I say. Any decent gentleman would be able to supply one for your Lucy should she require one!"

Faster than the eye could follow, Oberon produced two brightly colored bits of silk, and presented one to Lucy and the second to Diana. The girl giggled, while the young woman turned a lovely shade of pink.

For Rowan, there was nothing. Though she told herself that he was halfway across the room, that he was doing her a favor by not paying her undue attention, she felt perversely slighted and then annoyed. As he continued to ignore her,

Rowan's contrition began to dissipate. How dare he kiss her? What right had he to make her feel so utterly . . . confused.

"Does your mama know that you spend your days upon such nonsense?" Lady Stanhope asked, singularly unimpressed by the trick.

"She is well aware of my peculiarities, Lady Stanhope," Oberon said with a half smile. "And if it is any comfort to you, milady, she is no more pleased with how I choose to while away my time than yourself."

"Obviously, your mama is a discerning individual. Far better to spend your time in your family seat at . . . where did you say that your family resides?" Lady Stanhope raised her lorgnette as she posed the question.

"I did not say, milady," Oberon said pointedly.

"And Adam Chapbrook is your friend?" she asked, her disapproval patent. "Spends his time tilting at windmills, is what I hear, but there is no doubt that the man is among the cream of the ton. Recently married, they say, something about the bride's family, odd kick to the gallop I am told."

"I have the honor to call Brand my friend, Lady Stanhope," Oberon interrupted. "But at present, 'tis best if I remain incognito." He turned to Rowan once more. "If we might discuss the matter at hand, Mrs. Penham. I have offered to tutor Sir Hector in the art of illusion. However, he has requested that I instruct the children as well."

All eyes, censuring and hopeful focused on Rowan. Magic lessons . . . her breath caught in her throat.

"I certainly hope the governess has the sense to put a period to this lunacy before it starts," Lady Stanhope said, fixing Rowan with a basilisk stare.

Oberon walked over to stand before Rowan. "I would not wish to interfere with your regime, Mrs. Penham. So I suggested that it would be best to apply to you first."

"Lessons in illusion?" she asked. Only years of hard-learned control kept her from quivering like a dowsing rod that has found water. She searched those enigmatic eyes and found them carefully guarded.

"Exactly," Sir Hector said enthusiastically. "But only if you give your agreement."

"It is entirely your choice, Mrs. Penham," Oberon agreed.

Rowan wanted to laugh. Her choice! Choice was only illusion, as were all her hopes and dreams. But while she had always known that her fate had been etched before her birth, her loneliness and desperation had never driven her this far before. That an Outsider would invade her fantasies was the outside of enough, but to react to his presence like a witchling at her first Beltane was beyond belief.

Perhaps her capricious imagination had focused upon him because she owed him so much, but she knew that her thoughts had been bent in his direction before her life debt was ever incurred. Since that first meeting on the road, he had haunted her. *And before that,* her private voice reminded her, *you have dreamed of this man before, always.*

"And what would you teach them, sir?" she asked, trying to silence those absurd secret murmurs, telling herself that Oberon's kiss had come more out of scorn than desire. She reminded herself of his friendship with the illustrious Lord Brand, whose name alone was enough to send Lady Stanhope into a social twitter. Oberon probably thought himself well above a mere governess' sphere. Still, although she ought to have felt relief, she once more felt a peculiar disappointment.

"I would be instructing them in simple skills, really. Vanishing coins, kerchiefs, and hoops, nothing that might be beyond the capacities of a deft child," Oberon explained.

Envy shot through her. *Simple skills,* he called them. These younglings would soon have the very bread and butter that she had long starved for. *And they will be with him,* her inner self whispered jealously. But any impulses to deny Lucy and Davy's obvious wishes died at the sight of the hope on Davy's face.

"Yes," she agreed with a sigh. "I will allow magic lessons."

"I told you, Oberon!" Davy whooped. "I told you that she was a great gun, didn't I?"

"But there is one provision," Rowan added, raising her voice above the din.

The children eyed her anxiously, and Oberon regarded her with a wary expression.

"You may only learn magic after your regular lessons."

Rowan paused, as two heads nodded solemnly. She tried to swallow her resentment at the unfairness of fate. For these little ones, the achievements of her birthright would be nothing more than an amusing diversion.

"Well, I suppose that is settled," Sir Hector said, starting to seat himself at the desk.

"Not entirely," Lady Stanhope said. "Who will be supervising these lessons? Surely, you do not intend to leave your dear children in the care of a man who, after all, refuses to reveal his identity. He could be an absolute bounder."

"Mama!" Diana said, stricken. "What of the letter of introduction that Sir Hector was given?"

"From this trickster's own hand? Letters can be forged!" Lady Stanhope declared in the sonorous tones of authority. "Now, if Master Oberon would simply tell us his family name, I am quite certain that we may be entirely assured of his veracity." She raised her lorgnette and peered at Oberon. "If the governess will remove the little ears from the room, you can utterly rely upon our discretion, sir."

"There is no need for Lucy and Davy to leave, Mrs. Penham," Oberon placed a restraining hand on Rowan's shoulder.

Though the touch was but a brief one, Rowan tried to analyze the effect, like a bellows upon a fire, stirring embers to flame. *Take care, lest you burn yourself by coming too close,* she warned herself.

"I fear Sir Hector will have to make his decision without those facts in his possession, Lady Stanhope," Oberon said.

Though his tones were measured and polite, Rowan could sense the anger beneath, held carefully in check.

"I will superintend the lessons, if that would help," Rowan offered quickly before her instincts for self-preservation could come to the fore. After that searing kiss, the less that she saw of Oberon, the better. Yet Rowan could no more resist the opportunity than a toper could forego a bottle. "Will that not satisfy propriety?"

Relief and disappointment warred with temptation. Although Damien had disliked the idea of using the children as a source of information, the opportunity that Sir Hector had inadvertently given him was too fortuitous to reject. Often, the activities of a household, its comings and goings, however concealed or denied, would be well-known to a child. In their youthful candor, Lucy and Davy were not likely possessed of much discretion.

But with the governess hovering in the background, there would be precious little opportunity to direct the conversation and revelations to his purposes. Given what had just occurred in the nursery, the possibility of spending time with her each day was only slightly less hazardous than puffing a cigar in an armory filled with powder kegs. Even now, though she wore her dowdy guise, he could see the sea-drenched Siren lurking behind the panes of those spectacles. Those wondrous gray eyes regarded him with a direct gaze.

"It would be too much to ask of you, Mrs. Penham," Damien forced himself to say as he tried to dispel the memories of that kiss. "I had not even considered the boredom you might be subject to, watching the constant repetition of simple sleights of hand."

"To the contrary, sir," Rowan replied, her tones pert. "I should be glad to learn alongside my charges. A governess can never have too many skills inside her carpetbag."

"Well, then," Sir Hector declared, "we are all agreed."

"Not all!" Lady Stanhope's chins quivered in indignation. She rose from her chair, like a ship of line whose sails have caught the full wind. "Do not say I did not warn you, Sir Hector, when this ends in disaster."

"Mama!" Diana looked at her mother in exasperation. "You must excuse her," she addressed the company, "the heat has overset—"

"You will not make my excuses to a governess and a charlatan, my girl," Lady Stanhope bellowed. "As for Sir Hector, if he will not heed good advice, then I wash my hands of this matter entirely! Come, Diana!" She sailed from the room, leaving a wake of dismay behind her.

Diana burst into tears and rushed out toward the terrace.

Sir Hector looked toward the door, then out toward the garden, his face stricken with indecision. "If you would excuse me," the baronet murmured, rising hastily to follow the weeping young woman.

"Lady Stanhope was not nice to say such things," Davy

said. His lower lip began to tremble as if he was about to weep himself. "And she made Diana cry."

"Lady Stanhope is worried about you and Lucy, Davy," Rowan said quietly, cupping the boy's chin in her palm and smoothing back his hair. "Because you have no mama, you see."

Damien listened to her mild reply in surprise. The old termagant had insulted the governess, not to mention himself, yet he could detect no indignation in her voice.

"But why did Diana cry?" Davy asked. " 'Tis not at all her fault that her mama was a rudesby."

"Sometimes children tend to blame themselves for their parent's shortcomings," Damien said, putting a hand on the boy's shoulder. "The young lady is embarrassed that her mama chose to express herself in an unseemly manner. Perhaps she felt that she might have prevented Lady Stanhope's outburst."

"But what could Diana have done?" Lucy asked doubtfully.

"Nothing," Damien said, bending at the knees until he and the girl were eye to eye. "Lady Stanhope chose to act as she did. Parents are responsible for the choices that they make, Lucy, remember that. We are not to blame for what our parents do."

He looked into the puzzled child's face, and felt a stab of regret for the innocence that was soon to be lost. Once Sir Hector's web of intrigue was sundered, these children would inevitably be sullied by their father's treason. What expectations could there be for the son and daughter of a traitor? Their lives would be shattered, and he would be the instrument of their doom. "It is not your fault," he said softly. "Always remember that you are not to blame for your father's failings."

"We are not speaking of Sir Hector's imperfections," Mrs. Penham admonished sharply. "But whatever our family's faults, society will forever judge us in the shadow of our loved ones, fairly or not. If that day should come, keep your lip stiff, Davy. Never show them tears, Lucy, and hold your head high. Do not allow them to discover your weakness . . ." Her voice trailed off, the adamant tone fading as her eyes met Oberon's.

Mrs. Penham's cheeks blossomed in color, and Damien glimpsed the remnants of deep pain beyond those concealing lenses. She had been hurt, badly hurt, and her description of the feral nature of society was bang upon the head of the nail. There was something fleetingly forlorn about her, but as quickly as it came, that momentary fragility faded.

"Run upstairs, now, children, and continue the essays that I set for you yesterday. If you wish to begin those magic lessons tomorrow, then you had best show me that you can have your work finished before dinner," she said, a wistful half smile taking some of the bite from her command. "I will be along soon to read what you have written."

Even as she spoke, Damien could almost see her rebuilding her barriers. The lines on her forehead smoothed, the gray sadness in her eyes sank back into the hidden depths. One by one, all signs of emotions disappeared, like the view behind a frosted windowpane. She turned, ostensibly to watch the children leave, but Damien knew that she was trying to regain her control.

He sauntered to the bookshelf and pulled a title at random, giving Mrs. Penham some time to recover her composure, waiting for her to speak. As he leafed through the pages, he wondered who had taught the governess those hard-learned lessons, to keep all vulnerability hidden, to take shelter behind the fragile shield of pride. *"I am not usually such a watering pot,"* last night's words reverberated in his mind. No wonder, if she had been taught to dam her tears lest they reveal weakness.

"I hope that you will forgive that last outburst, Oberon, and the one in the nursery as well," she said, softly. "I did not sleep too well last night. I owe you far too much to make such baseless accusations."

"I am not wholly blameless, Mrs. Penham," Damien said, shutting the tome with a snap, unaccountably pleased that she too had spent a restless night. "If anything, it should be myself begging for your understanding, and though I did not sleep much either, 'tis no excuse for my behavior."

"No, it is not," Rowan agreed, trying to keep from smiling

at his look of surprise. "Shall we call it pax for now, since we are bound to work together, and try to start anew."

"One may forgive, Mrs. Penham," Damien said quietly. "But forgetting, that is somewhat more difficult."

"Perhaps it is best not to forget," Rowan countered. "If we forget, then we repeat our errors."

"And you never make the same mistake twice, I remember," Damien said, setting the book on the table.

"And you are 'forever repeating them,' " Rowan recollected.

"So you did hear what I said on the beach," Damien said with an amused smile.

"You forget, Oberon, a governess's ears must be extremely sensitive, so that she may hear the hushed voices of her charges plotting against her," Rowan replied, relaxing slightly.

"You seem to have the children well in hand," Damien commented. "You care for them."

" 'Tis no less than the terms of my employment," Rowan said, trying to deny.

"No, 'tis more than that," Damien said, searching her face. "You appear to honestly care for their welfare, else you would never have spoken as you did." She shrugged and said nothing. "I have been down the pike often enough to recognize the voice of experience when I hear it. What you told Davy and Lucy was no less than the truth," he added. "Society is a pack of jackals that preys on the weakest of the herd. But a continuous pretense of impregnability is far too much to expect from a child."

"Is it?" Mrs. Penham asked, her eyes silvering into mirrors that seemed to reflect his most hidden thoughts. "Illusion is the only defense of the powerless, Oberon. A child will pretend that the blow does not truly hurt, though the pain makes her head reel. A wife will smile and dance with the man who causes her to lose her fear of hell, since his anger can always burn hotter than Hades itself if she fails to fool the public. An inferior servant will swallow every slight and galling insult with a deferential smile, lest she offend and lose her place."

Frustration grew within him, rage at a desire he could not seem to control. "And what of pride?" Damien asked, mar-

veling at her containment. Her voice did not falter or tremble, her countenance was a blank canvas, yet somehow he
knew that she was speaking of herself. She was that child and
wife as well as the servant. For a flickering second, banked
embers burned in the ashes of those eyes, and he wondered
how it was that she had not been wholly consumed in the
conflagration of her life.

"Pride, sir, is a luxury that only the powerful and the
wealthy may afford," she said, with a smile that held no
humor.

The concept was a difficult one for Damien to comprehend. Price was all that he had now that he was a mage no
more; pride and the slender hope that his Gifts might someday return. How could one survive without pride?

"Ah, poor Oberon!" A ghost of a smile touched her lips.
"Are you one of those mighty oaks, sir, who has never had to
bend before a powerful wind? I can well believe you are a
pink of the ton, despite Lady Stanhope's doubts." Her voice
held a hint of laughter.

"And you, Mrs. Penham?" Damien asked. "What tree are
you, then?"

"A middling sort of tree that bears fruit that no one in his
right mind would savor . . ." Her voice trailed off as if she
had unwittingly revealed too much.

Though the timbre of her tone was matter-of-fact, he
wanted to gather her into his arms, to soothe away those
long-ago hurts. But he could not touch her; he dared not after
what had just happened upstairs. "Not a willow, then?"
Damien was curious, but before he could question her further, Sir Hector returned to the terrace door.

"Ah, Oberon, Mrs. Penham, so glad that you waited," Sir
Hector said.

There was no necessity for Rowan to touch the baronet's
mind to discern what had occurred. His cravat was crumpled,
and the damp stains upon the linen caused her to suspect that
the waterfall knot had assumed a function in keeping with its
name. Still more indisputable was the look in Sir Hector's
eyes. A curious combination of guilt and glory was manifest
in his expression, like a child who has raided the pantry and
found the jam jar.

Far more successfully than any charm that Rowan could
have uttered, the encounter in the garden had encouraged the
romance between Sir Hector and Diana. Silently, she vowed
to do all that she could to help smooth the girl's path to Sir
Hector's heart. It would be Rowan's parting gift to the
Southwoods, a means of compensating for causing Lucy and
Davy to care for her. The children would need a mother, and
Rowan acknowledged a certain degree of satisfaction in seeing Lady Stanhope's grandiose schemes for a more exalted
alliance confounded.

"I was admiring your excellent library, Sir Hector,"
Damien said, turning to the baronet with relief. "You have
quite a collection here, I see." He picked up the book that he
had been browsing.

Relief flooded Rowan that the conversation had turned
from trees. Why in the world had those words spilled so
heedlessly from her mouth? A little more description, and he
might have guessed that she was speaking of a rowan. Even
for an Outsider, a name could be a thing of power. To reveal
her true name under the circumstances would be foolish beyond permission.

"This edition of Durien is quite rare. He was a contempo-
rary of Nostradamus, if I recall." Damien said, handling the
vellum-covered volume reverently.

Rowan's head jerked up. Durien! A Du Le Fey seer. What
was a book of Durien's prognostications doing in Sir Hector's library?

"Indeed." Sir Hector pulled another book from the
shelves, cradling a white vellum-covered folio. "I would
wager that you could not tell me what this is, Oberon, for all
that you seem quite knowledgeable."

Rowan stifled a gasp. *The Grimoire for Novices.* All these
weeks, the book that was the primer for every mage and
witchling had been nestling on the shelves in plain sight. Her
attention had focused instead upon the section that dealt with
the knowledge required to maintain her charade. Eagerly,
Rowan scanned past the men into the corner of the library
that she had never bothered to peruse.

The comte had placed his entire library under a binding
spell, effectively locking those books against her, but these

were not sealed by magic. Her fingers curled into fists as she forcibly restrained herself from reaching out to touch the knowledge that she had long hungered for. Here were grimoires both modern and ancient, books on magic and illusion, volumes upon philters and alchemy. All had been mutely waiting if only she had thought to look for such treasures in the possession of an Outsider.

"I believe that is *The Grimoire for Novices,*" Oberon answered readily, to Rowan's surprise. "Also quite rare."

"Lucky I did not place any money upon your ignorance," Sir Hector said with a guffaw. "Yes, this is an exceptional example of a grimoire and quite genuine, I assure you, though you can see that the writing appears wholly unintelligible. Supposedly, it is something of a primer for young witches, if you would believe that. According to lore, the printing would be entirely readable if one has magical powers."

"Indeed," Damien said, the corner of his mouth lifting slightly. "That is said to be true of some grimoires. However, I am sure that you have found that there are many that are comprehensible, although cryptic."

Rowan moved closer, peering over the baronet's shoulder. *"Spelle for freshening drye cowe"* the page was titled, but before she could read any further, Sir Hector closed the folio. Her hands fairly itched with longing to grab it from him, to touch the heritage that had been denied to her for so long. Her patrimony, in the hands of an Outsider who could not even read it!

"I was told by the seller that any witch who could not interpret this grimoire was put to death," Sir Hector said, setting the volume reverently in its place.

"From what I have learned, such witches merely found it difficult to marry among their kind," Damien said, looking up at the shelf as he recalled his sister's plight, a woman of the Blood without magical skills. Could Miranda have been happy with a mage? Would a husband born of the Blood have looked down upon her for the skills that she lacked? But Damien's musings ended when he saw a spine of scarlet amid the bindings. He whistled softly. *"The Black Grimoire . . ."*

Involuntarily, Rowan stepped back. She had hoped to never see the obscene horror of that bloodred cover again. If *The Grimoire for Novices* was the primer for the magic of Light, this was the ultimate text for the deacons of the Dark. Fortunately, both men were so intent on the book that neither noticed her reaction.

"Just what is lacking in my collection, Sir Hector," Damien said, watching warily as Sir Hector casually pulled the volume from its place. "Would you be willing to part with it for say . . . a thousand pounds?"

"I am not certain, Oberon," Sir Hector said, frowning as he leafed through the pages. "To tell you the truth, I paid less than a hundred for it, and I have kept it on my shelf solely because of its rarity."

Damien stared at the volume. He had to gain possession of *The Black Grimoire* at any price. "As you say, it is not an oft found book. I will pay you fifteen hundred for it."

There was a stubborn set to the illusionist's jaw, and Rowan held her breath, praying that Sir Hector would refuse to sell and that the ancient receipt for evil would remain forgotten and unused in the dark recesses of the library.

"If you want the wretched thing, I will gladly give it to you," the baronet said with a sigh. "Though I cannot discern the scratch of the writing, I vow that there is something about this book that disturbs me."

Rowan listened in silent horror. Yet another black grimoire was about to move out into the unsuspecting world. As Sir Hector had sensed, the evil volume had its own aura, a power that could agitate or fascinate. In the hands of an Outsider, it could cause no harm, but in the hands of a dark-driven child of the Blood, it could become a deadly force. It was the one book that the comte had never barred to Rowan, for it served but one master, its lawful owner. The grimoire changed hands only upon purchase or death, usually the latter. Rarely did a master of that grimoire die of natural causes.

"I insist upon paying you for your costs. 'Less than a hundred' I believe you said?" Damien pulled out his purse, and swiftly began to count before the baronet had a chance to change his mind.

"Totally unnecessary," Sir Hector murmured. "But if you

wish, I will accept your money. It may sound strange, Oberon, but I feel almost as if I have cheated you."

"How so?" Damien asked, his head inclining slightly in curiosity as he laid down the last of his ten-pound notes.

"Having paid good money, I could not bring myself to throw that bargain of mine away, but I confess that I will be glad to have it out from under my roof," Sir Hector said, with a nervous chuckle, putting the money into the drawer. "I vow that I feel almost giddy with relief to have it gone."

Oberon threw Sir Hector a look of patent puzzlement, and Rowan wondered how the illusionist could fail to feel the raw evil emanating from that scarlet cover, a binding dipped in blood, if the legends were to be believed. Sir Hector was entirely correct, Oberon had gotten the bad end of the bargain. For one who could not use it, the volume served as a disturbing influence, a magnet to misfortune.

"I will take it with me when the camp moves on, if you would not mind," Damien said, holding the volume gingerly and putting the filthy thing back in its place as swiftly as he could. He had hoped that his magical impotence would dull the book's sorcerous effect, but his arm felt as if it was afire and beneath his shirt, his band was like a burning brand. He was hard-pressed not to scream with the pain, but there had been no help for touching it. It was part of the ritual of possession. "My wagon is not quite the best storage for a rare volume."

Sir Hector waved his hand with a smile. "Please feel free to take it any time that you choose and avail yourself of the rest of my library if you wish."

"Until tomorrow, Mrs. Penham," Damien said with a bow, trying to keep his teeth from clenching. "Would four o'clock be acceptable?"

It took Rowan a moment to realize that he was asking her about the magic lessons. "Yes," she agreed, "four would be a good hour."

Chapter 5

Take me with you ... take me with you ... As Damien left through the terrace door, the echoing demand faded. Despite the hot sun beating down upon his head, he shivered. Now the book was his.

Horror mixed with a perverse thrill, and he felt almost like a little boy, playing with the contents of his father's gun case. But no matter how great that temptation, Damien knew that he dared not touch the trigger. That same breathless sense of danger urged him on even as his common sense warned him away. In that brief touch the insidious darkness had called to him, promising him pleasures beyond imagination, strength beyond ken.

Damien knew that he had to destroy it as soon as he could, but a book spun of dark magic could be undone only by sorcery. Though his own powers were gone, Midsummer Night was fast approaching, a time when the old magic was strong in the earth. Fire and the light of a midsummer moon, would provide the force needed to end *The Black Grimoire*.

When he reached the edge of the forest, Angel raced toward him, barking a greeting. Damien was about to pet the mastiff's silky head, but his hand stopped in midair.

"Sorry, my girl," he said, reaching down to wipe his palms against the fabric of his trousers. No matter that the book had been in his hands for mere seconds, he felt as if he had wallowed in unspeakable filth. Living water was the only thing that could cleanse him. "Tell Tante Reina that I will need fresh clothes, and if she can make one, a charm to protect me against the influence of *The Black Grimoire*. I have just purchased one."

Angel bayed mournfully.

"There is no help for it, my friend," Damien said. "I had

no choice. Unfortunately, I am presently as helpless as a newborn witchling with not a spell to protect myself from its evil, so whatever Tante Reina can provide will have to do. You will find me down at the beach."

As Angel loped toward the Gypsy camp, Damien sped toward the ocean. Taking the stone stairs almost too swiftly for safety, the mage began to peel away his clothing. Hopping along the pebble-covered strand, he shed his boots and plunged into the surf. Over and over he submerged himself, letting the waves clean away the foul taint until he felt the miasma of the book dissipating. Finally, as he floated to the surface, he allowed himself to think.

Of all places to find a Black Grimoire . . . Even Sir Hector had noticed the loathsome taint of evil . . . a puzzling notion. With all the corruption rampant in the world, there were precious few Outsiders who could still sense a baneful presence. Yet the baronet had somehow felt The Black Grimoire's pollution so keenly that he had been veritably eager to rid himself of the ancient volume. Surely, the man was no mage, else he would never have sold away a source of awesome power. Moreover, Sir Hector had been willing to give it away and then reluctantly accepted a Petticoat Lane price.

There were many more pieces to this jumbled puzzle than Wellington had imagined. But as Damien tried to fit those segments into place, not a one seemed to fit. Certainly, any man who had supposedly sold his honor for France's coin would not whistle fifteen hundred pounds to the wind. And if the legends associated with the grimoire of shadows were true, the ability to recognize its depraved nature was seemingly an indication of purity of heart.

The task that Wellington had set forth in Adam's library had seemed absurdly simple: bring the traitor and his cohorts to justice. But now Damien knew that the innocent would suffer along with the guilty. Still, mage or not, so long as Damien wore Albion's band upon his arm, he was bound to protect England's interests. Yet the image of the jovial baronet dancing on the gallows for the amusement of a hanging day crowd filled Damien with a profound sadness.

Remember your duty, he told himself. *Think of something*

else . . . anything else . . . With every stroke images of Mrs. Penham filled his mind. *Dark hair spilling across his shoulder in a silken cascade, catching upon the bristle of his unshaven face, every sensation alive to the touch of her, the taste of salt upon her skin, upon his lips, moon and cloud, darkness and light, the anticipation of the storm, rain falling in needles upon his skin as he watched for the light in her window, her fear, her despair, the shudder of her warm soft body in his arms.*

In vain he tried to summon other images, to conjure up memories of other women whose favors he had enjoyed. But his efforts were like a spell gone awry. Each one of them wore her face, their hands became her hands, hair blond, brown, or copper swirled into a screen of ebony that cloaked his skin in a sheet of heated sensation.

Damien swam deeper, trying to make himself one with the rhythm of the tides, but even in that shadowed fluid world, her image haunted him. She floated before him, those full lips curved into a sad semi-smile. *You are the chief mage of England . . .* In the uncanny silence of the deep, his mind repeated the words like an incantation as if he could banish her presence with the reminder of who he was, what he owed his family, his Blood. *She is an Outsider . . . Outsider . . . Outsider . . .* But no matter how many times he intoned those silent phrases, that ache of longing remained, and the knowledge of his loneliness gnawed at him even as his hunger for her grew.

Rowan stared out the nursery window, scanning the skies with longing. Although she knew that Mignon would not return for another day, she could not help but yearn for the small bird's companionship. Since Rowan's coming-of-age, the merlin had served as her confidant, adviser, and friend. Even the comte had not dared to deprive her of the animal companion. Yet, although the merlin was wise in many ways, Rowan doubted that she would be able to explain her extraordinary behavior.

What was it about Oberon that banished her discretion? Never before had she been so loose of tongue, divulging far too much of things felt, but best left unspoken. Life's hard schooling had taught her the necessity for concealment. Information was a weapon, and a revealed vulnerability was a flaw that would inevitably be exploited. Yet, whenever he was about, she found herself violating those laboriously learned lessons.

Lucy groaned, and Rowan turned to see the girl grabbing for the sand to blot an ink spill. She smiled, and though Rowan tried to maintain a frown, her lips tilted inexorably upward.

"Nearly done, Mrs. Penham," she said.

Rowan nodded, her throat tight as the curly head bent back down to concentrate upon the paper. She reminded herself that any attachment could be dangerous, be used against her. Her husband had always watched carefully for any incipient signs of fondness, and utilized that affection to punish and manipulate her.

When she was newly wed, there had been one roan stallion that she had particularly favored. No one, not even the comte had been able to break his spirit and tame him. Every morning Rowan had gone to the stables, bearing gifts of sugar and carrots in an effort to win Falada's wild heart. Day by day she had spoken to him, worked to gain his trust until he had finally allowed her into the saddle. How proud she had been, how foolish . . .

Unwillingly, her mind went back to a long-ago night. Her first mission, the first time her husband had demanded that she prostitute her powers for him. In her fear she had failed to get all the information that he wanted. However, to her surprise, when she returned to the chateau, the comte had neither ranted nor raved at her inadequacy. Instead, he had smiled and dismissed her.

The next morning she had gone down to the stable, and there, stretched upon the wall, was Falada. The stallion's skin had been flayed from his body, his head, still dripping blood, was mounted above it, staring sightless in silent rebuke. She had turned, ready to run, to scream, but the comte was standing behind her, smiling. No words were spoken, but she fully understood his mute message.

There were faint marks still upon her knuckles, impressions of her teeth as she had bitten deep into her own flesh to keep those cries of horror sealed in her throat. From that day forward she had worked to quell any sign of affection, any chink in her walls of indifference. But Giselle's birth had given him the ultimate weapon, the perfect lever to force her into . . .

"Mrs. Penham?" Concern laced Lucy's voice. "Are you well?"

"You look white as a ghost," Davy added anxiously.

"Just the heat, I suppose," Rowan said, swallowing the bitter taste of her memories. "Are you finished yet, with your essays?" The two children nodded.

"Then we will go down to the beach for a while. Would you like that?" Rowan asked. Perhaps she might be able to find some momentary peace in that tranquil place.

"Oh, yes," Davy said, "that would be splendid."

Damien slipped the clean shirt over his head, trying to keep hold of some measure of patience. As he dressed, Angel yipped incessantly, scolding her master in a worried whine.

"I swear you must be the reincarnation of a nanny," he said at last. "You must think me little more capable than a child."

Angel growled a rejoinder.

"Kind of you to remind me," Damien said, slipping on trousers over his small clothes. "Yes, I know full well that as a mage, I am impotent. Yes, I am quite aware that *The Black Grimoire* might easily come to possess me, but in order to destroy it, I have to own it. Though Tante Reina's magic might not wholly counteract the book's influence, whatever she may contrive will have to do, I suppose."

Angel lay down on the pebbled strand with a whine, covering her muzzle with her paws.

"I know what *The Black Grimoire* can do to me," Damien said irritably. "I also know the havoc it can cause in the wrong hands."

He bundled the wreckage of his hastily shed garments into the sack that Angel had carried, and tossed them out into the waves, watching them sink into the deep. When he washed his hands once again, he felt cleansed at long last.

With a sigh Damien bent to stroke the mastiff lightly on the head. "I have to find my way on my own now. You cannot treat me like a blind-eyed newborn pup forever."

Angel nuzzled him gently, whimpering in apology.

Damien smiled. "I know that you worry, Angel. In fact, I confess that I am a trifle nervous myself these days. Stay here and stand guard; I want to have a look down the beach.

Damien set off along the strand, looking for signs of a hiding place. Last night's storm had carried off the bit of driftwood that had been Mrs. Penham's seat. He shook his head, trying to bring his mind back to Wellington's business. The sooner he put an end to it, the better. Just offshore, there were some openings that might lead to caves. He was about to explore further when he heard Angel's warning barks. A woman and two children were just down the path. From the hound's hasty description, it was Mrs. Penham and her charges. "Let them come, Angel," he commanded.

Davy came down the stairs first, scrambling at a little-boy pace that had Damien's heart in his mouth.

"Careful, Davy," he called.

"Pooh!" the child said as he jumped the last three steps. "You sound just like Penny." His eyes widened as he saw the black mastiff standing at Damien's side. "I thought that I heard barking, but I wasn't sure. Is she yours, Oberon? She is very beautiful. What is her name? May I pet her?"

Damien laughed. "I vow, lad, you question faster than a barrister before the bench."

"Davy, remember your manners," Rowan remonstrated as she and Lucy followed the boy down at a less hazardous pace. "If Oberon finds your conduct unruly, he might not be so willing to teach you magic."

"Beg your pardon, Oberon," the boy immediately declared. "Didn't mean to be rude."

Damien suppressed a smile at the boy's face; though the tone was sincere, there was more than a bit of rebellious devilment in his eyes. "Yes, it was my dog that you heard. I agree, she is a beauty. Her name is Angel, and she enjoys being made much over if you are gentle about it, and if Mrs. Penham agrees, you may both pet her."

Davy looked at his governess, and she gave a curt nod.

Both children moved eagerly toward the mastiff. Damien watched to make certain that the two were not plaguing his familiar, but Angel's eyes were alight with canine ecstasy. As a mage's companion, the Gypsy children treated Angel with distant respect. It had been a long time since there had been younglings to properly adore and rollick with her. The trio were soon running along the shore, whooping with glee as Angel chased after Davy's ball, rounding the rocks. Their governess began to go after them.

"There is no need, Mrs. Penham. Angel will keep a watchful eye on them. She has the instincts of a nurserymaid when it comes to young ones," Damien said as the breeze made her dress billow softly, playing with the tendrils of her hair. "I take it that the essays are done?"

"They were almost finished by the time that I came up to the nursery," she said, her hand going up to shade her eyes as her charges disappeared from view. "It would seem that you were able to work magic without even being present, sir. And now you have caused Davy to apologize without a minor tantrum."

"Ah, so now you know the extent of my power, Mrs. Penham," Damien said, willing her to turn, to look at him.

Her gray eyes were turbulent, haunted, but in a blinking, all signs of disturbance were gone, like ripples caused by a breeze across a placid pool.

"I can only guess at your power," she said, her Welsh lilt flavoring the words. " 'The wisdom of the ancients,' I believe you said. That and the width of your purse make you formidable indeed. Fifteen hundred pounds is quite a sum, sir, more money than most people see in a lifetime, much less expend on a single book that cannot be read by most mortals."

"By most mortals . . ." Damien picked up the last phrase and examined it. "Do I take it that you believe that the grimoire *can* be read by some? Do you place credence in magic, then, Mrs. Penham? Not the tricks of hand that any trained idiot can manage with a modicum of skill, but real magic?" Even as those last questions slipped out, he wished them back between his teeth. What right had he to question her about her beliefs? As if it mattered whether she put faith in magic or not. Yet, as he waited for her answer, Damien found that it mattered very much indeed.

She hesitated. "I do not think that Sir Hector was wrong about the book that you purchased, Oberon." The governess spoke slowly, choosing her words with obvious care. "For all that you were prepared to pay a fortune for it, it is still a Dutch bargain, an object of evil that will do you no good."

A paradoxical glow of satisfaction lit within him. Outsider though she was, she was sensitive to the evil grimoire's emanations. He bent down and picked up a pebble, hurling it into the waves. "And what would you have me do with my valuable purchase, then?" he asked.

"Throw it into the depths, like you did that rock," she said, with a vehemence that surprised him. "Burn it if you can, but do not keep it, Oberon, if you value your peace."

Once more, he caught a glimpse of embers that flamed and then were abruptly extinguished in her eyes.

"Now you must believe me a superstitious fool," she murmured, looking down at her shoes, "in addition to being a reckless one."

"No," Damien said. Though he knew that he ought not to touch her, he reached out to cup her chin in his palm. Gently, he raised her head until her eyes met his. She blinked rapidly, as if trying to stem a tide of tears. His fingers traced the ridge of her cheek. "I do not think you a fool. You feel something that you cannot explain or touch, but unlike most, you do not attempt to dismiss or deny. You risk ridicule and attempt as a friend to give me warning. It is I who would be the fool, if I rejected your well-meant cautions."

"You understand."

There was audible relief in her whisper, but he could feel her tension. Damien knew that his touch was the cause, but he could not bring himself to let her go. He could feel the pounding of her pulse as his heart began to hammer a counterpoint. She cared enough to express her feelings about the grimoire and chance his mockery. Gratitude? Or could there be something more?

Did she share this strange bond, like an invisible cord, drawing him closer? The light puff of her breath upon his wrist stirred him until the urge to kiss her was almost unbearable, but he resisted, trying to break the spell with words as he forced his hands away. "As for your supposed recklessness, I account it no crime to seek a respite from this wretched heat, any more than I blame Neptune for trying to snatch you."

A smile lit her face, utterly transforming her countenance.

"Neptune has poor taste, it would seem," Rowan said with a wry smile.

"To the contrary, Mrs. Penham," Damien said. "The sea god is known to be most discerning."

"And just what would Neptune have wanted with me?"

Perhaps just what I am beginning to want. But Damien was not doltish enough to utter that thought aloud. "Have you ever wondered why the gods would always be trifling with mortals? I have always thought it because they could never quite trust their own kind. There was not much in the way of friendship up on Olympus or under the waves."

"So you believe that Neptune was seeking a friend?" Rowan said, amused. Friendship . . . she understood the relationship in theory, but other than Mignon, she had never experienced that type of connection, a companion who did not demand as due, an equal who might give without thought of gain. Was this, then, the power of a friend's touch, this strange communion without words?

"I cannot answer for Neptune, but I can ask for myself," Damien said. "Shall we be friends, then, Mrs. Penham?"

"Why?" Rowan asked, unable to accept the invitation at face value. Her thoughts twirled like a carousel as she searched for some reason for his strange request. "I am a governess, a nobody, and I really know nothing about you, beyond the fact that your purse outstrips your common sense. Likely you are a scion of some exalted branch of aristocracy, far above the likes of an upper servant like myself."

He regarded her intently, saying nothing. Obviously, he had been swimming, for the sweep of quicksilver hair across his brow was still wet, and his patches of damp caused his clothing to cling tight to his body. Rowan forced herself to focus on his face. Although the change in his demeanor was minute, a sudden glimmer of his jewel eyes sufficed to confirm her words. "Is this some part of your game, Oberon, to bemuse foolish mortals as did Shakespeare's King of Faerie, your namesake? Come to think of it, I do not even know your real name."

She took a step back, forcing herself to move away from the reach of those caressing fingertips, fighting this dangerous compulsion. Her dreams came to the fore with tantalizing force, and she ached to touch that sun-toasted skin, to kiss those sensuous lips with all the strength of sudden craving. She had never desired a man before, never felt this confusing longing that overwhelmed all good sense. But that was not what he professed to want from her. Friendship . . . "True friendship is a rare commodity, sir, a gift that I have experienced only once in my lifetime. If you mean this as a jest, it is a poor one. I ask you once more—'why?' "

Bewilderment passed like a cloud across his face, the arches of his eyebrows knitting as he seemed to struggle for words.

"There are some things that are difficult to explain, Mrs. Penham," Damien said, trying to elucidate something that he did not quite understand himself. "All that you say is true, and I cannot for the life of me think of a way to make you believe me. I suppose that I am luckier than yourself, for I have found more than once that which you rightly call a most precious gift."

Sun touched the heart of his jade eyes, coloring them with an amber core as he met her quizzing gaze.

"I suppose that I could attempt to convince you with platitudes. However, that would be less than honest, nor do I think it would persuade you. Though we have known each other for less than two sunsets, I feel something, a link that I cannot quite fathom myself." He brushed the wet silver of his hair back from his cheek and took a step toward her, leaving less than the breadth of a palm between them. "Perhaps it is because we nearly died together last night, but whatever the reason, I cannot deny it." He lifted his hand as if to touch her once more, but let his fingers fall limp to his side. "Can you gainsay it, Mrs. Penham? Or is this connection entirely a product of my own fancy?"

Every instinct demanded that she contradict him. All her years of training told her that the only safety lay in a total refutation of his absurd assertions. Irrational to admit that she shared this madness, but the appeal in his eyes was too strong. "I am told that there are many friendships forged on the battlefield . . ." she began.

"Just so," Damien agreed. "I have seen it happen very often."

"You were a soldier?" Rowan asked in surprise.

"Aye, there is blood on my hands," he answered, the aching look of guilt in his eyes matching the pain in his voice. Rowan knew at once that she had discovered one part of the unseen wall that guarded him against a Mindwalker's touch. Horror and remorse were securely mortared into a barricade beyond her ability to penetrate. Though she had never taken a life with her own hand, she knew what it was to be an instrument of destruction. How many men had died based on the information that she had provided for the comte? How many more would die when she provided Etienne with the means to free the Corsican from his cage?

Perhaps this was the source of the current that flowed between herself and the Outsider, a connection far deeper than the momentary attachment of shared danger. They were two lonely citadels built upon a river of pain and suffering. Once again Rowan contemplated the full magnitude of her debt. He had given her life; could she deny him compassion?

Tentatively, she reached out and put a hand upon the illusionist's shoulder. "No matter what fine names they put upon it, 'patriotism,' 'honor,' 'duty,' it is always so, Oberon, blood is always the currency of war," she said softly.

Damien's hand came up to cover hers, squeezing her fingers with tender pressure, letting her solace penetrate the wounds he had guarded for so long. Even as her touch comforted, it filled him with shame. Friendship was all he could honorably offer, but he wanted more, far more.

"I am beginning to believe that no one is wholly in league with the legions of heaven or in collusion with cohorts of hell; right or wrong are based upon a biased point of view," he said sadly.

"In the end, though, we all do what we must to survive," Rowan said.

"Survival?" Damien made the word into a question. "Is that enough?"

"No." She shook her head, and her smile was rueful. "But sometimes it is the best we can do, my friend."

My friend . . . Sympathy flowed from her, a healing unguent upon those invisible hurts that had festered for so many years. Beyond the gray veils of her eyes, he caught a momentary glimpse of an anguish that mirrored his own, a need that was all the more aching because he felt its throb within himself.

His hand rose slowly to smooth back a stray lock of hair from her forehead as he sought for an answer in her eyes. The curtains of her lashes parted, revealing puzzlement, pain, and wonderment. Her fingers rose to touch his cheek, all the permission that he required as he bent his head.

Though Damien had shared many a night with muslin company, he had never bared anything more than his body. The darkness that had tormented his being for so long, the stains upon his soul, had always been his alone to contemplate, to mourn. Even among those who loved him, no one else knew, except perhaps, for Angel. However, for all the dog's intelligence, an animal mind could not comprehend the moral dilemma posed by war. In a mastiff's view of the world, the death of the weaker was only to be expected. Kill or be killed was a credo that a hound might easily understand.

Even as their lips met, Damien was still attempting to deceive himself, trying to persuade himself that he was doing nothing more than returning the favor that she had granted, solace for solace, friend to friend. But beneath the simplicity of flesh upon flesh was a burgeoning demand.

His arms slipped around her neck, and he clasped her to him as if he could somehow absorb her into himself. The throbbing ache of his past calmed for the first time in memory, banished beneath the total assault of his senses. All at once dream and reality melded into one, but this was no phantasm in his arms.

Her lips were soft and yielding, but she responded with the shy innocence of a green girl. With reverent wonder Damien deepened the kiss, questing once more, as if he could somehow find the source of this mysterious peace. Slowly, the emptiness within him was replaced with an emotion that he had never before experienced outside the bliss of his magic . . . pure, unadulterated joy.

Rowan was drawn into a whirlpool of sensation. She tasted the salt on his lips and savored the clean sea scent in her nostrils. As he pressed closer, a dozen years of memories flooded her mind . . . men . . . all the force of their lechery as they tried to seduce her . . . use her . . . all their pretenses of civility crumbling before their basest longings. Would the wall in Oberon's mind hold strong against this tide of feelings? Or was she alone driven by this swift, relentless current?

Rowan braced herself for the impact of unshielded emotion, but the Outsider's fortress did not yield. Relief was tempered by disappointment. She had half hoped to catch a glimpse of the person who hid beyond that wall. Perhaps then she might rid herself of these extraordinary notions and exorcise him from her dreams.

After all, he was just a man, like any other, driven by lust. But even though she could not touch his thoughts, she knew that there was more to his caress than the urges of the male appetite. For the first time in her life, Rowan tasted sweetness in a man's kiss. Cold fear melted in a wave of engulfing heat, setting her alight from within. His touch was gentle even as it threatened to shatter her to the core.

Her husband had often likened her to an ice woman, incapable of warmth. Now Rowan knew that this too was a lie among so many others. The comte himself was the winter that had frozen her heart. With this gift of friendship, Oberon had given her a promise of spring, and with that thaw came a hope that she dared not admit, not even to herself.

All of her life, she had dreamed of being held thus, with a tenderness that made her feel both fragile and strong. A lifetime of caution urged her to end this madness, but her body would not bend to the will of reason. Her fingers rose to twine themselves in the tangled damp mass of his hair. She leaned against him, letting his arms support her as she gave way to her secret fantasies, knowing that from this day, the phantom of her nights would have a face, Oberon's face.

The fine linen of his shirt, the azure sky, the cry of the gulls, the flavor of his mouth, his scent, Rowan sketched it all upon the canvas of her trained memory, determined to savor this moment forever. Though she knew that no man would ever touch her again, hold her this way, she would have this scrap of time and the knowledge that she was capable of passion.

A sharp bark echoed in the rocks. "Penny! Oberon! Come quickly!"

Rowan broke guiltily from Oberon's embrace just as Davy came running around the outcropping.

"Lucy has cut herself, Penny, and it's bleeding ever so much." Tears of fear were streaming down the child's face. "She fell on a rock, and it is all my fault."

Before the boy finished, Damien was sprinting across the strand, leaping boulders with the power and grace of a stallion. Rowan held Davy in tow and followed the illusionist to find him already kneeling by the weeping girl's side.

" 'Tis far better than it looks, Mrs. Penham," Damien said, hastening to reassure her. "These surface wounds tend to bleed prodigiously."

"I should have been with them," she groaned, looking at the flowing scarlet gash. "If I had only—"

"This would likely have happened anyway," Damien cut her off, unable to bear the guilt in her eyes. "My Mama would say that children are required to eat a peck of dirt and bleed at least a pint before they pass into adulthood. Lucy is just taking care of the latter requirement."

"It is not your fault, Penny, but mine," Davy said, starting to cry again. "I was chasing Lucy about with a crab I found, and she ran, and she fell and . . ."

"You are going to help make it up to her now," Damien said, nipping the tears in the bud. He reached up to unbind the loose knot of his neck cloth, then with his teeth, he started a rip in the fabric. "If I had become the watering pot every time my sister had come to grief through my plaguing, I would have cried an ocean. Stop the tears and give us a hand, lad."

With a sharp pull Damien tore the cloth in half. "Go dip this into the water, Davy," he commanded, giving the boy a piece of the linen, "and hold it high as you bring it back. We need to clean off some of the dirt and gravel."

Davy ran and returned quickly with the dripping cloth.

"It hurts," Lucy wailed. "It hurts so much."

"And this may make it worse for the moment," Damien said, smoothing the child's forehead, wishing he could use the tools of his magic. A simple sleep spell, and she would feel nothing, but he was as helpless as any Outsider with no power to ease Lucy's pain.

"Take my hand, dear," Rowan said, the pebbles digging into her knees as she knelt at the girl's other side. "While Oberon binds you up, let us pretend, Lucy. Make believe that the pain is going through you, and you are giving it to me to hold."

"Like a package?" Davy asked.

"Like a package," Rowan agreed, reaching for the red writhing knot of hurt in Lucy's mind.

Damien watched as the child sniffed doubtfully through her tears, but she slipped her fingers into the governess's palm. Mrs. Penham stroked the girl's cheek and began to sing a Welsh song. Though he did not understand the words, Damien could feel the current of calm in what was obviously an ancient lullaby. Beneath his hand he felt the girl's tension ease with the soft, lilting rhythm.

Taking the cloth from Davy, Damien swiftly began to cleanse the grit and dirt from the wound. To his surprise, Lucy did not flinch away beneath the sting of the saltwater as he wiped the crusting blood.

Mrs. Penham's voice faltered for a moment, and he glanced up to see that the color had drained from her face. The governess bit her lip. "Go on," she whispered hoarsely. "Go on. I shall be fine."

Damien set the torn slice of skin back into place. "You are a lucky girl, Lucy," he said as he wound the dry cloth around the child's knee. "That rock cut like a razor, and you might not even have so much as a scar to show for this."

"It hardly hurt when you cleaned it," Lucy said.

"We magicians are known for our light touch," Damien

said, tousling the child's hair. "But you, mademoiselle, are a most extraordinary patient."

"You're a great gun, Lucy," Davy agreed, bestowing his highest accolade. "Why, Penny looks like she had worse of it than you did. I would have been screaming bloody murder."

"We do not curse, Davy," Rowan said, her voice faint as she struggled to manage the burden of Lucy's pain, to extricate herself from the girl's jumble of emotions, but Rowan was tired, her own feelings in too much of a turmoil.

Damien glanced at the governess and saw that the boy was entirely correct. The woman looked as if she was about to keel over.

"The sight of blood, I am afraid," Rowan explained with a weak grimace. "Give me a moment or two to get back to myself, Oberon."

Damien nodded and turned his attention to the cliff stair, glad of the fine weather and the daylight. Lucy would not be able to walk, but the child appeared to be an easy burden. It was the woman that concerned him. "Get help, Angel," he said softly. The mastiff barked and raced up the stair.

"Up with you, little one," he said, lifting the girl carefully. "Let us see if you are as light a bit of thistledown as I think you are."

As he rose, Lucy clutched her governess's hand, nearly pulling the woman up with her. But Rowan could not scramble to her feet quickly enough to maintain the child's grip.

"Ohhh." Lucy sighed, her eyes fluttering closed as she went limp in Damien's arms.

Rowan gasped sharply at the tug of Lucy's consciousness before it snapped, releasing Rowan's mind from its grasp.

"I am surprised she did not give it up before now, poor mite," Damien said, shifting his burden over his shoulder. "Now, do not dare to faint on me, mermaid, else you will disappoint me. I had not supposed you to be a milk-and-salt-water miss."

"I would not dream of causing you disappointment, sir," she said, taking a deep breath as she drew herself upward.

In the space of a few seconds, her color had vastly improved. Still, there was an unhealthy pallor to her cheeks and a strain lurking about the corners of her eyes.

"You need have no fear about having to carry us both up the stairs. 'Tis Lucy that must concern us now. The sooner that she is seen to, the better I shall feel," Rowan added.

Damien nodded, assessing the rapid change in Mrs. Penham's countenance until he was satisfied that she had recovered sufficiently to make the climb. "The Gypsy camp is nearer than Southwood Manor, and I would sooner trust Tante Reina's healing abilities than the skills of the finest Harley Street quack."

To his surprise, Mrs. Penham made no protest at his choice. Slowly, they made their way up the stone steps.

Chapter 6

Halfway down the cliff path, they were met by a group from the Gypsy camp. At the lead was the man who had shared a wagon seat with Oberon the other day. Rowan dredged his name up instantly. Dominick.

"Tante Reina is waiting," Dominick said, carefully taking the small burden from Oberon's hands.

Rowan's brow rose in puzzlement. How had they known the situation? But as they reached the caravan, anxiety overshadowed all questions. A small wizened woman approached hastily, beckoning them toward a shaded spot where blankets had been spread. Though her brown eyes were rheumy, there was an air of calm competence about her as she directed the placement of her patient. Rowan relaxed marginally.

"Slow, slow," the Gypsy woman instructed, bending to place a rolled blanket beneath the girl's head. With a gesture she dismissed the members of the tribe. "Tell me all."

"It is my fault!" Davy said. "I was chasing her, and she slipped on a rock and her knee was all bloody."

"Nonsense, Davy," Rowan said. "I should have been watching you both more carefully. If it is anyone's fault, it is mine."

"And you, boy?" Tante Reina asked, her gaze fixing on Damien. "I know better than to believe you will take any share of blame, eh? What part do you have in this?"

Oberon's face flamed red, and Rowan knew he was recalling those moments on the beach. What would have happened if Davy had not come running, she wondered? In all her days she had never so utterly lost control of herself. She could feel her cheeks beginning to burn.

Tante Reina eyed both of them with a shrewd gaze and

nodded toward Damien. "Never did this one accept blame, missus, in all his days. You would do well to know this," she said, addressing herself to Rowan as she undid the bandage. "Always, always, poor Miranda, she is left to take scolding."

"His sister? He said that he tormented her," Rowan said, seating herself on the ground next to the Gypsy.

The old woman's brow wrinkled. "Told you of Miranda, did he?"

"I have admitted some of my sins, Tante Reina," Damien said, with a sheepish twist of his lips.

"A good beginning! A good beginning!" Tante Reina exclaimed with a cackling chuckle, but she fell silent when she looked at Lucy's wound. She clucked softly. "Poor little one. Is well-done, the cleaning, the binding. The pain must it have been great. No wonder she faints."

Damien nodded. "She was far braver than many a soldier that I have seen. I must admit, it surprised me that she remained conscious through the whole. It was not until I was entirely done that she swooned."

"But Penny nearly fainted!" Davy piped up.

Tante Reina turned her assessing eye on Rowan once more, and the young woman nearly wilted beneath that frank appraisal. Lucy's pain transference was already taking its toll. Only rarely had Rowan ever before called upon this aspect of her Mindwalker's Gift, for the risks were considerable. If Death came to call when two were mind-bound in pain, both members of the link would perish.

While Rowan could not actually heal a wound, she could diminish the pain, but only by taking it into herself, feeling the agony as if the injury was in her own flesh. Although there had been little chance of such dire consequences in Lucy's case, if the child's grip had not loosened, Rowan would likely have fainted along with her.

"The blood," Rowan murmured by way of explanation. Even though she knew that the dull throbbing in her knee was merely a phantom remnant of Lucy's hurt, it made it feel no less real. "The heat."

"True enough, Tante Reina," Damien corroborated Davy's observation, still concerned by the governess's wan countenance. "Of the two, I could have sworn that Mrs. Penham was the one more in need of sal volatile."

"Aye, maybe the blood," the Gypsy said sotto voce, returning her attention to her patient. "All that can be done, done it you have, boy, and done well."

Once again, Rowan wondered about Oberon's identity. Without question the man was a product of the world of privilege. While clothes and mannerisms could be easily acquired or feigned, his unconscious hauteur, his air of command attested more certainly of his connections than a page in DeBretts. Yet his face lit with pleasure at the Gypsy's praise, like a little boy who has been unexpectedly complimented by a strict schoolmaster. This old woman had obviously known him from childhood.

"Sir Hector? You sent word of his daughter?" Tante Reina asked as she gently wrapped the wound again.

"No," Damien said, worry furrowing his brow. "I wanted to wait until I heard what you had to say before I dispatched the news to Southwood. Quite frankly, I am not certain if it is a good idea even now. Perhaps we can wait and bring her directly back to the manor."

"You fear how Sir Hector will feel if he knows I care for his child?" The old woman asked, with a shake of her kerchiefed head. "His wife, came to me for herbs to ease her pain. Help her, I did, when no Gajo doctor could. For this service, Sir Hector gives this camping place to my people. Lucy's father will not be angered by you bringing her here. Go, milord, and tell him that all will soon be well."

The Gypsy's casual use of the title was yet another confirmation of Rowan's suspicions, and Oberon's rebuking frown was again one more. Milord . . . mentally Rowan added a rung upon the ladder of hopelessness that separated her from Oberon. But though he was as far removed from her sphere as Hades from heaven, she could not deny her bemusement.

Oberon . . . how fitting that he had chosen to hide behind a name from Shakespeare's tale of magic and benighted lovers. Rowan had always had great sympathy for the queen of the fairies, vengefully enspelled by her husband and the roguish Puck, but in that sympathy had been a small measure of scorn. Now Rowan knew what it was to have her senses stirred by a man who was no more suitable to her than Shakespeare's humble mechanic, Bottom, had been for the Faerie Queen.

At least poor Titania was excused for her unseemly choice by reasons of ensorcellment. However, try as she might, Rowan could pretend no such extenuating circumstances for herself. Any enchantment was of her own weaving, the product of her fantasies and emotions.

Unlike the bard's unfortunate queen, there was no happy ending waiting for her, neither forgiveness, nor redemption, nor joyous celebrations would be Rowan's lot. For her, there would never be a mate, a lover who would open mind and heart to her in complete union. At best, if she fulfilled her task, she would have her daughter back and perhaps a measure of peace. But as she watched Oberon leave the camp, she knew that peace was too much to hope for, and happiness was impossible. She could ill afford to play the role of Titania.

Damien sprinted across Sir Hector's lawn, Angel loping along at his side. Although his walk to Southwood Manor had been accomplished at a deliberately leisurely pace, the dash would achieve the effect of a hasty run. While Tante Reina was entirely confident in the continuity of the baronet's goodwill, Damien was less than sanguine. Any promises made by Outsiders to Gypsies were usually contingent upon whim, and since Sir Hector was a known traitor, his ability to honor his bonds was already in doubt.

At this juncture the last thing that was needed was for Sir Hector to chase the lot of them off his property with a kick for a "fare-thee-well." Damien had little doubt that the child would recover as Tante Reina said. However, Damien thought it far better that the baronet find his child conscious and coherent. With any luck at all, Lucy would have had sufficient time to return to the waking state before her father appeared on the scene.

The terrace doors to the library were open. Briefly, Damien hesitated, wishing that he had one of Tante Reina's charms to counter the influence of *The Black Grimoire*.

Even upon the threshold, wisps of its baneful presence were already hovering at the edge of the mage's mind. Unfortunately, the reality of present circumstance would not be changed by mere wishful thinking. Sir Hector was visible at his desk, and there was nothing to be gained by further delay. Damien rapped upon the glass, effecting an audible pant as Sir Hector waved him in.

"Take a good sniff about, Angel," Damien quietly told the mastiff before pulling the door open.

"What brings you running neck or nothing, Oberon?" the baronet asked, rising in apprehension. He walked to the sideboard and poured a glass of brandy. "Tell me what is wrong, man, and then take a drink, for from your face, I would guess that you might need it."

"Your daughter has been injured," Damien said.

"Lucy!" Sir Hector's florid face blanched.

"Just a gash upon the knee, that is all and bound up quickly," Damien hastened to reassure him.

"Where is she? I must go to her at once!"

"Mrs. Penham is with her, Sir Hector," Damien said, keeping his tones soothing. "We took her to the Gypsy encampment, since that is nearest."

"Is the old woman they call 'Tante Reina' still dispensing her nostrums?" the baronet asked.

Damien nodded cautiously. "Aye," he said, and took a sip from his drink.

Sir Hector relaxed visibly. "I could not want for a better physician. Nonetheless, I will go right away. But first, I must tend to these." He gestured toward the desk and hurried around it to gather up a pile of papers.

There was no need for Damien to see the seals upon the documents to determine their origin; a mound of dispatches from Whitehall. Wellington had planned to increase the amount of information being sent to the baronet. The more that Sir Hector received, the more likely that he could be caught in the act of passing them on.

"Why not just leave them, Sir Hector?" Damien asked. "Surely, no one will disturb them while we are out?"

"To be sure," the baronet agreed. "Nonetheless, I cannot allow these to be lying about."

"Of a sensitive nature?" Damien inquired, taking another sip of brandy as he gauged the man's reaction.

Sir Hector smiled stiffly. "Bluntly, yes. I hate to ask, Oberon, but if you might wait outside for a moment, I shall join you directly."

Damien inclined his head, telling Angel with a look to keep her eyes open. "Of course, Sir Hector. Despite Lord Brand's recommendation, I am, after all, unknown to you. I shall wait on the terrace. I will take this with me, if you do not mind; t'would be a shame to let it go to waste."

Brandy in hand, the mage exited quickly, ignoring an impulse to detour to the bookshelf. *The Black Grimoire* was whispering again. As he went through the glass doors, Damien's heel touched the frame gingerly. The door swung slightly inward, changing the angle of the glass. No backward look was necessary to know that Sir Hector was observing Damien's exit. He strolled toward the shaded part of the terrace, causing his boots to strike the stone in a deliberate stride.

The mage leaned casually against the balustrade, savoring the brandy as he watched the angled glass. As he had hoped, the reflective qualities of the polished surface afforded him a fair view of the activities in the room. If Fortune favored him, any activities that were beyond Angel's line of sight would be visible to him.

Sir Hector had already gathered up the jumble of papers and headed for the bookshelves. He looked pointedly toward the terrace door before fumbling at his neck cloth. Pulling forth a gleaming key, the baronet reached up above his head and pulled a volume forward. Slowly, a section of the shelf swung away.

Sir Hector's bulk blocked the rest of the procedure, but it was simple enough for Damien to determine that there was a hidden vault behind the shelves. An examination of the baronet's private papers might be exactly what was needed to bring matters to a close. Damien was facing the lawn when Sir Hector came out the door. Turning, the mage placed his empty glass upon a stone table. *The Black Grimoire*'s call seemed to grow louder, and his head began to

ache with the whisper that now seemed to grow to a muffled
roar.

"My apologies, Oberon, but . . ." the baronet began with
a shamefaced expression.

Damien waved his hand in a gesture of dismissal. "Think
nothing of it," he said. "Only a fool would take offense at a
justifiable precaution."

"Good thing, then, that you ain't a fool," the baronet said,
running down the steps with surprising speed.

Rowan dipped the cloth in cool water. Through the fog of
pain, she reached for the girl's mind, sending her sweet
dreams of swimming in the ocean and raspberry ice. Lucy
smiled, and Rowan felt a growing sense of satisfaction. *This
was what I was meant to do; this is the true purpose of my
Gift.* Davy's head lay in her lap, hiccuping sobs disturbing
his slumber. Despite all assurances, the poor boy continued
to blame himself for his sister's injury. Weariness notwith-
standing, Rowan gently slipped amid the tangle of Davy's
guilty thoughts, and planted a seed of solace. *Lucy will recover,* she told him silently, *there is no need to fear.*

A gnarled hand came to rest upon Rowan's shoulder.

"You are worn out, missus," Tante Reina said, her hoary
eyebrows knitting in concern. "Here, drink."

Rowan started at the unexpected touch, bracing herself
for an onslaught of Outsider thoughts as she quickly
shielded herself. But the only emotions that the witch could
discern were plain upon the wizened woman's face.

Rowan recalled once again the reasons for her late husband's fear of the Romany. Their minds were inscrutable,
and they were possessed of a magic that was all their own.
Rowan took the mug gratefully, sipping the hot sweet liquid.

"Rest," Tante Reina said, shaking a scolding finger.
"What good will you be to little ones if you are spent?"

"I must be here when Lucy wakes," Rowan said, fighting
to hold her eyes open. A night without sleep and the events
of the day were finally taking their toll.

"Call you, I will," Tante Reina promised, "soon as she
stirs."

The thought of stretching out was almost irresistible. "No," Rowan shook her head. "I could not."

"Only a step away is empty wagon." The Gypsy woman folded a blanket and smoothly shifted the little boy to the makeshift pillow. With unexpected strength Tante Reina tugged at the governess's arm. Reluctantly, Rowan rose, wincing as needles of inactivity pricked at her legs.

"But what if they wake while I am away? They are among strangers." Rowan said, recalling her first waking away from home. The comte standing over her bed . . . staring at her like a ravenous animal . . .

Tante Reina shook her head. "Strangers we are not. Sir Hector's children know us well. 'Tante Weina,' the boy calls me when he learns first words." The old woman's lips curved in a coaxing smile, as she urged Rowan along. "See how close is wagon."

Rowan was surprised to find that she was standing at the wagon's stair. Indeed, it was as the Gypsy said, no more than a few steps away from where Lucy slept.

"I call; is promise," Tante Reina said, noting the wavering expression in the young woman's eyes. Though the tea that she had prepared was only mildly soporific, its effects were magnified by weariness. She helped the governess up, ushering her in to the dimness of the wagon.

Inside it was surprisingly cool, the open doors in back and front letting the breezes waft through. With a sigh she settled herself upon an inviting nest of blankets, letting herself drift. Just as she was about to cross the border between sleep and waking, she caught a familiar scent, the faint odor of soap and cigars that was almost like a physical presence. . . . Oberon . . .

With an effort Rowan forced her eyes open once more, scanning her surroundings in the haze of half-light. Hung upon pegs were a variety of men's garments, colorful Gypsy garb side by side with Bond Street's tailored splendor, strands of silk kerchiefs, and shining brass hoops adorned the walls. Oberon's wagon. His shirtsleeve stretched across the pillow, its linen folds brushing against her cheek.

Rowan tried to compel herself to rise, but her limbs felt as if they were filled with lead. It was dangerous to be here, surrounded by his belongings. But the bliss was already upon her, filling her with its comforting glow, restoring the well of magic used in the service of the Light. With a soft sigh she put her head down and surrendered to dreams.

Tante Reina dipped a cloth into a newly drawn bucket of spring water. Lucy's eyes flickered open.

"Tante Reina," the girl whispered in confusion. "Mrs. Penham, where is she?"

"Now, I will fetch her," the Gypsy woman said, rising to her feet.

"Please," Lucy said, grimacing as she attempted to move. "I want her to take away my pain again. My leg aches so."

"Take away pain?" the elderly Romany queried, a hoary brow rising in question.

"It sounds foolish, but when she holds me, 'tis as if she is taking the hurt from me," Lucy whispered, self-doubt in her voice. "She told me to give the pain into her hand. I thought that was silly, but it hurt so much . . . so I pretended to pass it along to her, and somehow . . ." The girl's forehead wrinkled in puzzlement. "But that cannot be, can it?"

"Many things may be." Tante Reina glanced toward Damien's wagon pensively as she considered the mage's account of the accident. The governess had nearly swooned, but the child had not reacted. Was it the power of a clever suggestion that had relieved the girl's pain, or was there another force at work?

Tante Reina muttered to herself, remembering Damien's face as he had looked upon Mrs. Penham, the hunger within the glance that he had tried so hard to hide. The Great Witch Hunt of King James had nearly destroyed the Blood, driven many into hiding their Gifts. Many such secret witches had married outside the covens. No wonder, then, that traces of Merlin's heritage occasionally surfaced in unexpected places. If this woman was one of those lost children of the Blood . . . ?

But even if by some chance there was magic flowing in the governess's veins, it was tainted, weak, insufficient. The covens would never abide such as a mistress of witches, especially if Damien's powers were gone forever. Tante Reina clucked sadly, deciding to keep her peace. Far better it was not to give Lord Damien hope where there was none.

She bent to wipe a smudge from Lucy's cheek before she spoke. "A draught I will give you, to dull the knife of your pain, Lucy. Then I get Mrs. Penham for you."

As she was getting to her feet, Angel streaked into the clearing, barking sharply. Within a few seconds Damien followed hard on the hound's heels. "Sir Hector is not too far behind me. Though he is a substantial fellow, I vow his feet can devour ground," he said, smiling when he saw that Lucy's eyes were open. "How is our patient faring?"

"Just waking," Tante Reina said. "Mrs. Penham is in your wagon. Now I go to wake her."

"She is sleeping?" Damien asked, surprised that she had allowed herself to be separated from Lucy.

"One of my resting teas, I gave her, else she would be with the girl still," the Gypsy explained. "Poor woman is spent. I would let her sleep, but I make promise to call her when Lucy wakes."

"Best that you be with the child when her father comes. I shall wake her," Damien said, climbing the steps of the wagon. Gradually, his eyes adjusted to the dim light.

Damien's breath caught in his throat. Mrs. Penham's hair had come undone, spilling across his bed, framing her face like a dark nimbus. In sleep the strained line of her mouth eased into soft fullness. Caution and care were wiped away, hidden behind the dark lashes that curtained her eyes. Her glasses sat upon the shelf, filtering a stray ray of sun into fragmented rainbows.

With quiet tread Damien crossed the short distance to kneel at her side. Gazing down at her, it took every ounce of his control to keep himself from stroking the velvet softness of her skin, from gathering the silken spill of her hair into his hand and letting it flow against his cheek. Fantasy supplied images of her, turning to him with open arms, invitation in her eyes. What would it be to wake up to this face each morning, to watch the sun rise above the trees together?

She moaned softly, reality momentarily melding with

imagination, but Damien soon understood that there was no desire in that mournful sound.

"No," she whimpered, her voice oddly childlike. "No, please don't hurt me, please."

Damien watched as she curled in upon herself in a defensive posture, her fists balled, clutched to her body, her knees drawn inward, like a threatened hedgehog.

"No . . . I beg of you . . . no . . . don't touch . . . me . . ." Her voice rose fractionally with each word.

"Mrs. Penham," Damien said, as he shook her gently. "Mrs. Penham, you are having a nightmare."

She came awake with a jolt, snatching his hand away. Bolting from him in a scrambling movement, she pulled herself to a sitting position in the corner of the wagon. "Where?" she asked her eyes wild and disoriented. "Who?"

"Oberon," he said, watching as her expression changed from frantic desperation to embarrassment. "Tante Reina sent me to wake you."

"Lucy? Is she conscious?" Rowan asked, averting her eyes from his. She rose to her feet and smoothed her gown.

"Lucy is doing quite well. Tante Reina is taking excellent care of her," Damien said. "However, it would seem to me, Mrs. Penham, that you need a bit of concern yourself."

"I have always taken care of myself, Oberon," Rowan said, a chill in her voice. She snatched her glasses from the shelf, jamming them onto the ridge of her nose. What had he heard? she wondered. She had been dreaming about the crossing to France, the morning that she had lost all innocence, all hope.

"Have you ever truly taken care of yourself, Mrs. Penham?" Damien asked, doubt flavoring his words.

The tone of sadness in his voice drew her eyes to his face. Even in the dimness, she could detect compassion in his expression. "Yes, I have," she said, her posture stiffening in defiance. She did not want his pity. Her fingers mechanically shifted to her hair, combing it for loose pins. Swiftly, she twined the strands into a knot and jabbed it into place. "No one else ever has considered my needs."

"Not even your husband?" Damien asked, hearing a venom that was almost palpable. Strange how the simple act of straightening her hair became inherently sensuous, stirring him almost to the boundaries of his control.

"My husband?" She laughed, the sound holding no trace of humor, and her eyes became a gray wasteland, giving him a brief glimpse of an arid past. "My husband least of all. The only thing that he ever gave me was a child."

Once more, Damien caught an odd thread of nuance. "You have children, Mrs. Penham?"

"A daughter," she said, her expression softening with obvious affection. "She is eleven years old."

Eleven. Damien drew a sharp breath as he concluded a rapid mental calculation. "Thirteen," he murmured. "You were no more than a girl yourself. What manner of man would . . ."

"An evil man. A cruel one . . ." She shook her head as if the action would somehow dismiss the memories.

Deep within those smoky eyes, Damien saw incredible wellsprings of pain. He found himself hating the late Mr. Penham with a startling passion. In light of this revelation, her broken pleas made in the midst of sleep gained a haunting new pathos. "And your daughter?" he asked. "Where is she?"

The governess turned away, her fists clenched at her sides. "With his family," she said, her voice barely above a whisper. "I had no choice . . . no choice at all." She whirled abruptly, the shimmer of dammed tears in her eyes. "But I doubt that you could understand that, could you? Being who you are."

"And just who am I?" Damien asked.

"A man, strong, with obvious wealth and power behind the name that you hide," she said, frank appraisal in her scrutiny. "You must care very deeply for your family if you hide your identity to protect them from embarrassment. There is love in your voice when you speak of your mother, your sister. You have the freedom to take to the road and play at magic. You go where you will, do what you will . . ." she trailed off as he moved closer.

Damien held himself in check, but he could not resist a touch. "No," his voice was harsh, though his fingers brushed tenderly against her cheek, "not what I will, Mrs. Penham, though you have much of it right. My heritage and name bind me, more surely than any chains of iron. In truth, I do love my family, and I have already failed them once; I have vowed never to do so again. Amazing as it might seem, Oberon the Magnificent cannot always have whatever he desires, for all his illusion of wealth and power."

His lips came down upon hers, but there was no demand in his kiss, just a bitter sweetness, tinged with regret. Her arms crept around his neck, demanding more of this strange communion, to find that touch of magic once again.

To Rowan's bewilderment, he broke away, holding her at arm's length, searching her face, his expression mournful. "And you, Mrs. Penham, who are you behind your illusion?" he asked.

"Illusion?" Her eyes narrowed, the bilious taste of fear rising in her throat. "Illusion, sir? That implies that there is more to me than meets the eye."

"We all create our own illusions, Mrs. Penham," he said. "The image that we project to the world is as much a trick as this." He plucked a silk flower from the air and tucked it behind her ear. "Or these." With his other hand he reached up to snatch the spectacles from her eyes. "You have no need of lenses, Mrs. Penham, any more than I do. Your impromptu swim last night was extremely revealing. I have more than a fair idea of what lies beneath these layers of fabric." He grabbed a handful of the stuff of her gown. "Why do you hide your glory, Mrs. Penham? You are a beautiful woman."

The last vestiges of sleep vanished, seared away in a blaze of anger. Fury glowed within the granite forge of her eyes.

"Beautiful!" The word was like an epithet as she wrenched herself out of his grasp. She confronted him defiantly, her fingers balling up as if she was planning to land him a blow. "It would seem that my illusion is a rather poor creation, sir, if you can pierce my guise so easily. How safe is a beautiful woman without power or family to support her? Do not think that you flatter me, sir, by commenting upon beauty, when my looks have been the cause of most of my life's anguish."

Rowan drew a ragged breath and turned away, staring

blindly out the back door as the words tripped out in a stac-
cato rush. "Do you think me easy prey now, because of what
you heard? I know the script of my nightmares well as Kean
knows his Shakespeare. Had I come to the rape scene yet? I
doubt it, since my throat is not nearly raw enough for it. I
usually wake up having screamed myself hoarse. Ask no
foolish questions about my disguise, sir, when it is men like
yourself who make sport of pursuing a pretty face." She
turned to confront him accusingly.

"Men like me?" Damien said, his blood chilled, as the
meaning of what he had heard seeped in slowly. "You are so
certain you have my measure, Mrs. Penham. I am candid
enough to concede that I want you. And I suspect, if there is
a shred of honesty within you, you would not deny your own
desire for me. But do I truly deserve to be compared to the
beast who wed you, the monster who apparently raped a
child bride?"

Rowan's face flamed in shame. "No," she admitted.
"What you have taken, I gave willingly enough, and if honesty is what you crave, then I confess that this strange bond
between us is beginning to frighten me. What magic do you
possess, Oberon, that utterly confounds my common
sense?"

"I do not pretend to understand this any more than you
do," he said, his hand running through his hair in a gesture
of confusion. "If it is any comfort at all, Mrs. Penham, I find
myself equally ill at ease with my feelings. Call it what you
will, but neither one of us can afford to surrender to this
madness. You merit far more than I can offer you." He
stepped back toward the door. "Sir Hector will be here in a
moment or two. Best for your employer to find you with
your charges. There is a mirror by the door that might be of
some use."

Rowan watched as he parted the curtain and slipped into
the daylight. Hesitantly, she walked to the small glass in the
corner. Her fingers rose to take the silken flower from her
hair. Rowan stroked the delicate petals.

"Beautiful . . ." she had heard that empty compliment so
many times in uncountable fulsome variations. Yet, ironi-
cally, this time she could neither dismiss it nor forget it. He

spoke of her beauty as if it were a temptation to be resisted and this passion as an insanity that had to be rejected.

If there is a shred of honesty within you, you would not deny your own desire for me. To gainsay this sudden awareness, this sudden need to be near him, to touch him, would be a lie. Although Rowan had often played the role of seductress, she had never allowed herself to be seduced.

You merit far more than I can offer you. At long last she had met an honorable man, a man who was unwilling to use her for his own satisfaction, someone who believed that she deserved to be treated with integrity. He was entirely correct: capitulation to this inexplicable craving could cause nothing but grief. Why, then, was there a part of her that was damning him for his virtue? Swiftly, Rowan repaired the damage to her coiffure, straightened her clothing, and went to join Lucy and Davy.

Chapter 7

The curtains were wide open, and the library of the Chateau Du Le Fey was flooded with sunlight. Two golden heads were bent studiously over an ornate onyx chessboard. Giselle was biting her lip as she picked up her queen and took his pawn.

"Are you certain that you wish to move your lady there, little one?" Etienne asked the little girl before she removed her fingers.

She cocked her head sideways, large gray eyes openly inquisitive, all signs of fear gone now. It had been a difficult task indeed, to gain his sister's trust. No wonder at all that, when one considered that she had been snatched from her mother without so much as a farewell and delivered into the hands of a brother that she had never seen.

His resemblance to the comte had further complicated matters, sending the girl into spasms of terror as she feared that the old devil had risen from his grave to plague her and her mother again. Even when those apprehensions had been laid to rest, her confidence had been a long time in coming.

"You think only of what is here at this moment, *cheri*," he said, pointing to the board. "Contemplate the next move and the move after that. What would you do if you were in my position and I in yours?"

Her tongue flicked to the corner of her mouth as she concentrated, so like her mother. That simple gesture took him back through the years to a vision of a girl, ungainly, swollen with child. Etienne could only be grateful that his father's jealousy had brought about his exile from the chateau. He had little doubt that he might have killed the old man had he been forced to be a silent witness to that charade of a marriage. Through Giselle's ingenuous chatter, Etienne had been able to paint a fairly full picture of the hell his stepmother had endured.

"Your knight!" Giselle crowed. "You have only to bring up your horse next move, and you force me to sacrifice my queen to save my king."

"*Très bien, chéri, très bien*; you begin to see the whole board," he said, tousling her curls. "It is a terrible waste to give up your queen for so small a gain."

She smiled up at him, her gaze adoring, and Etienne felt an unfamiliar pressure in his chest.

"By Hades!" The library door burst open, and Claude came barreling into the room, waving a sheaf of papers. "She has betrayed us, Etienne; the bitch has betrayed us."

Giselle scrambled to Etienne's side. He rose from his chair, his arm automatically circling her shoulder in a sheltering gesture, holding the trembling body close. For his sister's sake, the mage kept his tones calm. "You upset the child, Cousin," he said, contained anger expressing itself in every measured word.

"Ah, by the Merlin, I did not see you, Cousin," Claude said, his manner changing instantly to ingratiating unctuousness. "How beautiful you look today, my dear. Did you get the roses that I sent to you? Did you like them? Give Cousin Claude a little kiss for thanks, eh?"

Etienne felt the girl's shudder. "A simple *merci* will do, Giselle, and then you may go seek old Beatrice for your rune lessons. We shall finish our game later."

"*Merci*, Cousin Claude," Giselle murmured softly, shooting her brother a grateful look before excusing herself with a quick curtsy.

Claude followed her with his eyes, devouring her every movement until the door closed behind her. "Why do you send her to Beatrice to learn? Your father had the right way of it, Cousin, I would prefer to be my future wife's teacher, in all things," he said with an unpleasant chuckle.

"The betrothal was only a threat against Rowan, Claude; not a promise to you," Etienne said wearily, reining in his disgust.

"The time has come to make good on those threats, Etienne," he said, scattering the chess pieces as he slammed the sheaf of papers onto the table. "Look at this. I knew we could not trust her, so I contacted one of our agents at Whitehall."

"An unnecessary risk," Etienne said coolly.

"Unnecessary, eh? Look at these figures," he demanded, poking a finger at the place. "Not quite the same as your *belle-mère* has provided, are they, eh? She has deceived us, Cousin, and she must pay the price for her broken vow."

"If the vow is truly broken," Etienne said, containing a frown as he compared the contents of Claude's documents to the estimates that he had just received from Rowan. The numbers were indeed different. Though there was not a great deal of variance in the details, the shifts were significant enough to require an alteration of plan. How could they facilitate the emperor's escape without adequate knowledge of the forces arrayed against them? His grip upon the papers tightened.

" 'If,' you say?" Claude railed. "Are you fooled by that pretty face? Your father was her pimp, Etienne, and her master. No doubt she is as greedy as any demimondaine upon the Boulevard. Perhaps England made her a better offer, and she has crawled into bed with the enemy. Do you defend a whore's honor?"

In answer Etienne raised his left hand. His shirtsleeve snaked down to his shoulder. The gold band on his arm glistened in the sunlight, cool blue fire forming on its surface. "I defend the honor of the Du Le Fey, Cousin, and she is a Du Le Fey. You would do well to remember that we made her into what she is. And though I admit that my father used his wife shamefully, it would seem that you and I have merely taken his place as procurers, *n'est-ce pas?*"

"But she has betrayed us," Claude whined, cringing before the show of power.

"If she has broken her vow, she will pay," Etienne agreed, his mouth hardening into a tight line. "But it is I who shall determine that price, Claude, not you."

The old oak beams of The Ram's Head were blackened with nearly two centuries worth of smoke. Gasps of awe were followed by shouts of approval as a pure white dove flew up into the rafters to perch and survey the crowd.

Damien bowed. "Your cap, Freddy," he said, handing the old man his weather-beaten hat with a theatrical flourish.

The wizened codger took the brim gingerly, squinting as he peered inside trying to determine where the bird could possibly have been hidden.

"Checkin' t'see if yer got any more squabs in yer chap-oh, Freddy?" Tess, the barmaid, teased, sidling closer to the mage. "Mebbe yer might find a thing or two in my pockets, Oberon," she said invitingly, patting her ample hips languorously.

"Ain't nothin' in Tess's clothes what nobody here ain't seen before," one wag declared.

"Better'n what yer cuddlin' in th' dark, Sam Chaney," Tess retorted raucously. "An' far as I know, yer ain't held nothin' o' late what don't go 'oink' or 'moo.' "

As the room filled with laughter, only Damien noticed the quick flash of hurt in her eyes.

"To the contrary, Sam," Damien said, slipping a hand into her pocket. "I find that women are always full of surprises." He pulled out a bright blue silk kerchief. Tied to its corner was a pink one and to its end yet another. Orange, red, green, yellow, purple . . . silk followed silk in a seemingly endless succession.

"Cor!"

"Will yer lookit that!"

"Why, Tess, how many of these have we here? I count ten so far." He twined the kerchiefs around the barmaid's neck as the patrons began to count along with him. "Fourteen . . . fifteen . . ." her expansive bosom was covered with the silken chain. "Twenty-two . . . twenty-three . . ."

"Twenty-nine . . ." Damien pasted a look of astonishment on his face as he pretended to encounter some resistance . . . "Ah, this one is a bit stubborn, I might need a bit of help here . . . if you would all rise from your seats, gentlemen, and give me a rousing chorus. I think that 'G-d Save the King' would be most appropriate."

There was a sound of scraping and shuffling as the audience of household servants, farmers and fishermen got to their feet. As they began to sing the anthem, Damien tugged the last kerchief. No small flimsy scrap this. He drew the moment out until the first stanza was finished, unknotting the last silken twist, and unrolling the tightly wound fabric to reveal the Union Jack.

"No wonder it was so contrary," Damien said with a broad grin, undulating the silk banner so that it seemed almost like a living thing. "I give you England, my friends, long may she wave. Shall we drink to the king and country? I am buying."

His last announcement caused a cheering rush for the bar. Damien folded the flag carefully and put it on the table.

"Here, Oberon, these is yers," Tess said, beginning to untwine the garland of kerchiefs from her neck.

"Keep them," Damien said. "After all, they did come from your pockets. If you do not mind, though, I shall keep the Union Jack as a souvenir of the evening."

Tess laughed. "Aye, sounds more'n fair ter me. Got ter give John a hand wiv th' drinks at th' bar, luv, but I'll be back ter give yer my thanks." The look on her face made it clear exactly what kind of thanks she was offering.

Damien gave her a smile. As he packed up the accoutrements of his illusions, he kept his eyes and ears open. For just over a week now, he had been coming regularly to The Ram's Head. Small and slovenly as the inn was, around these ramshackle benches and tables were gathered the heart of the community. A few tricks and a few rounds of drinks, and he had these stout yeoman in his palm.

One toothless old gaffer extended him a grin and his hand before making his way to the bar. Damien accepted them both, along with the smiles and nods of the crowd. Little more than a seven-day, and they had taken him into their embrace without question or reservation. The lack of novelty in their lives made them ridiculously easy to please. Yet, somehow, the praise he received for the few effortless tricks that he performed for them acquired a meaning well beyond face value.

As Lord Wodesby's son, and later when he had assumed his father's title, Damien was accustomed to deference. When he had attained the position of Wellington's pet sorcerer, awe had been flavored with hearty measures of fear and disdain. In this small smoky hole, he was accepted, admired for his own achievements, not the accidents of blood or birth.

Tess brought back a brimming mug, and Damien raised it high. "The king and England!" he declared.

"The king and England," they echoed, downing their drinks as if they had not spent half the night with bent elbows.

Damien put the remnants of his ale down on the table as Tess twined her arms around his neck. With all the room suddenly watching, there was little choice but to take the kiss that she so blatantly offered. Clearly, his carefully woven reputation as a lady's man was in peril.

Tess was pretty in her own blowsy way. Her hips moved against him, telling him that with minimal encouragement he could have far more than a mere kiss. Perhaps he ought to take Tess up on the invitation, Damien thought as he bent to meet that rosebud mouth. The barmaid was as unlike Mrs. Penham as chalk to cheese. Possibly the reality of another female would serve to exorcise the dark Lilith that was haunting his nights.

Damien closed his eyes against the leering faces. Sounds of knowing guffaws and catcalls faded as he consigned himself to the realm of pure sensation. The odor of stale spilled ale mingled with the scent of inferior perfume as Tess pressed herself closer. He tried to concentrate on the here and now, the soft willing woman in his arms, but his imagination betrayed him.

In his self-imposed darkness, Tess's blond curls were transformed into a smooth curtain of raven's wing. Blue eyes changed to a stormy sea of gray. Her lushly padded charms became elegant curves. Beneath his fingers, the barmaid's coarse countenance altered into the delicate fine features that were forever branded in his memory. She was his mermaiden, his desire. All his longing, his passion were poured into that one kiss.

It took a virtual chorale of whistles and whoops to break the spell. Tess sagged weakly against him, her eyes dewy and bedazzled. At that moment revelation hit Damien with blinding force. He could not take Tess, not while he was under this strange enchantment.

Magic, this was, yet wholly unlike any magic that he had ever known. Although he could practice no sorcery, he would be able to detect the telltale assault of a spell cast upon him as easily as a fist in his face. Was this his destiny, then? To be forever haunted by Mrs. Penham? Dark or fair, short or tall, would they always become her phantom?

With a sigh of regret he untangled himself from Tess's embrace. Holding one woman in his arms while making love to another in his mind would be an abomination to Venus and to himself. Gently, he tweaked one of the barmaid's bright curls and produced a coin. "No wonder golden hair is my weakness," he said, opening the fold of her pocket and dropping it in to clink against the other coins there.

"Did yer Frenchy lady have golden hair?" one of the men asked.

"Like spun sunlight," Damien replied, entirely willing to embellish the penny broadsheet tale that he had been feeding the patrons of The Ram's Head in dribs and drabs. "But her eyes were not nearly as blue as our Tess's. Still, I was in love with her, but she belonged to another. I never gave her more than a kiss."

"Iffen it was like unto what you gave Tess . . ." One man began with a leer.

"Gives me shakes just t' think on it. Th' Frenchy kilt his wife for nothin' more'n a kiss." Tess added to the now familiar narrative, touching her necklace of scarves with a romantic sigh.

"Think her husband is still after yer, Oberon?" Another questioned eagerly.

"The old man vowed vengeance," Damien said, his eyes resting on each avid face in turn. With the honed instincts of a showman, he paused, letting the impact of the statement sink in. "I offered to duel him, but coward that the Frenchy was, he refused."

There was a hiss of breath, and not even the clink of a mug marred the silence.

"He's not above sending out henchmen to do his dirty work," Damien added as his pièce de résistance. "I would not be afraid to face him man to man, but that doesn't seem to be the Frenchy's way. There have been a few close calls in these past few months, I'll tell you. He might even try hiring an Englishman to try to get at my back."

A murmur of disapproval rippled across the room at this dastardly possibility. "Ain't seen no strangers of late, Oberon," the old codger said. "Then, there ain't no sayin' what them sneaky Frenchies might do, even wiv Napoleon under lock n' key."

"Aye, heaven's own truth that is," John concurred from his place behind the bar. "Seems ter me 'tis no more'n our dooty to be lookin' out fer Oberon here. Any man jack what sees a stranger, Frenchy or other, yer be lettin' me or Oberon know."

Heads bobbed in unison, and Damien was humbled and shamed by the adamant promise of their defense. It was an odd feeling to be the protected instead of the protector. Even as a child, he had spent considerable time shielding his defenseless sister against taunts and magical pranks. For most of his adult life, it had been Damien's task to be the defender, the champion of his family, of the covens, of the Blood, of England itself.

Upon less than a week's acquaintance, these stout yeomen had closed ranks about him, claiming him for one of their own. He was manipulating their sentiments, and though it was for England's good, he could not help but feel remorse for using them so.

"Thank you, all of you," Damien said, his gaze sweeping those reddened weathered faces. "I am deeply touched by your offer of help. Certainly, I may sleep more secure in my bed tonight knowing that my friends are on the watch."

He whistled softly, and the dove fluttered down to perch on his hand. "Good night," he said, gathering up his pack. Tess followed him to the door. He bent to give her a regretful brush of his lips.

"Still love her, don't yer?" Tess asked, her question masked beneath the rising hubbub of the tavern. "T'was her yer thinkin' of when yer kissed me, wasn't it?"

Damien nodded.

"Poor man," she said, her gin-roughened voice subdued by melancholy. "T'be in love with a woman yer can't never have."

"Yes," Damien admitted. "I love her, and there is not a damn thing that I can do. It would not be fair, Tess, not to you, not to me."

She nodded in understanding. "Fair or not, if yer change yer mind. I'll be waitin'."

Damien mounted his horse and rode toward the Gypsy camp. Near the cliff path, he heard the soft deep hoot of an owl and echoed the call with one of his own.

"The cove?" Damien asked the swiftly approaching shadow.

"Nothing," Dominick replied in disgust. "Calm sea and sky, enough moon for light, yet we see nothing. Not even smugglers."

"And those casks that your son found in the sea caves?"

"Old," Dominick told him. "Older than me or you, I think. Whoever hid them has long forgotten them, my friend. And strangers, have any been seen?"

Damien shook his head. "Not that my net of John Bulls has detected. How in Hades is he doing it, Dominick? Just this afternoon, Wellington sent confirmation that the last batch of documents has swum the Channel, under our very noses, I might add. As His Grace pointed out, it is only a matter of time before his cohorts discover the discrepancies in the information that we are feeding to the baronet."

"Hard to believe that Sir Hector deceives us with such ease when I have never seen a man so clumsy," Dominick said, his dark eyes mournful. "The automatons that belong to your sister's husband will never be the same. Why do you bring Sir Hector to the camp for his magic lessons, Lord Damien? Better to bring him simple tricks to Southwood, things which he cannot break so easily. For your sake, I will try to fix Adam's machines . . ." The Gypsy sighed and raised his shoulders in a gesture of hopelessness.

"Damn Adam's precious automatons. He is the one who has gotten me into this detestable tangle," Damien said in a burst of temper. "Why could my brother-by-marriage not be content to become a father in absentia like the rest of his fellows in the Outsider world?"

"It is the woman. You avoid her," Dominick said wisely. "When you love truly, you wish to be near, just as you do, my friend. You wish to be near your woman, but you fear to love her."

Damien looked silently out at the sea, the light-tinged edges of the horizon that were the harbingers of dawn. "Yes," he admitted. "Now, more than ever, I fear it. With or without my powers, I am Lord Wodesby, Dominick. On my shoulders rests more than a thousand years of tradition, responsibility. Once before, I denied the obligation that is part of the Wodesby heritage, its blessing and its curse, and because of that, my father is dead."

"And if it was murder by magic, as you believed, perhaps you too, would have been destroyed?" Dominick suggested.

"Perhaps . . ." Damien said, "or perhaps my father now might be waiting for his first grandchild to be born."

"All is fated," the Gypsy said.

"Aye, that is so," Damien agreed. "But I shall not fail my name ever again, Dominick. I cannot. That is why I am trying to keep my distance from Mrs. Penham. What honorable end can this have?"

"I know not," the Gypsy said, sympathetically. "But like it or no, you will have to face her. Tante Reina says that tomorrow young Lucy's bandages will be gone. The magic lessons that you have promised are due to begin."

Damien dug his heels into the side of his horse, and rode into the night like a madman.

Clouds were gathering outside the nursery window as Tante Reina unpacked her embroidered bag. Lady Stanhope's daughter, Diana, had insisted upon being present, and Rowan noted that Lucy was gripping the younger woman's hand as the Gypsy set out an array of vials and ointments on the stand near the child's bed.

"Will we be taking the bandage off today?" Lucy asked plaintively. "It has been nearly a week now."

"Patience, Lucy," Diana advised. "You want it to heal properly, without any scarring."

"Pooh!" Lucy said. "What matter is a little bit of a scar? Davy has two of them already on his knee, and no one made him stay abed!"

"It is different for a woman," Diana said. "Anything which

may affect looks are very important for a female. Is that not so, Mrs. Penham?"

"I will not say that appearance is meaningless, Miss Stanhope," Rowan concurred, catching the wistful flavor of the younger woman's words. "But sweetness of temper and kindness also have a great deal to recommend them."

"Your own beauty you have, Miz Stanhope," Tante Reina agreed as she set her bag down. "To come see the child every day, as you do, read, play cards, make her happy so she will stay abed. A beauty of spirit I see in you."

Diana's cheeks turned pink with pleasure. "It is kind of you to say, Tante Reina. But I am told that only that which I may see in the mirror will be of use to me in the future. According to Mama, looks and fortune are all that matter in the marital Tattersall's of the ton. Unfortunately, I have only the latter," she said with false cheer.

The old woman shook her head. "More than you know, child, you have. In your hand I could see it, if you will allow me."

"Tante Reina can see the future," Lucy stated confidently. "Last year, she told Felicity Rhode that she would be wed before Christmas, and it was just as she said."

"Would you read my palm for me, Tante Reina?" Diana asked, putting out her hand hesitantly. "I have some money . . ."

"No silver," the Gypsy said, taking up the young woman's hand. "If I read, I do it for your kindness to Lucy. But do you wish others to hear your fortune, Miss Diana?" She inclined her head meaningfully toward Rowan and Lucy. "What I see, I must say."

Diana gave a nervous giggle. "I doubt that I shall have another such opportunity. You must forgive me for saying so, Tante Reina, but Mama is not fond of Gypsies. She would be scandalized if she knew that I was here with you, much less even considering having my fortune told."

"I won't tell," Lucy said stoutly, "cross my heart." She looked pointedly at her governess.

"Nor I," Rowan agreed, curious to hear what the old woman would reveal. Never before had she heard of a Gypsy who would wave away an offer of payment. "I will say nothing, Miss Diana."

With a nod Tante Reina led Diana to the table in the center of the nursery and motioned toward a seat. With a nervous smile Diana sat down and extended her hand.

"The left," Tante Reina corrected as she seated herself. "Closest to heart." Diana placed the correct hand in the old woman's palm, and waited while the Romany began to trace the lines.

The nursery became uncannily still, the atmosphere redolent with an acrid scent, like the aftermath of lightning. Gypsy magic. Although many Romany fortune-tellers were naught but frauds, Rowan quickly knew that Tante Reina was not one of those charlatans. Tension built to a crackling intensity as those gnarled fingers traveled the mapped pathways of the young woman's hand.

"Choices," Tante Reina muttered. "Too old, he thinks himself, too old to win a girl's heart. Greatly he cares for you, enough for your good, to give you to another. See here where it leads, if you choose to deny him? Marriage you will have . . . children, but no love." She shook her head sadly. Silently, she followed the alternate trail of the life line, stopping with a hissed breath. "A shadow threatens, though not directly upon you. Betrayal, sadness but at the end love may be found."

"May be?" Diana asked.

Tante Reina folded the young woman's fingers upon themselves. "Many futures there are in every hand, Miss Diana, always changing they are from day to day. Choices we make, directions we take, altering the course of life. Tomorrow I may see different than I do today, because of your choosing, one path clearer than another. But now I see this."

"He loves me?" Diana whispered, her countenance glowing with wonder.

The old woman smiled. "Aye, a love that would sacrifice. Rare. Precious beyond measure."

"He would give me up because he feels himself unworthy?" Diana asked.

The Romany nodded.

"Well, we shall see about that," Diana said, rising from the chair, rebellion brewing in her eyes. "We shall see about that."

"And you, Mrs. Penham?" Tante Reina's brow raised in inquiry. "Your fortune would you have told?"

Rowan felt the tug of temptation. To know where it all would end, to gain a sense of direction when her life was all awhirl, was tantalizing indeed. "I think some futures are best left untold," she said quietly.

Tante Reina shrugged, as if in acquiescence, but her gaze was questioning. Nonetheless, she rose and went back to Lucy.

A contrary twinge of jealousy bit Rowan as the girl reached for Diana's hand. In the past few days Rowan had deliberately promoted the affection between Lady Stanhope's daughter and the children. Not that it had been difficult; Lucy and Davy were already fond of Diana and the young woman's devotion to Sir Hector's offspring had been easy to nurture. Not even a trifling nudge of witchcraft had been required.

Still, as Tante Reina unwrapped the length of linen bandage, Rowan wondered if it had been a good idea to solicit Diana's presence while the wound was being tended. If there was pain to be dealt with, Rowan could scarcely snatch Lucy's hand away. Luckily, the fabric peeled off easily.

"Is good," the elderly Gypsy pronounced, gazing with satisfaction at the crusting scab on Lucy's knee. "I think there will be no scars."

"Then, I can play out-of-doors again?" Lucy asked. "And Davy and I can begin magic lessons, for Papa would not let us start until it was all healed."

The old woman nodded.

"Thank you, Tante Reina!" Lucy said, pressing a kiss on the Gypsy's wrinkled cheek.

"Is not me you should be thanking," Tante Reina said, with a toothless smile, "but your Missus Penham. She has a healing touch, healing hands."

"Thank you, Penny," Lucy threw her arms around the governess and hugged her tightly. "Thank you for taking the hurt away."

"Shall we go tell Davy and your papa?" Diana suggested.

"Yes, let's do. They will be ever so happy," Lucy agreed. She raced out the door with Diana close behind.

"Ladies do not run," Rowan called, leaning against the doorsill, her cheeks still pink with the afterglow of Lucy's display of love and admiration. It was the first time that the girl had ever called her "Penny." Rowan turned to find the old Gypsy eyeing her curiously.

"Children," Rowan said dismissively. "I thank you for your commendation, Tante Reina, but Lucy's recovery is entirely due to Oberon's skills and your excellent nursing."

"As you say, missus, as you say," the old woman nodded as she began to pack her vials and powders back into her bag. "The little one, she tells me before that you take her pain from her."

"A child's fancy," Rowan said stiffly, reaching to pick up a vial from the nightstand. She had hoped that Lucy's remark would pass unnoticed. "Sometimes the imagination can overcome the pain of reality." Rowan held the vial out to the Gypsy.

"Sometime," Tante Reina agreed, her dark eyes glowing bright as she reached past the container to catch the younger woman's wrist. "Sometime more there is than we would wish others to see."

Rowan tried to snatch her hand back, but the old Gypsy's grasp was like a vise.

"Read for you, I would, missus. No silver do I ask to cross my hand, but as gift to another who has a Gift."

Rowan shook her head, clenching her fingers into a fist. "No need to offer again," she whispered, "it is not necessary, truly."

"No palm must I behold to know that you have great sorrow. Seen it I have in these past days, like a shadow it hangs above you," Tante Reina said, kindness in the earthy depths of her eyes. "No lines must I read to know that worry dogs your footsteps. Your future I offer to help you if I can, child. You need a friend, and this would I be for you. No one else is here to listen. What I say is for you and you alone."

Slowly, she brought Rowan's fist to her lips, brushing the clasped knuckles with a papery touch.

Like a flower unfurling, Rowan's fingers opened. The old

woman peered into her palm, tracing the web of lines with a gnarled finger.

"What do you see, Tante Reina?" Rowan asked as the silence lengthened. "Can you find the answers that I seek?"

The Gypsy woman enclosed Rowan's hand within her own. "No, child," her brightly kerchiefed head shaking as she emphasized the negative, "in these lines, few answers can I find. Love, I find, but if past or future, I cannot say. A magic of your own, you have, unlike mine. Your pathways of mind, of heart, change constantly with that power in your veins. What is to come is written here in a language I speak not. But I do not understand why you do not know this already? Never have we Gypsies been able to tell fortunes for those of the Blood," she said, regarding the young woman in puzzlement.

Rowan pulled back, trying to hide her fear, but the old woman's grip held fast. "The Blood? What manner of nonsense is this?"

"Like a drum, your heart beats, child," Tante Reina said, her gaze suddenly keen and appraising. "There is much you do not know, this I see now, else never would you let me view your hand. Before, I think there is some Blood in you, maybe, but enough of an Outsider's palm lines so I may read for you. Is not unknown for this to be. But too much of Merlin's kind are you, child, of the Blood born, for me to read fully. The love I spoke of, I see in your eyes, not your hand."

"You speak foolishness," Rowan said, her voice rising in anger and fear.

"Do I?" Tante Reina's fingers clasped the pulse in Rowan's wrist. "Mention the Blood, and you throb like waves at flood tide, daughter of Merlin. Let there be no lies between us. With me there is no need to hide your magic."

"You must speak to no one of this," Rowan commanded, her free hand fumbling for the chain at her neck and pulling forth the badge of her office. "By Merlin's—"

"Seek not to bind me, Lady," the Romany's bent back straightened, her mien changing all at once. She raised her chin, her countenance radiating regal confidence, even as the telltale glow of witchfire began to radiate about the twined snakes.

"A Gypsy cannot be ruled by your magic. A great lady witch you are, yet, you do not know this? Truly this confuses me," Tante Reina mused aloud. "You possess one of Hecate's most powerful talismans, yet you know not the simple rules that every witchling learns before she utters her first spell?"

There was no anger in the old woman's tone, only mystification and concern. Rowan began to tremble at the Gypsy's lack of fear. Without a means of coercion, Rowan had nothing more than the Romany's word to shield her. "Please," Rowan pleaded hoarsely. "I beg of you, tell no one. My daughter's future depends on it."

"You are ignorant, indeed, child, if you know not the sacred bond of a true reader. What I see in your hand only you may reveal. I am bound to silence, unless you say otherwise." The Gypsy spoke soothingly, as if to a frightened child. "I can help you and your daughter. Friends have I of the Blood."

"You ask that I place my trust in one of the Blood?" Rowan shook her head vehemently. "Who, Tante Reina? My dear departed father, who sold me into a hellish marriage out of jealousy and greed? My kin, who never bothered themselves about my welfare when I needed them most? My late husband's family? Who do you think holds my daughter, like a sword above my head? By Hecate, I would as soon wager my child's future on the throw of a crooked die as put my faith in the integrity of the Blood."

The Gypsy squeezed Rowan's hand. "I cannot force you. You must decide for yourself, but there are those worthy of trust. I will not betray you, but I have fear for you."

"Why?" Rowan asked suspiciously. "Why should you care about me? And what reasons do you have for your worries? Are you concealing something from me, old woman? Something you have seen in my lines?"

"What I see, I tell," Tante Reina said, a flash of anger in her eyes, as she let go of Rowan's fingers. "Your fear, I can touch, hold in my hand, feel its breath upon my neck." Her expression grew less harsh.

"What you say in ignorance, I forgive, child." Tante Reina shook her head sadly, a tear trickling down her weather-beaten cheek as she contemplated the tangle of secrets that bound her.

"My apologies, Tante Reina," Rowan said, that single tear affecting her far more than a raised voice, causing her to gentle her words. No one had ever wept for her before. "There have been pitifully few things in my life that have justified my faith, and sometimes, it is difficult to believe the truth when I hear it. I am sorry to draw you into this muddle."

"Help you, I will, if I can, but mighty powers you trade with, forces you do not understand . . ." Tante Reina said, contemplating the implications of this new twist of events.

"That may be true," Rowan said, watching the chase of emotions across the old woman's face; fear, sadness, confusion, followed by the eventual triumph of resignation. "I can only assure you that I mean no harm to you and yours."

"Oberon, I consider one of mine," Tante Reina challenged, carefully watching the witch's reaction. Deep in the agate of the young woman's eyes, the Gypsy found the answer that had been hidden within the palm's lines of the witch.

"I owe your Oberon a life debt," Rowan answered, trying to conceal her anguish. "And even if I did not, I would not hurt him."

"You love him, lady?" Tante Reina asked, a forlorn hope rising in her breast. She recalled the look on Lord Damien's face when he had emerged from his wagon on the day of Lucy's injury: hunger, need, and unbearable anguish. He believed Mrs. Penham to be an Outsider, but she was not! By Hecate, she was not!

"How could I care for him?" Rowan asked, questioning herself as much as the old woman. "Love? 'Tis an illusion, a young girl's fantasy; I learned that long ago. And were I to be so foolish as to give my heart away, I would not toss it to an Outsider."

"Indeed no," the Gypsy concurred, delighted by the girl's obvious effort at dissimulation.

Though Tante Reina seemingly agreed with Rowan, the Romany's toothless smile was knowing, infuriating. "Even if I was doltish enough to think my affections engaged, it would be of no consequence," Rowan added angrily, stuffing a vial into the Gypsy's bag. "Your Oberon has made it very clear that he could not waste himself on a mere governess, so you need have no fears for him. In this modern day and age, a few kisses means nothing."

"Nothing," Tante Reina echoed, slowly weaving the bits and pieces of evidence and conjecture into a coherent tapestry. As a reader of fortune, she knew that every happening, great and minor was a part of the pattern. *A few kisses, eh?* "Much surprised am I, though, to hear this. Never was he a man to take such things lightly." She watched the governess's lip curl in disbelief, though her eyes lit momentarily in what might have been hope.

Silently, the Gypsy cursed her aging memory. She was missing something very important, the thread that would weave these disparate snatches of fate into a coherent whole. Eagerly, she waited for the young woman to add more wool to the spindle of information, but the door burst open and the children ran in.

"We are to have a fair, Penny!" Davy shouted excitedly.

"And a ball," Lucy added, "a midsummer ball, Papa says. And the Gypsies will play music. Diana has promised to help us. And I am to have a new dress for the fair."

"She acts swiftly, Lady Stanhope's daughter," Tante Reina murmured in amusement.

"And Papa says that there will be races and prizes," Davy added.

"At the ball?" Rowan teased.

"A novel idea, Mrs. Penham," Damien said, sauntering into the room. "Do you think that we might match Lady Stanhope against the rector's wife? Although, I might be hard-pressed to guess which one has more wind to her, and as for legs and chests, I would say—"

"Pray, do not, sir," Rowan scolded, trying hard to look stern, but the children's giggles proved to be her undoing. The very idea of those two redoubtable matrons racing neck or nothing across Southwood's vast ballroom was too humorous to resist. Despite all her efforts, laughter swelled in her throat, bursting forth in a wave that carried all the force of her tension and fear.

All of Damien's resolutions were washed away in the tide of her laughter. At this moment the fact that his investigation was at a standstill did not seem to matter. Wellington's worries, Adam's broken automatons, Southwood's schemes seemed to dissolve before the genuine glow of merriment in Mrs. Penham's eyes. Tears of laughter began to stream down her cheeks, and though his jest had been a weak sally at best, Damien found himself carried away in the current of her delight.

Never had she seemed more beautiful, more desirable than at this slice in time. He laughed along with her, his gaze locking with hers, sharing without words the ludicrous picture that he had verbally painted. And as their laughter liquefied into chuckles, he found that he could not look away. Chuckles faded to chortles, and all his carefully crafted explanations and excuses sank like stones in the depths of those quicksilver pools. Gradually, they fell into breathless silence, and he found himself desperately searching for a clever phrase to break the tension.

It was as if the week of separation had never been. Day by day, Rowan had almost managed to persuade herself once again that her feelings were nothing more than the creations of a lonely woman's fantasy. Now, standing before Oberon, she knew that she had lied to Tante Reina, to herself. Will or nil, he beguiled her just by his presence. Like the willow to water, she was drawn, wondering if his touch would bring that same sweet longing once more, and if the taste of his kiss was still a potion that could heighten all of her senses.

Carefully, Tante Reina watched, feeling the current between the two spouting like the meeting of wind and wave, watching them fight against an elemental pull that seemed as strong as the force of fate itself. With a sigh she put the last of her salves into her bag and fastened it around her waist. No temporary fascination this, but destiny.

Utterly unconscious of any tension, Lucy added her news to the pot. "Papa said we may stay up late and watch from the minstrel's gallery. It will be ever so nice."

"That sounds lovely," Rowan agreed, seizing eagerly upon the child's statement. "Perhaps we can persuade Cook to give us a tray to bring up with us."

"Oh, no, Penny," Lucy said, her curls bobbing. "Papa says that you must come to the ball too."

"That is most kind of him," Rowan said, her guilt growing as she acknowledged Sir Hector's generosity. If only he were an evil man, her deceit would be so much simpler. "But I have no gown to wear to so fine an event. I would be just as happy watching from above, and no one would tread on my toes."

"From what I have gleaned, it is to be a costume ball, Mrs. Penham," Oberon said. "Surely, something can be contrived."

"There is no need for your kindness," Rowan said, her tone feigning an indifference that she could not feel. "To what purpose would it be for me to pretend that for one night I am a guest in my employer's home? No matter what fine feathers I might wear, come morning, I will still be as I am."

"Please, Penny, you could be a princess," Lucy suggested.

"Pooh!" Davy said, wrinkling his nose. "A pirate."

"There are no lady pirates, Davy," Lucy said, her nose rising in superiority.

"There are too!" the boy challenged.

"Are not!" his sister replied.

"Papa says that Mrs. Armistead is a pirate with what she charges for beeswax candles," Davy said authoritatively. "Oh, do be a pirate, Penny. Avast me hearties!" he cried, swiping at his sister with a feigned sword. Lucy shrieked in mock terror and glee, running toward the stair.

"She's better!" Davy declared with a grin, and charged after his sister with a robust "Aargh!"

"So it would seem that Lucy is not suffering any lasting effects from her fall," Damien said, his brow rising in amusement. "Are you going to follow Davy's advice and be a female buccaneer, Mrs. Penham? I vow, it would be fitting, for you are one of the most dangerous women that I have ever met."

"Perhaps it is you who ought to play at pirate, Oberon," Rowan said, imagining him in sailor's garb, his hair blowing in the winds. "It would suit you."

Once again, the look exchanged between them served to underscore that far more was meant than said.

"And shall I kidnap you and carry you off in my ship?" Damien asked softly. A sudden cloud crossed her face, her eyes darkened abruptly, and he once more glimpsed the shadows of old pain.

"This is foolishness," Rowan said, trying to banish the sudden rush of memories, the rocking of the boat, the long-ago fears of the girl she had been, carried far from home, helpless, hopeless. "I have never quite understood the attraction of grown men and women dressing up in ridiculous costumes."

"Have you never pretended as a child?" Damien asked, puzzled by the sudden change in her demeanor. "I suppose that we all have a bit of a wish in us to go back to those uncomplicated times. With a stout stick and a bit of string, we could create a bow and imagine ourselves in Sherwood Forest with Robin Hood. Or with a feather in the hair, we became Indian braves in America. 'Tis much the same thing, I suspect, the desire to be other than the prosaic people that we are. Except we need more in the way of accoutrements as adults to create our illusions."

"Yes, but in the end, we are neither princesses nor fairy queens. We open our eyes and see that the only thing that has changed about our lives is the hour on the clock. Those who did not love you, still care nothing. If you began the pretense alone, you end alone," Rowan said, remembering that she would be leaving Midsummer Night. The charade would end, and the illusion that was Mrs. Penham would vanish into a memory. It was all for the best.

The gray of her eyes turned to quicksilver as she regarded Damien sadly. He tried to imagine a life that was composed entirely of harsh realities, an existence without the solace of hopes and make-believe.

"Dreams never last, Oberon," Rowan added, with a melancholy tilt of her lips. "And they leave us hoping for things that we can never have. In my life, I have yet to see any happy illusions triumph. Now, if you will excuse me, I must see to the children before they get wholly out of hand. The servants have set a table on the terrace for your props."

She turned, and Damien took a step as if to follow. For a brief instant Tante Reina saw his heart as clearly as the lines upon an Outsider's palm. Love was written plain in those emerald eyes. And despair.

Chapter 8

The afternoon sun had slipped to the west, casting South-wood's terrace into shade. Rowan seated herself to the side, the better to observe Oberon's secrets. It was rather disappointing to see that he had brought few things with him for this first lesson in "magic." He began with coins, the art of palming an object. Golden guineas jumped from hand to hand, vanishing into the air only to appear behind ears, under teacups.

Damien could feel her eyes upon him, and began to act like a greenling mage. For her, he made every pass perfect, performing with a smooth dexterity that was almost as satisfying as real magic. Seamlessly, trick flowed into trick. From her soft gasps, he knew that he was successfully weaving a veil of visual deception.

In the corner of his eye, he could see the wonder mirrored in her rapt gaze. There was a part of him that wanted to shout, "This is not real! This is not magic! Once I could have filled the sky with rainbows or command the lightning to duel in the heaven. Once I could have made the wind sing your name." It was entirely absurd, and Damien knew it. Yet he still wanted to dazzle her, like a peacock fanning his tail. Instead, he made the coins fly hither and thither, forced to content himself with mere illusion, displaying the only modest part of his plumage left to him.

Swiftly, Rowan understood that there was naught that was simple about the skills needed to produce even false magic. The fleeting sleights of hand to make a coin pass unseen required more than mere dexterity. There was a grace of movement, an exquisite sense of timing that made all the difference between the fumbling efforts of Sir Hector and the fluid fantasies of eye that Oberon created.

"How did you do that?" Lucy asked, clapping her hands in glee as he peeled back the petals of a hothouse rosebud to reveal the missing guinea.

"What people believe, Miss Lucy, is as important as what they see, if not more so," Damien explained, casually flipping the guinea from hand to hand.

"But how is that, Oberon?" Davy said testily. "Show us how to do it and let us try."

Damien flipped the coin into the air and caught it.

"Choose the hand that holds the guinea, Davy, and you may keep it," he said, holding out his pair of clenched fists.

"That hand!" Davy laughed, and pointed to the illusionist's right. "That is the hand that has the guinea. 'Tis as easy as falling off a chair."

In answer Damien opened his left fist. There, gleaming in the center of his palm, was a golden guinea. Davy groaned.

"How did you do that?" Lucy asked, her eyes widening. "I saw you catch it with the other hand."

"Indeed you did, Lucy," Rowan said, her excitement rising as realization dawned. "Your other hand, if you would, Oberon."

Rowan warmed beneath his smile of approval.

"I should have realized that it would be difficult to fool you, Mrs. Penham." His right hand unfurled to reveal a second gleaming guinea.

"I was right!" Davy crowed. "I was right after all."

"You were," Damien said, flipping the coin to him, "but I made you doubt the evidence of your eyes. Belief, lad!" He tossed the second coin in the air and caught it left-handed. "Belief will triumph over logic nine times out of ten. In the normal course of events, I would have casually put my hand in my pocket and thus relieved myself of the second guinea. But your Mrs. Penham was observing very carefully. I imagine that you get away with little mischief when she is on watch."

"Can't get away with nothing, with her around," Davy agreed with a giggle.

"Anything," Rowan said, correcting him automatically.

"You see!" Davy complained, trying to palm his prize as the illusionist had done.

"I shall show you again, lad," Damien said, smiling at the child's fumbling efforts. "But first, I've promises to keep." He bowed before Rowan, plucking another gold coin from the air with a flourish. "Yours, I believe, Mrs. Penham."

"Whatever for?" Rowan asked. It seemed as if her heart had abruptly taken up residence in her throat.

"You are as deserving as Davy," he said, the approval in his voice almost like a caress. " 'Twas you who figured out the trick, after all."

"I want nothing from you," she said, trying to keep her tone too low for the children to hear.

"I know," he said, the green of his eyes deepening to the verdant shade of a shadowed forest. "Perhaps that is why I want to give so much. In my experience, most people want something, the only difference between individuals is the subtlety or lack thereof with which they present their demands." He picked up her hand and pressed the coin into her palm. "Practice, Mrs. Penham," he told her aloud. "Practice the trick, and we shall see who can do better, you or your pupils."

"Show me, Oberon," Davy entreated, tugging at the illusionist's shirtsleeve. "Show me again."

Rowan's fingers closed about the gold piece, unconsciously savoring the lingering remnants of his warmth.

"Use your fingers like this," Damien said, bending at the knee to the children's level, silver head meeting the two fair ones as he adjusted coins in their hands.

With a seemingly endless supply of patience, he showed them the trick over and over again. He would make an excellent father, Rowan decided, picturing him surrounded by a circle of children. *His children, not mine, not ours,* she reminded herself. *Why do you persist in torturing yourself with the never-can-be?*

Forcing her attention away, Rowan turned her back on the trio and practiced manipulating the coin. Over and over again, she repeated the motions until they were fluid.

"I did it!" Lucy cried.

Rowan turned as Lucy ran to her side.

"Watch me, Penny! Watch me!" she demanded.

The girl looked up at her governess, her piquant face shining with pride as she slowly repeated the trick.

"Well-done, Lucy," Rowan said, a catch in her voice as she thought of Giselle. *Soon, soon,* Rowan told herself. *Soon I will teach this to Giselle. She will never be shamed, as I was.*

Every night for the past week, Rowan had been spending hours in the library, devouring the contents of *The Grimoire for Novices.* Thus far, she had succeeded in freshening one of Southwood's dairy cows and used a locating charm to discover Davy's favorite toy soldier in the corner of the nursery. Each time, the bliss had touched her like a mother's hand, gentle and approving as she used her power in the service of others.

"I can do it too, Penny," Davy declared, in rising excitement as he demonstrated his newfound skill. "Look at me! Look at me!"

"A master and mistress of illusion," Rowan said. "Your Papa will be very proud."

"We must show Papa," Davy insisted. "He is down by the stables. May we go do the trick for him, Penny, please?"

"Oh, yes, Penny," Lucy added her plea to her brother's. "He will be ever so proud."

Rowan nodded. "Very well, but come right back children. Your grammars are waiting."

Lucy and Davy groaned in unison.

"Do you think that you might teach us to make books disappear?" Davy asked, a mischievous glint in his eye.

"Off with you youngling," Damien said with a chuckle. "And make certain that you return promptly for your lessons. No trouble for Mrs. Penham, else you will learn no more magic from me."

Davy gave a reluctant nod of acknowledgment. "Race you to the stable, Loo!" he challenged, shouting the last words over his shoulder.

"Cheater!" his sister called, sprinting off after him.

"Lucy! Ladies do not—" Mrs. Penham began, but Damien cut her off.

"Let her go, Mrs. Penham," he said, watching the children disappear across around the corner of the garden. Once more, Damien tried to banish the pangs of guilt. Wellington had sent a message with his decision. Whether Damien succeeded in breaking the ring or not, Sir Hector would have to be taken into custody. The last tick of the clock would come just after the midsummer ball. "Let Lucy have a memory of dashing across a lawn to show off to her papa on a summer's afternoon. Society will put a bridle upon her all too soon."

"And it is my task to accustom her to the bit, Oberon," Rowan said, trying to keep annoyance from her words. "Unless she is reined in gently now, she will taste the whip of general disapproval later. Far better a mild rebuke from me, than a lashing humiliation in the future."

"Once again you speak from experience, I take it," Damien said, discerning an underlying bitterness.

"My mother died when I was three," she said, her eyes mirroring long-ago hurts. "My father made no bones about his disappointment. Had I been the son that he longed for, perhaps it might have gone differently. But since I was eventually destined for some other man's home and hearth, my father left me much to myself."

She leaned against the stone balustrade, outwardly serene, as she described the disaster of her childhood. Only the changing shades of gray in her eyes, and the rapid flutter of the pulse at her throat betrayed her.

"Consequently, I grew up wild. I could swim like an otter and handle a boat on a stormy sea, but the art of managing a household or a husband, the simple skills that were necessary to be of value . . ." She shook her head. "Those I was never taught."

Damien wanted to hold her, to soothe away a child's bygone pain. But there was something in her demeanor that warned him away, told him that his gesture would be less than welcome. He thought of his early years surrounded by his family and a seemingly endless supply of magical uncles, aunts, and cousins. For all their squabbles and petty annoyances, he had never considered what it might have been to grow up alone, unwanted. "But you learned . . ." Damien said, trying to substitute words for a touch.

"Indeed, I did." Her syllables were clipped, harsh. "To flee my father's indifference, I consented to marriage. However, during the journey to meet my betrothed, my father-in-law-to-be decided that he would much rather have me for himself."

Thirteen . . . she had been only thirteen . . . the icy hand of recollection touched Damien. Pent memories of terror drifted in her eyes like smoke across a mirror, a soul-searing horror that was beyond his ability to imagine, much less comprehend. "And your . . . father?" He choked out the words.

She shrugged, the casual resignation on her face made him want to weep.

"My father had what he wanted, an immediate settlement to stave off his debts . . . his unwanted daughter off of his hands . . . Of what import is it now?" she said, masking her emotions with a tight smile. "The past is over and done."

"But we can learn from the past," Damien said.

"I have, sir," she said, opening her hand to reveal the marigold that he had given her. "In my case, the past has been a most demanding master." Before his eyes, she adroitly palmed the coin. "As you can see, I have learned to pay close attention to the lessons that life offers." Casually, she reached up to smooth her hair, and the guinea reappeared. "You are a most excellent teacher, Oberon. But what I told you before has not changed. I try not to repeat my mistakes."

She flipped the coin into the air, and Damien caught it automatically. "I am already beholden to you, Oberon, keep your guinea and your pity, for I have no need of either." She turned to go.

"Mrs. Penham, wait," he said, putting a restraining hand on her shoulder.

"Why?" she asked quietly, her back stiffening with annoyance. "Has this become some manner of game to you, despite your protestations of integrity? Any hope of salvation that we have lies in resistance. Why do you persist, Oberon, in making this harder for us both?"

"I don't know," he whispered, his fingers straying to a tendril of hair at the nape of her neck. "I wish that I could understand. You have done naught to encourage me . . . to the contrary, and yet . . . During the day, it is not half so bad.

I try to keep myself busy." He willed himself not to bend, not to kiss that tempting hollow below the mass of her hair. "Always you are there, at the back of my mind, and I conjure you up from my thoughts. But at night, Mrs. Penham, at night my mind roams free, beyond all control, and you are there with me."

Gently, he turned her to face him, and the bewilderment upon her countenance was a reflection of his own. "Do you dream of me, then, as I dream of you? Do we inhabit this same strange vision in the darkness?" His hand rose to stroke the nape of her neck.

"No," she murmured, heat creeping slowly up her cheeks.

"Liar," he whispered. "You dream as I dream, feel as I feel . . ."

"This is absurd," Rowan said, trying not to shudder as his fingers traced their way to the tip of her spine.

"I have found, Mrs. Penham, that I cannot kiss another woman," Damien said. "She becomes you."

His eyes were as dark and mysterious as a forest at nightfall. Rowan tensed at the thought of someone else being held by him, kissed by him. "What a great disappointment that must be for you, to have your women turn into prim-and-proper governesses!"

She pulled herself away, her mouth thinning in disapproval as she stepped back. "I take it, then, that you have made a conscientious effort to verify this unfortunate development? No doubt, that is what kept you busy this past week."

"You have been counting the days, Mrs Penham. How flattering," Damien said, his mouth twitching with humor, inordinately pleased by the jealous flash in her eyes. "I might almost say that you were angry and perhaps a trifle envious."

"You may almost say anything you wish, sir, and it will matter very little to me. However, you are right on one of those counts, and it is certainly not jealousy," Rowan said, biting off each word as it came out of her mouth. "I wish you good fortune in your continued experimentation. No doubt you will find some female who will suit you, if you try enough of them. I wonder if I shall have a similar difficulty the next time I kiss another man? I suppose I shall have to find someone as unlike to you as possible."

"Then, I must give you an adequate basis of comparison, Mrs. Penham," Damien said, pulling her back into his arms.

He crushed her to him, oblivious to windows, heedless of the soon-to-be-returning children, unconscious of everyone and everything but the woman in his arms. Another man . . . he was well aware that she had deliberately sought to taunt him. Yes, there would doubtless be someone else. Yet some perverse part of him wanted to imprint his brand upon her, to haunt her as she was haunting him.

All at once he was submerged, lost in the kaleidoscope of a thousand shattered mirrors, her eyes, staring back at him in a myriad of moods, wonder, fear, anger, hope, smoke, quicksilver, granite, and steel. In those shards he saw his own reflection, despair, passion, hope, and rage. The fragments melded, merged until he scarcely knew what feelings were his own. He felt his and her emptiness, the great void of need that yawned like a gaping wound. Beyond, something beckoned, something bright and wonderful shining at the bottom of that dark chasm. If only he dared to reach for it.

Rowan felt raw emotion bursting through every crevice and chink in the fortress of his mind. She recognized the battering of lust, the burning oil of desire, but knew that part of the assault came from within herself. But even as she felt his mind walls begin to crumble, her own defenses were falling, those carefully constructed shields yielded against the fierce charge of passion. Her heart pounded, a traitor at the gate, trying to release the bars, to let down the bridge and allow the enemy to invade. *But he is an Outsider,* Rowan told herself, *an Outsider . . .*

Outsider . . . Outsider . . . , Damien's thoughts echoed as he pressed her against him, as if he could somehow erase the future and the past. Here . . . now . . . no beyond or before. Her soft moan drowned out the litany of duty and obligation.

She will remember me, by the Merlin. She will remember me, the words reverberated between them as the boundaries of their minds blurred. *Outsider . . . Outsider . . .*

A child screamed deep within her, like a battle trumpet,

rallying all the memories of terror, a call to arms to defend the citadel of her being. *Remember,* that younger self cried, *remember what it was to surrender your every thought to him. Remember what it was to have your mind share his, to see the darkest realms of a man's spirit, to reveal the deepest secrets of your soul.* Oberon was no mage, yet, that longburied spring of fear welled up suddenly. "No!" she cried, pushing her hands against his chest. "No!"

Deep within the whirlpool of sensation he heard her, felt the chilling current of her terror. Her fists flailed at him, trying to force him away. Her eyes were wild and fearful, and somehow Damien knew that she was not seeing him, but some other time and place, some other man.

A cry echoed from above. Only his native prescience caused him to duck away, narrowly avoiding razor-sharp talons aimed at his face.

"Kek, kek . . . kek . . . kek!"

From beneath the shelter of his forearm, Damien saw the small hawk wheeling overhead, gaining momentum for another strike. He pulled a knife from his belt, readying himself for the attack.

"Get back, Mrs. Penham," Damien called. "Run into the house, before it tries for you. That lady's hawk may seem rather small to you, but those claws can do damage. It must be mad." He moved toward her, prepared to push her indoors and defend them both.

"Just keep your . . . distance . . . Oberon," Rowan ordered, her words chopped and breathless.

"I am not going to kiss you again, woman," Damien growled. "But unless I am mistaken, that bird is about to try its talons once more. I have never seen the like of it."

"You are not in error," Rowan said, raising her hand into the air. "However, it is you that she will strike, if she perceives that you are attacking me again."

"Kek, ek ke ek," the hawk cried out once more, but to Damien's surprise, the raptor landed gently on Mrs. Penham's shoulder. It turned its beak toward him, regarding him with a baleful cere stare.

"My husband's family had no desire to care for Mignon,"

Rowan stated the bent truth as she stroked the bird's ruffled streaked black feathers.

"An unusual pet," Damien murmured.

Rowan nodded. "I was fortunate indeed that Sir Hector was kind enough to allow me to keep her with me. She does tend to be somewhat protective, though."

The merlin cocked his head, as if in challenge.

"Mrs. Penham, I . . ." Damien began.

"Do not," Rowan said, her stomach tying itself into a knot of fear. She wanted to despise him, but how could she? Despite her decidedly mixed emotions, she longed to step back into the shelter of his arms, to lose herself once more in his kiss. "Do not begin an apology you do not mean, or make another protestation of your honest intentions. Do not ask me if I dream of you, or if I feel the world exploding when you touch me. Do not tell me of your newfound failings with other women, or expect me to sympathize with you for your sufferings. For though you have witnessed war and destruction, I doubt that you have ever known what it is to stand entirely alone."

She blinked, fighting against the sudden stinging in her eyes. "Soon you will go back, Oberon, to the bosom of your family, your friends, your world, and find some woman of your own kind."

He stepped forward, opening his mouth as if to protest. Mignon spread her wings and screeched a warning.

"I suspect that as time passes, my face will fade from your memory," Rowan said, trying to keep herself under control. "For both of our sakes, I hope that our dreams will soon be our own once again. And if, by ill fortune, your woman still chances to wear my face when she lies in your arms, then treat her with kindness, Oberon."

This time he made no move to stop her. She walked, keeping her shoulders steady, placing one foot before the other until she was out of sight and up the stairs.

Every day was an exquisite form of torture. The lessons in illusion continued, but Rowan was not foolish enough to allow herself to be alone with Oberon. Still, like a starving pauper with her nose pressed to the bakery window, Rowan surreptitiously feasted her eyes upon him, knowing that she would never go beyond that invisible pane. She was torn between relief and despair when Oberon announced that he could no longer give any more magic lessons until after the fair.

Even now, she lingered at the window, telling herself that she was watching the sunset, when she knew that she was seeking a glimpse of him. Down below, through the open terrace doors, she could hear the sound of his laughter floating on the evening breeze and the scent of cigar smoke drifted up like incense in the gathering dusk.

Rowan forced herself to go back to the nursery even though she knew that Lucy and Davy were both fast asleep. A full day of activity had exhausted them both. Gently, Rowan uncurled Davy's fingers, removing the red silk kerchief from his grasp. Cheap dye from the wisp of fabric smeared his palms. No wonder, since he had been practicing with the garish square constantly in the hours since this afternoon's lesson.

With a careless flick of her hand, Rowan made the cloth vanish and then reappear before folding it and placing it on the nightstand. She had learned a bit of illusion these past few days and a good deal more about herself. Unfortunately, though she could now credibly make a kerchief or a coin disappear from sight, Rowan had not yet succeeded in banishing her emotions. The sound of Oberon's voice, a chance touch was still sufficient to send her heart leaping even as her head declared her the veriest mooncalf.

"Kekkk-kekk-kek kek!" With a rush of wings, Mignon flew onto the nursery sill, flapping agitatedly as she sidled back and forth.

"Hush! You will wake the children," Rowan warned as she hastily poured water into the washbowl, urging the distraught hawk to drink. "Whatever possessed you to return so close to dark, foolish one?" she scolded, smoothing back the raised pinions. "I was not expecting you back from France until the morning."

The raptor cocked her head from side to side, fixing a glaring cere eye on Rowan as she gave her report.

"Claude? At the Chateau Du Le Fey? Are you certain that

it was he that you saw talking to Giselle?" Rowan leaned against the bedpost as the bird cawed indignantly. "No, I suppose that it is difficult to mistake him. Did they know that you saw?"

"Kee," the small hawk responded, indicating a negative.

"But Etienne would not dare to violate his oath . . . he swore . . ." Rowan began.

"Ke ek, Ke ek keee!" Mignon crackled, lifting a clawed foot.

Rowan closed her eyes in pain. " 'An oath is as strong as its maker,' " she repeated softly. "Aye, of all people, I should be aware of that truth. If only I had some way to protect her!"

Friends, I have, of the Blood . . ., Tante Reina's words echoed in her mind. Briefly, Rowan considered the idea and immediately discarded it. Experience had taught her that she could rely on no one but herself. If Etienne meant to somehow circumvent his oath, knowledge was her only weapon, her only hope. He could not suspect that she had nearly completed *The Grimoire For Novices.* But that primer did not contain the information that she required. There were powerful spells that could be invoked against oath breakers . . . spells that could be found in the library downstairs.

"Tonight," Rowan promised herself softly. "Tonight."

Damien drifted toward the open doors of the terrace, lifting his brandy glass to his lips, but taking the most minute of sips as he looked up at the darkening sky. He could see a candle burning in the nursery window, and Mrs. Penham stood for a moment limned against the light. Even though he knew that she could not see him, he retreated into the shadows, like a lovesick schoolboy.

"A pity that you cannot continue the magic lessons," Sir Hector said mournfully, picking up the decanter to pour himself yet another brandy. "Davy's become a dab hand with those coins and kerchiefs, far better than his Papa, I must admit."

"You have improved quite markedly, Sir Hector," Damien assured him, "But with the fair in another two days . . ."

The baronet sighed. "Aye, I know. And I'm grateful for the bit of magic that you have given us Oberon, but not so much for me as the children. I vow, I haven't seen the little ones so happy for a long time."

And now it was nearly over, Damien thought, the summer afternoons on the terrace with Davy giggling as he ran around and around Lucy, twining her in an endless garland of kerchiefs, Sir Hector, fumbling every trick with amiable goodwill, and Mrs. Penham . . . Damien looked up to the window again, but she was gone. Mrs. Penham with her mercuric eyes, watching Damien's every move. Since that last shattering kiss, she had been as distant as a cloud.

Not that he could blame the woman. Thus far, it was Mrs. Penham who had shown herself to be the possessor of good sense. Far better to put an end to the matter before honor went entirely out the door. His actions had been inexcusable, against all propriety, against all logic. Yet, maddeningly, the sound of her footsteps on the stair still caused him to stop. The husky lilt of her laugh still haunted his nights, and the memory of her in his arms made those dreams seem all the more real.

I should never have involved myself with the Southwood family, Damien thought, staring up at the familiar stars. *Two nights hence, and their lives will never be the same. And mine, mine has changed forever.*

He fingered the two blocks of wax in his pocket. A new set of dispatches had arrived from Whitehall just this afternoon and were doubtless on their way to France. However, they had yet to discern just how the baronet had managed that trick. The contents of that safe might be their only means of discovering the man's methods.

Damien could only hope that some definitive evidence of Sir Hector's perfidy was locked in that vault; ciphers, names, anything that might lead them to untangle the web of intrigue. At least, with conclusive proof in hand, this niggling feeling of guilt would end, and the farce could be brought to a mercifully early close.

"Moon will be nearly full tonight," Damien called, deliberately spilling a bit of brandy on his neck cloth. Thus far,

the baronet had filled both glasses four times, and to all appearances, the mage had matched his host drink for drink.

The mage eyed the amber liquid mournfully; the best
brandy he had ever tasted, yet he dared not drink more than
a trickle. Tante Reina had warned him that liquor might mit-
igate the effects of her talisman. Damien touched the charm
beneath his shirt for reassurance. It had taken the Gypsy
woman well over a week to gather all of the necessary in-
gredients, but despite the power of her magic, she could not
altogether shield him against *The Black Grimoire's* influence.

Even with his mind wholly unclouded, the siren call of his
newest possession hovered on the edges of his consciousness like a garbled dirty word. Despite his lack of power, it
screamed at him, promising all manner of delights, pledging
to renew his magic. Nonetheless, it was critical that he
maintained the illusion of drunkenness. Every mage was
trained to understand the importance of appearance in ritual.
And this, the most basic of all male friendship rites, was no
different. A man who held himself back from the bottle in
the *tête à tête* of a binge was not to be trusted.

Surreptitiously, Damien tipped the balance of his liquid
into the bushes. As he turned back toward the half-foxed
baronet, Damien could almost swear that the chorus of
crickets had grown decidedly more raucous.

Putting on a mild smile, he went back to the decanter.
"Ex . . . excellent," Damien complimented, with intentional
hesitation, as if his thoughts were fuddled. He poured himself another helping of the amber liquid, almost missing his
glass entirely. "Sorry . . ." he murmured. "Comes from making . . . a pig of m'self. Hard to find good French brandy
during the war."

"To the contrary, it was all too easy," Sir Hector declared,
his florid face ripening to a cherry of inebriated indignation.
"So many people of our class were wholly unwilling to give
up their foreign luxuries, even though smuggling put English gold into the Corsican's pockets."

He leaned forward in his chair with the earnest countenance peculiar to a man who was half-seas over. "You may
think me foolish, Oberon, but I would not even serve French

brandy until Napoleon was sent to Elba, even though my father laid this batch in Southwood's cellars before King Louis lost his head. How many magistrates have sent men to perdition for smuggling when they themselves create the demand for that ill-gotten fruit, I ask you?"

Newly acquired of course, since the peace. Ruefully, Damien thought of his jesting remark to Wellington on the very night that he had become mired in this affair, and recollected the duke's knowing smile. Sir Hector's remarks were no more than the truth, but scarcely the kind of truth that Damien had expected from a traitor's lips.

The baronet's look of righteous indignation demanded an answer. The mage shrugged. "Ladies would have their fripperies, I suppose, and you cannot expect the ton to drink water," he said.

"Drinking English blood more like . . ." Sir Hector murmured morosely. "How many of the Corsican's cannon and rifles did we pay for, I wonder, for our silks and brandies?" He stared into the empty hearth and shook his head. "But it is over now, thank heaven. It is over."

Damien watched the baronet's countenance with concealed amazement. Although the mage could swear that Sir Hector was fully foxed, every word had the ring of sincerity. Through the bleary look of the truly jug bitten, Damien saw a light of genuine indignation.

Yet, Damien thought, there was no other possibility. No one else had access to the doctored information that had been making a rapid transit to the Bonapartists. With a wobbly hand the baronet poured himself yet another glass. No doubt about it, he was not feigning his drunkenness.

The mage allowed himself another minute sip as he speculated. He had long subscribed to the ancient Hebrew adage that the true nature of a man is oft revealed by how he behaves when he is in his cups. But though Sir Hector's tongue was well-oiled by brandy, not a foul or mean word had escaped his mouth. To the contrary, until this moment, the baronet had seemed to be in charity with the world, exuding an aura of kindly goodwill that Damien could swear was unfeigned.

Sir Hector sighed. "I wish my Mary had lived to see

Napoleon's downfall, to know that all that time spent away
from her . . . from the children was not in vain . . ."

"You were involved?" Damien asked, rejoicing that the
conversation was finally heading in the right direction.

The baronet nodded. "Indeed, I had some trifling part in
the effort, the paper-shuffling side of the war, the offices of
Whitehall."

No brandied braggadocio, just a modest statement;
though, from what Damien had been told, this man was well
entitled to boast of his role in the war effort. It did not fit, by
the Merlin, it simply did not fit . . .

"Too much time . . ." Sir Hector said softly, his eyes dark
with sorrow. "And Mary did not let me know that she was
ill. She thought that what I did was important y'see. She was
like that, my Mary, rest her soul . . ."

"The Gypsies remember her fondly," Damien said.

"Everyone does. My parents chose well for me, Oberon,"
he said. "We grew very exceedingly fond of each other,
Mary and I, a good woman . . . an excellent woman . . ."

"An arranged marriage?" Damien asked, eager to keep
him talking. Bitterness at the governmental demands that
caused a man to neglect his sick wife was a spurious moti-
vation, but by now Damien was willing to seize upon anything that would help him make sense of this jumble.

Sir Hector nodded his head with the jerkiness of a puppet
on a string. "Our lands marched, we'd known each other
since leading string days. T'was a comfortable life we had
together, and I was well content . . . but now . . ."

"Now?"

"I am a fool, Oberon . . . the greatest fool there is," the
baronet confessed, his voice dropping to a whisper.

Damien leaned forward, awaiting the bombshell, trying to
keep his eagerness in check. Perhaps if Sir Hector confessed, agreed to turn the tables on his French partners, there
might be room for mercy. "Indeed, Sir Hector, I cannot believe it, you seem a most sensible man to me."

"I was . . ." the man said with a gusty sigh, "but I do believe that I have fallen in love. What could be more ludicrous, I ask you? A man my age, acting like a veritable
greenling."

A woman, of course . . . *cherchez la femme.* Empires had been won and lost for a woman's sake. Damien's host rose unsteadily from his chair to lean against the mantel, his florid countenance the very picture of woe.

"Devil of it is, it wouldn't suit, wouldn't suit at all," he said. "Too many differences between us . . . too many . . . our stations . . . age. Time and again, I have told her, yet she don't seem to think it matters."

Differences . . . our stations . . . age . . . even as Damien waited for further disclosures, he felt a vague unease.

"Wouldn't think of it to look at her, at first. But she's a pretty little thing," the baronet rambled on.

The disparate fragments of information began to assemble themselves into a discomfiting whole.

"And, of course, 't is plain as a pikestaff that the children adore her," he added, seating himself back in his chair.

Mrs. Penham.

With unheeding haste, Damien gulped down the remnants of his glass, letting the liquid fire ignite as rage filled the sudden cold hollow at his core. *I am a fool . . .* Sir Hector's words echoed mockingly back at Damien. Images of Mrs. Penham and Sir Hector crept obscenely into his thoughts, laughing, kissing . . . lovers.

And you believed her . . . you believed that she was being honest, virtuous, but she was laughing at you . . . laughing. All the time she was warming his bed . . . his lover . . . the traitor's lover, the voice in Damien's head mocked. *You loved her, and she has made a fool of you . . . a fool.* He crossed the room, towering over Sir Hector. Words began to buzz in the mage's head, like the hum of flies around a rotting corpse. *He deserves to die . . . the traitor must die. No magic necessary, no kill the traitor, kill!* Damien's hands reached around the baronet's neck.

"*Hhhhunzzzzz!*" Sir Hector's snore was loud and throaty, sending a warm brandy blast wafting into Damien's face.

The Black Grimoire! Damien stepped back, aghast at what he had nearly done. The deadly combination of liquor and the heat of his jealous anger had made him especially vulnerable to the pernicious influence of the cursed book. Sweat damped his brow as he beat back the grimoire's assault upon his will. When its rasping demands were muffled to a dull whine, Damien bent once again. Gently, he eased Sir Hector's key from around his neck.

In rapid succession Damien took the two rectangular tablets from his pocket and laid them open on the table. Carefully, he pressed the key into the soft wax to make an impression for a mold. For safe measure he repeated the process with the second tablet to assure that Dominick would have at least one good form from which to fashion a duplicate.

For a moment Damien debated whether or not to try the vault then and there, using Sir Hector's own key. But it was early yet, and the servants were still about. There was a chance, however slight, that the baronet might rouse himself.

More menacing still though, was the insinuating force of *The Black Grimoire* urging at the edge of his consciousness, seeking to drive him once more into a state of frenzy. The risk that he might be goaded to act as judge, jury, and executioner was still too great. He decided to return later with the duplicate key.

With conscious restraint he slipped the key back around Sir Hector's neck, easing the chain into its former place beneath the folds of the baronet's neck cloth. Next, he went to the terrace doors and worked the latch carefully. To a casual tug, the entry would appear locked, secure enough to fool an unwary servant shutting the house at the end of the day. But with a little bit of force, the rigged mechanism would easily give way.

Let me help you, master . . . help you. The grimoire wheedled.

As the words formed themselves in Damien's mind, he felt an odd combination of disgust and awe. It was almost like a living thing. With each contact, the tendrils of evil became more lucid even as its efforts to insinuate itself into his good graces grew in deviousness. He felt an almost overwhelming desire to touch that scarlet binding, to open it, if only just to see for himself the pages that were the stuff of legend.

I can restore you, master, give you back your magic.

Damien stopped dead, realizing that his hand was only inches away from the book. "A few days more," Damien said under his breath. "Less than a week, and I will rid the world of you."

You need me. England needs you. Shall I tell you what Mrs. Penham does here at night, massster? . . . Destroy the traitorsssss . . . The grimoire hissed malevolently.

Rage and curiosity warred within him at this seeming confirmation of his suspicions. Hastily, Damien crossed the room and tugged at the bellpull to summon the servants. Assuming his foxed mien once more, Damien had them carry the baronet upstairs.

"Are you certain that you do not prefer to stay the night, sir?" the butler asked, concerned.

Damien considered the idea and immediately discarded it. There was no telling what the grimoire might attempt were he to spend the night under the same roof. "Fresh air . . . will do me good," he said, waving cheerily as he wobbled out into the darkness.

Chapter 9

The house sounds had long since faded into silence. Wearily, Rowan pulled on her wrapper and picked up her candle.

Mignon cooed a question.

"There is much that I have to learn, my friend, and precious little time. Sleep must wait," Rowan said. With noiseless steps she made her way down the stairs to the library, setting her candle down in the sheltered alcove near the corner window.

Eagerly, she went to the shelves, her fingers brushing past *The Grimoire for Novices* with regret. She was so nearly done, but that simple primer did not contain the kind of wizardry necessary to deal with a mage of Etienne's caliber. Rowan briefly considered Lady Morgaine's ancient but concise *Practicum,* but that work dealt mostly with day-to-day household spells. *The Ars Magica* was what she sought. A seminal work on spells and charms said to be authored by the Merlin himself, the *Magica* dealt with some of the more demanding and dangerous arcana, the double-edged sorcery that could destroy both the object and the wielder.

Rowan reached the woad-colored binding, scrupulously avoiding grazing the bright crimson cover beside it. Even though she was not its mistress, *The Black Grimoire*'s touch was a thing to be avoided.

Rowan settled herself in the chair and began to search for material pertaining to promises and oaths, her fingers skimming "Philters and Potions" section. "*To Kindle Desyre . . . On the Nyte of the fulle moon shall ye gather . . .*"

And what if one wished to quench passion, to suppress longing? Rowan leafed quickly past the nostrums designed to rouse romantic interest. What she needed was the remedy for that peculiar disease of the heart, some mystical physic for the ache that gnawed at her soul. But now Giselle was her main concern.

With frantic fingers she searched the pages until at last, she found the reference that she was seeking, "Promises and Vows." Eagerly, she leafed through the section, skimming through assurances and guarantees to oaths to the harsh punishments reserved for the vile crime of oathbreaking.

"Take two pinches of elephant's horn, fresh is preferred, dried wille do . . ." she read. With a sigh Rowan turned the page.

Dominick's face glowed red from the heat of the concentrated coal fire. The smells of molten metal and burned wax mingled as the Gypsy cracked his mold open to reveal a precisely formed key.

"Is perfect!" Tante Reina gave her grandson an approving grin as he laid the newly made key beside its twin. "If one does not work tomorrow night, then you shall have another chance, Lord Damien."

"Not tomorrow, Tante Reina. Tonight." Damien picked up the keys and cursed as they slipped from his fingers onto the ground.

Tante Reina frowned, scrutinizing the mage with growing concern. A bad omen that the keys spilled, but far more dismaying was the change in his demeanor. Something had happened. But what could have caused his eyes to glow with this feral light like a panther in search of prey? The old woman moved forward grasping Damien's jacket with a bony hand as she sniffed.

"Pah!" she exclaimed. "I smell brandy. Did I not warn you, boy, of the danger? Yet you drink like a fool."

"There is more on me than in me, but aye, I am the fool you name me," Damien said, pulling the elderly Gypsy's hands away roughly. "She has us all fooled, I suspect, you, me, Sir Hector, every single one of us, by the Merlin."

"What do you mean?" Tante Reina asked.

Damien ignored her. "Tomorrow, Dominick, I want you to go directly to Adam. Wellington was satisfied with Mrs. Penham's references, but suddenly, I am not. I want her thoroughly investigated and discreetly, without those bumblers at Whitehall crying 'view halloo' and alerting the fox. Adam will know the best means. Have him find out exactly when these leaks of information began."

"You think that the woman . . . ?" Dominick began. "Then, Sir Hector maybe—"

"Is innocent?" Damien cut him off, reading the plainly hopeful look on his friend's face. "The kind of detailed knowledge that is being relayed to France cannot be obtained in the course of mere pillow talk. Whoever is responsible obviously has full access to the dispatches from Whitehall." His voice softened at Dominick's downcast reaction. "It might be possible that your Sir Hector is an unwitting dupe, though I would not sign White's betting book upon it. Certainly, it will not be the first time that a man has made himself a fool over a female, or the last."

"Missus Penham and Sir Hector?" Tante Reina asked incredulously.

"Sir Hector claims that he is in love with her," Damien said, with a sneer. "And Mrs. Penham apparently professes to return those fond feelings. The man is trembling on the verge of the parson's mousetrap. Not that he need ask her, mind you, for to hear him tell it, the governess has all but proposed to him."

He bent to retrieve the keys from the dust, sliding one into his pocket and absently passing the other from hand to hand, making it appear and disappear as he continued his mocking narrative. "The humble proper governess, so conscious of her place that a kiss could melt her, all those stories about her husband and her unhappy childhood, a mere ploy for sympathy. By the Merlin, Siddons ought to give her notice as England's greatest actress, and retire in Mrs. Penham's favor! All this time that she has been holding me at arm's length with her damnable nobility, she has been taking him to her bed."

"And Sir Hector, he told you this?" Tante Reina asked, her confusion plain.

Damien nodded, suddenly holding out both keys again. "There are any number of secrets within the dregs of a good bottle, and Sir Hector was quite forthcoming when he had seen the bottom of a few glasses. The boxwoods drank most of my meager portion, Tante Reina."

"But not all," she said pointedly.

"Not all," Damien admitted, guiltily recalling the glass he had downed in a single gulp. "I had to drink something, for appearance's sake."

"And Missus Penham, he mentioned her by name?" Tante Reina asked.

"Yes," Damien said, dredging up the details of the conversation, even as a part of him was trying to forget, to pretend that this night was part of a bad dream. "I mean no . . . he didn't mention any name. Sir Hector is far too much of a gentleman to divulge the lady's identity, but there was no mistaking his meaning. He spoke of the difference in their stations, the children's fondness for this woman that he professed to adore, and the fact that he did not realize her beauty at first. I know I didn't see it . . . not when I first met her." He tried to keep his tones even, disinterested. How had he been such a lackwit? How diverting it must have been to have two men both dancing on her string. "I wanted to kill Sir Hector," Damien confessed in an agonized whisper. "Though he is perhaps as much of a victim as I. I had my hands wrapped around his fat neck."

"*The Black Grimoire,*" Tante Reina murmured. "Weakened by spirits you were. Anger, disappointment, they make you easy prey to its evil, to its counsel that the one you love is false."

" 'The one that I love?' " Damien echoed, his voice thundering with the waves of pain that suddenly assailed him. "Love is a much abused word, Tante Reina. How could I possibly love a woman who is an Outsider and most likely a traitor and a whore?"

"Where we give our heart, we cannot always choose," Tante Reina said, her rheumy eyes filled with sadness. "You may close your eyes against the dawn, Lord Damien, but the light still shines, much as you wish to deny."

"And would you prefer I abjure my duty, Tante Reina?" Damien demanded. "Like my mother, like my sister?"

"Ever swift to the verdict have you Wodesbys been since Mordred's day, and quick to anger! 'Tis the bane of your kin, boy, to judge all harshly, yourself not least," the wizened Gypsy admonished, shaking her fist. "You think that their choices were easy? Your mother gave up love for duty! And your sister nearly died because she did not believe herself worthy of the Wodesby name! No right have you, to reproach them—now especially. You begin to understand their pain, their anguish, I think."

Earthen eyes pierced to his heart, and Damien was reduced to a child, caught at mischief once again. "Yes, I understand," he acknowledged, looking at the keys that gleamed dully in his hands. "And I cannot fault them. At least the Outsiders that Mama and Miranda chose were worthy and honorable. How can I possibly love her, Tante Reina, knowing what I know?"

"And what is it you know, boy? What *The Black Grimoire* whispers?" the elderly woman asked, aching at the anguish in his question. How could she ease his suffering, guide him, and still keep within the constraints that bound her as a reader? "When you laid hands upon that foul book, it read your heart, secrets hidden even from yourself. The darkness within you feeds it, gives it power. Remember this, Lord Damien, when you make reckoning. Remember, kernels of truth lie at the center of most strong falsehoods."

"And sometimes, Tante Reina, hard realities cannot be gainsaid, no matter how much we would wish it otherwise," Damien said, his mouth tightening into a grim line as he placed both keys in his pocket. "No matter where the truth may lie, no matter what I might feel, I still wear this."

He placed his fingers over the token of his office, stiff and unyielding beneath the stuff of his black shirt, like a shackle, tethering him with intangible fetters of duty. There would be no escape from the manacle of his obligation, not until his successor removed it from his cold, lifeless arm, as he had taken it from his father's.

Tante Reina placed a restraining hand on his sleeve. "Stay, boy, and tonight do not go back. Let the sun rise and set on your anger so you might see more clearly."

His palm slid over her fingers, gently brushing her aside. "There is no time, Tante Reina," Damien said. "You need not fear for me. The brandy's fire has long since been quenched, and I promise that I shall not touch another drop until *The Black Grimoire* is destroyed once and for all. Sir Hector's footmen have tucked him safely into his bed. That is why it is best that I go now. He is so cast away that he is unlikely to disturb my perusal of his private papers. Perhaps I will find what I need to damn him, and then this farce will be at an end."

She knew better than to plead. The stubborn expression upon his face was one that she recognized from boyhood. He would not be swayed. *"The Grimoire* is crafty," she warned him. "Wary, you must be. Your jealousy, your rage, leave them behind you."

"I will take care, Tante Reina. Have no fear," he said, with a futile attempt at a smile. He started toward the woods, summoning Angel with a low, deep whistle.

The elderly Romany woman crouched beside the mastiff. "Watch him," she told Angel softly. "Take heed of your master. There is much he does not know."

The dog licked her hand in reassurance before loping into the night.

Chapter 10

Two phantoms crossed the lawn of Southwood, skimming across the pool of moonlight before losing themselves in the shadows of the shrubbery.

"Stand guard, Angel," Damien whispered.

The hound growled a low acknowledgment as Damien made his way across the terrace to the library doors. With a sharp tug the lock clicked open, and he stepped into the darkened library, leaving the entry ajar behind him.

He paused near the threshold, letting his eyes accustom themselves to the dimmed room. To his relief, *The Black Grimoire* was silent, but the air was still pregnant with its malevolence, as if it was waiting.

Swiftly, Damien crossed to the shelves, placing himself approximately at the spot where he had seen Sir Hector stand, just in front of the bookcase. Angel had confirmed that the controlling mechanism had been somewhere just above the baronet's head. Unfortunately, one of the failings of familiars was their inability to read. Damien would have to search for the title that served as a lever.

His eyes swept the shelves, drawn despite himself to the scarlet bound volume, its gold-lettered title writhing across its spine. He glared at it defiantly, noting in passing that there was now an empty spot where *The Ars Magica* had been. Reaching up, Damien methodically tipped each book in turn until he reached *Solomon's Key*. There was a barely audible click.

Beware, Oberon! Beware! There was danger hiding in the dark, but he did not seem to hear her warning. She ran to him, and he turned, his arms opening to her, but as she reached the sanctuary of his embrace, his fingers turned to golden snakes, wrapping themselves around her throat. "All an illusssion," they hissed. "Tissss all an illussssion."

Rowan woke with a start, the mistress's talisman in her hand. Judging by the cold mound of puddled wax, her candle had long come to the end of its wick. By the faint glow of moonlight, she eyed the heading at the top of the page— "Rending the Oath Render." Unfortunately, like all of the other charms for redress that she had found, this one contained a key ingredient that was difficult to obtain: three hairs of a pregnant black cat collected on a Samhain night.

Disappointed, she tucked her chain of office back into the neck of her nightdress and closed *The Ars Magica*. There was no telling how long she had been sleeping, and with her head feeling as if it was stuffed with cotton wool, any further effort would be the waste of a good candle. It was time to seek her bed. She rose and stretched her arms, setting the book aside.

Staring through the glass out into the darkness, Rowan conjured Oberon from the fabric of the night, letting that vision fill the sudden emptiness within her. Why was it that she could recall every second that she had been with him, every word, trace the path of his hands, the nuance of his touch, the pressure of his lips? How could it be that she had felt his rage and bitterness, and at the same time feel a sense of belonging? Was it possible to drown in a morass of guilt and fear and yet glimpse the glory of the Light all at once?

She will remember me, by the Merlin! The phrase echoed in her mind. She shook her head in silent confusion. No, it could not have been his thought. Perhaps this too was the effect of her muddled emotions, mistaking her own feelings and the familiar witch's epithet for Oberon's. If this was the result when his mindwalls had barely been broached, she shuddered at the consequences of another encounter.

Only once before had another's mind fully joined her own, a rape of her soul forced upon her in the union of bodies. Rowan shivered at the memories of that invasion. Though the comte had been physically able to overpower her, he had never succeeded in subduing her thoughts. Indeed, the screaming force of her terror had kept him from her bed after that single night. Rowan had sworn it would not happen again, yet here she was on the brink of surrender, to an Outsider, a virtual stranger.

As she stepped from the nook, Rowan noticed a movement at the corner of the bookcase.

"Who is here?" Before she had a chance to think, the words spilled out of her mouth.

The intruder whirled to face her. Rowan felt a stab of dismay. How did the stone spell in *The Grimoire for Novices* begin; the one that rendered an attacker motionless? Tongue of frog? Or was it tongue of toad? As he advanced into a puddle of moonbeams, she released a relieved breath.

"Oberon, whatever are you doing here at this hour?" Was she still dreaming, or had she somehow managed to summon him from her thoughts?

"Sir Hector gave me the freedom of his library, if you recall," he said stiffly. "I was just seeking something to read. And yourself?"

"I fell asleep in the chair," she admitted with a sheepish quirk of her mouth, but her smile faded when she saw Oberon's look. Though his lips stretched, it was more a grimace than a grin.

His clothing blended with the darkness, and the harsh light illuminated the stark planes of his countenance, giving his face the eerie appearance of a marble bust, suspended in nothingness. She shuddered involuntarily.

"Cold, Mrs. Penham? Were you expecting Sir Hector to come and keep you warm?" he asked, openly mocking. "Unfortunately, I regret to inform you that your lover is besotted with the bottle tonight, so you will have to look elsewhere for comfort."

She shook her head in bewilderment as she took a step back. "I do not understand."

"Brava, madame, an affecting performance, as usual," he said, fixing her with a cockatrice stare. "How *do* you manage that air of innocence? Is that what you used to bring Sir Hector panting to your skirts? I know that it almost brought me to heel."

"You must be drunk. The filth that you utter is undoubtedly crawling from a brandied tongue," Rowan said, feigning an air of hauteur even as an icy feeling of apprehension crept up her spine. Although he made no move to touch her, he had the poised menace of an adder, coiled, waiting to strike.

"Unfortunately, I am entirely sober," Damien said, his eyes glittering with menace. "Much as I would prefer to be floating in the jug, I have temporarily sworn off liquor."

As he moved closer, Rowan could see that he was most definitely not drunk; the jewel-hard clarity of his gaze was far too focused, almost reptilian. He regarded her coolly, his aspect distant, calculating, sending a warning to all of her senses. Rowan eyed the door and turned, but he countered her quickly, cutting off escape.

"Leaving so soon?" he asked, the corner of his mouth curling in disdain.

"I could scream," she cautioned him, "and bring the household running."

"And I could say that you arranged to meet me here tonight, Mrs. Penham. How would your employer feel about that, I wonder? Cuckolding him before the banns are even read?" He advanced slowly.

"What in the world are you talking about?"

"Scream, by all means, if you are so certain of your power over Sir Hector."

"And have the servants find me alone with you?" Rowan groaned in despair. "I would lose my position."

"You might, in a manner of speaking. Not so sure that you can get him leg-shackled, Mrs. Penham?" he asked with a scornful leer. "He is smitten, I grant you, but Sir Hector might not be so enamored if he finds you in another man's arms."

"Sir Hector?" Rowan shook her head once more. "In love with me? Have you gone mad, Oberon? Or is this another one of your games?"

"No game, madame." His fingers struck out to encircle her wrist. With a sudden tug he forced her tightly against him. "How could I hope to compete against a premiere player such as yourself. All your pretty protests, your pretense. And you were laughing at me all the while."

In the ghostly light she could almost believe that she had gone back in time, to the library of the Chateau Du Le Fey, the voice of the old comte, ranting and raving, accusing her of all manner of infidelities, jealous because he dared not rape her again and risk the Mindwalker's rage that had nearly killed him.

Familiarity brought Rowan its own curious sense of calm. She had been here before, though not in this place, not with this man. Though she did not understand the cause of Oberon's transformation, she had ample experience in surviving the frenzied abuse of a madman.

Only moments before she had been dreaming of him, spent her waking hours recollecting his touch, the feel of his arms around her. Now the thud of Oberon's heart was a death drum, and the heat of his breath upon her cheek became an obscenity.

Yet strangely enough she could at last acknowledge the full measure of her feelings. Without Giselle's fate in the balance, Rowan knew now that she would have denied her Blood, forsaken her heritage, if Oberon had beckoned.

A part of Rowan wanted to fight, to weep, to rail against this injustice. But she shut that firmly away within the deepest chambers of her heart. Ruthlessly, she pushed aside fear and disappointment in favor of survival. The part of her that had endured as the Comtesse Du Le Fey came to the fore, emotionlessly calculated her chances.

Cry out, and the servants would come running. A governess in nightclothes, away from her bed, found in a man's arms? There was little question whose story would be believed. Just a day short of her goal, Rowan would be dismissed, and Giselle would be doomed to a repetition of her mother's hellish marriage. Nor would it pay to fight the inevitable, to seek mercy. Rowan could find no pity in the green glacier of this man's eyes, no warmth that would melt before an appeal to honor. He believed that she had no integrity, and she could expect none from him.

Kill him. The notion crept into her mind, gaining appeal as she considered the appropriate irony of that mode of revenge. It would require no more than a concentrated thought at the moment of intimacy, a lunge of focused anger and her attacker would be dead.

Kill him, Misuss Penham!

The exhortation echoed inside Rowan, startling her into

thought. Mrs. Penham? Never in the course of this charade had she thought of herself by her counterfeit name.

Kill him! You are witch . . . the grimoires, I see you read them. Kill him!

The demand grew in fury, like a scream at the center of her being, but now she recognized the thought as alien, coming from without . . . through Oberon.

Kill and I will be yours!

The Black Grimoire. It could not know Rowan's heart as it did the thoughts of its rightful master, but it obviously knew that she was using the baronet's magical library. Reluctantly, she raised her eyes to meet Oberon's. His wolfish leer chilled her, but the telltale tinge of ruby amid the brilliant depths of green froze her to the marrow.

Was Oberon of the Blood, but unaware? One of the Lost Ones who had denied the Gifts of their heritage as the price of survival? Only yesterday the thought would have sent her soaring, but there was no time to contemplate how or why. He was under *The Black Grimoire's* spell. Clearly, he did not have the means to protect himself from its influence, nor could she do it for him. And through him, the dark book was speaking to her.

Kill him . . . and I will be yours . . .

Though Rowan was ignorant, even she knew the ways of the legendary *Black Grimoire.* Usually acquired by murder or more rarely, by purchase, the book itself sought owners who were willing and able to utilize its power. Righteous intentions, worthy goals made no difference, for eventually the book became the true master, entwining its holder in its web of evil and violence.

Oberon's fingers rose, tangling themselves in her hair, forcing her head back. Rowan gasped with pain, and his eyes lit with unholy pleasure, a lust that demanded to be slaked. His obvious intent caused her to shudder, not just for herself but for him. If Oberon carried out the threat in his ravening gaze, he would be forever a slave to *The Black Grimoire's* depravity. Every spark of the Light, every hope of eternity would be ruthlessly quenched. Unless . . . there might be a way to save him.

Damien saw a glitter seeping from the corner of her eye.

"Tears, Mrs. Penham? From the woman who does not cry? I am honored." He trailed his hands along her hair, savoring the luxurious feel. Her eyes were wide with fear, like silver mirrors. He nuzzled the long graceful column of her throat, relishing the taste and texture of her skin. She trembled, and her palpable terror excited him strangely. He could feel her pulse pounding beneath his lips.

"Is this what you want, Oberon?" she asked.

"Yes," Damien whispered, "I have never made it a secret."

"Once again it would seem that I have little choice," Rowan said, with a sad wisp of a smile.

Her speech was toneless, almost entirely without emotion, but from the icy feel of her skin, he knew that she was not as calm as she pretended to be. "You made your choice, Mrs. Penham, you chose Sir Hector. You lied to me . . . You lied to me!"

"No, I never lied to you, Oberon." She spoke almost as if to a child. "But no matter what I say now, I will not convince you. You think me a whore, and obviously intend to treat me as one." Rowan swallowed convulsively, trying to speak as the lump in her throat threatened to choke her. "I owe you the debt of my life, sir, and presently have no means to pay it. Let us make a bargain, then. Perhaps I can salvage something for us both." She raised her head high.

He took her by the shoulders and shook her like a rag doll. "Do not try to make a fool of me again, woman!" he said. "I believed in you, I loved you, I was almost willing to lay aside my name, my honor for you, and you lied to me. Whore!"

"Whatever you might believe me to be, no woman deserves to be taken against her will," Rowan said, her whisper defiant, tears spilling down her cheeks. "I loved you, Oberon, though you may not credit it now. What you would take from me by force, I would offer you as a freely given gift."

I loved you . . . Her words penetrated, a tolling bell through a fog. Damien felt a strange disappointment . . . *freely given gift.* His tongue skirted his lips slowly as he considered. *Ssstrike her for her insssolencce,* the thing within him demanded. *Ssstrike her!* Damien's hand rose.

"Take me, Oberon," she begged him. "Take me here and now, like the light skirt that you assume I am. But take me willing, to keep the stain from your soul. Take me as the price for the life you gave back to me on the beach that night. Take me because I loved you."

Take me because I loved you. Something was not right. His hand drifted to her cheek, but she did not recoil as he touched the wet softness. Deep within a wild man howled, demanding to be let loose and bury himself in that soft flesh, even as another part of him quaked at the maw of darkness. Damien reached for that faint shimmer of light that was her voice, unintelligible before the demon wail that drove him, except for those few words, *I loved you.*

"I hope this taste of forbidden fruit will cure this madness of yours, Oberon," she said, standing before him, her head bowed. "And hopefully, this night you will succeed in making me loathe you. Perhaps, then I might be able to forget you."

Damien released her for a moment, stepping back to pull his shirt over his head as a sweet ache spread through his body. If she bolted, he could recapture her easily. He found himself half hoping that she would try to run away. But she just looked at him, her eyes filled with an ashen sadness, resignation and something else that he could not define. *I loved you, Oberon . . .*

"*Do not look at me,*" the demon within commanded, unable to bear that look of willing sacrifice. "*Do not look at me like that!*"

Obediently, she turned her gaze to the Turkish carpet. He let his shirt billow to the ground and reached for the neck of her nightclothes, ready to rend them from her back. But as he tugged at the soft fabric, the magic of her words echoed, rising above the mindless din in his head, causing him to hesitate. An unfamiliar warmth glowed at the base of his throat, and his hand crept upward to touch the rough canvas bag that held Tante Reina's charm.

Tosss it awayyy, the voice in the back of his mind urged. *I will give you back your own magic.*

Sweat misted Damien's brow as he blinked, trying to clear the red haze from before his eyes.

"You will be mine, tonight, mine," Damien said, letting her loose momentarily to jerk convulsively at the knotted leather thong.

You do not need it. Tossss it awayyy! The demand sounded more strongly this time, while in his heart he heard a still, small echo. *I loved you, Oberon.*

She liessss. She liessss.

His finger crushed the contents of Tante Reina's packet, sending a wave of fragrance wafting into his nostrils, verbena, lavender, rosemary . . . rosemary for remembrance. *Who you are, remember,* he heard the old Gypsy call. *What you are, remember.* The clean scent washed through him as the crimson haze that obscured his sight began to clear. Damien blinked, stepping back from the brink of the hellish void as the berserk within him bellowed with rage.

Mrs. Penham stood before him in her nightclothes. Despite the heat of the night, she was shivering, her head bowed, her shoulders bent in abject defeat. As the demonic din in his mind subsided, Damien felt a dawning horror. Wisps of memory pierced the fog of his thoughts.

"Mrs. Penham?"

Hesitantly, Rowan looked up. Dark strands of hair converged at his waist, contrasting sharply with the alabaster tint of his skin, moonbeams coated the living sinew with a quicksilver light, making him seem like a man poured from metal. Amid the sterling, the radiance of a golden gleam caught her eye. There upon his arm were runes carved in gold, the band of the mage of Albion, the talisman of the chief mage of England.

Friends I have of the Blood. Tante Reina's words echoed as a thousand questions raced through Rowan's brain and relentless answers paralyzed her. This could be no other than Lord Wodesby who stood before her, the man whose troth she had denied, and she had just promised herself to him without reservation.

It mattered not that Rowan's pledge had been made without knowledge of his identity. If Lord Wodesby took her at her bond, then the magic of his Blood would call to hers. Her soul would stand naked once more, vulnerable, all her secrets, her hopes, her deepest fears would be known to him, all that the comte had seen and more. But infinitely more horrifying was the fact that she had come to love this man.

Should he choose to wield that love as a weapon, she would be helpless against him.

What did it matter now? What did anything matter? Rowan closed her eyes, readying herself for the assault that was to come, preparing her mind and body for invasion and the inevitable loathing that would follow. As a mage, he would see what she had seen, know the degradation that she had known. How could he help but despise her?

"Mrs. Penham?"

He touched her shoulder lightly, and she opened her eyes, his face swimming before her. He shook his head, like a near-drowned man, struggling from the sea. Blinking through her tears, she could see that the crimson taint was gone from his look, and his brow was wrinkled as if in puzzlement.

"My head aches," he murmured. "This must be a nightmare."

"Yes," Rowan agreed, her voice breaking in relief. *The Black Grimoire's* hold had been shattered for now, but an oath had been made and the time for reckoning was nigh. "A nightmare, indeed. And in this hellish dream that we share, a bargain has been sealed. I am yours, Oberon, if you want me. I still offer you your pleasure for the life that I owe. If it is your wish, we can be quit of this debt between us."

In the ancient days, before the laws of the Blood had been codified, there had been freewill offerings of human life. Damien knew that those unfortunates must have stood thus as she stood before him now, ready, resigned to their fate. Beneath the tearful glitter, her eyes were dead, hopeless. Her face had the waxy, ashen cast of haunt's pallor.

Damien reached out to touch her, to smooth back a tendril of hair that had fallen to her face, and she flinched, then stood still, holding her breath, visibly willing herself not to move. He wanted to believe that he was sleeping, but the swelling rush of recollection would not allow him to deny what had nearly happened here.

Rape.

I loved you, Oberon . . . Impossible. Yet midst the dark miasma of his memories, those words had been his salvation. *Take me because I loved you.* Past not present, and from the stricken look on her countenance, there would be no future. If the love that she had professed had once existed, he had surely murdered it this night. His mind reeled in confusion, Sir Hector's drunken ravings, his own black suspicions, the foul cravings of his buried heart, and *The Black Grimoire*'s urgings all danced in a devil's waltz.

"Your answer, milord?" she asked dully.

Her tears had ceased to flow. Damien wanted her to rail against him, to lash out at what he had almost done to her, but this quiescent surrender was almost beyond bearing.

"There are no debts anymore, Mrs. Penham," he said, at last, pushing his hair back with a nervous hand. "How can I hope that you will understand what I hardly comprehend? Though it is no excuse, I was not myself . . . no . . . that is false . . ." He hesitated, his look bleak as he admitted the truth. She deserved that, at least. "In reality, I suppose that I was myself. I think that deep within us all lurks a monster, a part of us that is usually well confined beneath the facades that we build. Tonight . . ." he drew in a deep breath. "Tonight that fiend within ran loose . . . When I think . . ."

Damien searched desperately for words, wishing that she would react, give him some sign that she could comprehend and, perhaps, forgive. "I would have hurt you unpardonably, used you with all the force of that frustrated demon because I have fallen in love with you, Mrs. Penham."

There was no flicker of recognition amid the ashes of her eyes, only despair. She clutched at the neck of her night rail, pleating the folds of fabric closed, as if she still believed that he might tear it from her body. "All these years I had always wondered about love. Something of an academic interest, I suppose, for I knew quite well that my choices would be limited," Rowan said, without inflection.

She drew a ragged breath. "Love was never a possibility. Still, I persisted in dreaming of something that I could never have. You see, though I protest to the contrary, even I have some secret illusions."

Her look was both mocking and melancholy. "Childish of me, but dreams were all that I possessed, and of late, those dreams have been of you." Rowan's fists clenched as she fought against the pain of dying hopes, the flood of might-have-been happiness and regret. "You claim that you have fallen in love with me, but you do not know me, any more than I know you. These feelings are illusions, Oberon, as false as the silk flowers that you produce from the ether. We can offer each other nothing real, nothing lasting."

"No, Mrs. Penham," he said softly, "there is something more here, I feel as if I have been dreaming of you all of my life."

"The dream has ended," Rowan whispered. "Strange, I had never thought of love in terms of pain. Hate is a far simpler emotion, no everlasting needing, no wanting what you can never have, no emptiness or loneliness when the one that you despise is gone."

"I owe you—"

"Nothing!" she said, her voice rising. "There are no more vowels between us, Oberon. From this night forward the slate is wiped. Take me now if you wish it, or we are done!"

"Aye, we are done."

Rowan nodded woodenly and walked to the door, like a marionette on a string.

Damien watched helplessly as she reached for the knob. "Can you forgive me, Mrs. Penham?" he asked softly.

"Does it matter?" she asked, not bothering to look back as she closed the door behind her.

He wanted to run, to hide himself away. Damien snatched up his shirt, but the rigid shaft of metal in his pocket reminded him of his mission. He waited until he heard the sound of her footsteps upon the stair before turning back to Sir Hector's hidden vault.

The shelf swung easily on its hinge, revealing the keyhole of the safe behind it. With barely a jiggle, Dominick's key turned the mechanism. Damien opened the door to reveal a sheaf of papers. Rapidly, he searched through the heap, but it seemed that there was nothing there beyond the latest documents that Whitehall had sent the baronet. As he was about to replace the papers, Damien noticed a gleam of vellum toward the rear of the safe.

He reached back to find a small packet bound with ribbon. The delicate scent of lilacs drifted up to his nostrils as he carefully untied the bundle and unfolded the topmost missive.

"Dearest Hector,"

The schoolgirlish scrawl was plain in the moonlight.

> My papa will have no objection. As you know, 'tis
> Mama who nurtures great hopes for my conquering
> Society. Still, I shall marry no one but you. Courage,
> darling, when you come to beard the dragon in her lair.
> I am waiting.
>
> All my love,
> Diana

As *The Black Grimoire*'s laughter began, Damien's usual deftness deserted him. He fumbled, then refolded the letter with exquisite care, replacing all exactly as he had found it. The scornful snigger magnified to a mocking roar as he closed the safe and set things right. Damien clutched Tante Reina's talisman and ran into the night, barely pausing to shut the doors behind him. *The Black Grimoire*'s derision echoed in his ears as Angel yapped in concerned inquiry at his heels.

Rowan stood at the nursery window, watching dawn creep into the sky.

"I do not know why he is here," she said, answering Mignon's chittered question. "I have spent half of the night going around and around the possibilities in my mind. Why would the chief mage of England be playing at illusionist? Mere coincidence?" She shook her head. "I think not. He lacks a mage's ring, yet he wears a Gypsy charm around his neck. Why would he need such inferior protection when he wears a more powerful talisman? And how did a mage of his reputed power succumb to *The Black Grimoire*?"

"*Ke'ekkkk?*" Mignon asked.

"Fly?" Rowan began to pace as she mulled over the hawk's suggestion. "No, not just yet. Sir Hector was thinking that a new packet will be arriving from Whitehall tomorrow. Apparently, they are planning to move Napoleon to a new location. Less than two days, and the terms of my oath fulfilled. Giselle will be free, Mignon, free to love where she chooses."

The small hawk twittered joyously.

"Indeed, we will all be released from the grasp of the Du Le Fey," Rowan agreed with a mournful smile. "However, I doubt that I will ever be wholly free again."

"Kekkkk, kkkk!" Mignon threatened.

Rowan chuckled. "Ah, my fierce one, I have no doubt that you could poke Lord Wodesby's eyes from his skull, but it will serve no purpose. By Midsummer Night, you and I will both be gone." She turned from the window and gazed at the sleeping children. "They will miss me, I think, but not for long. When I touched Sir Hector today, I saw that he plans to ask for Diana's hand. She will make them an excellent mama, for she has a kind heart."

Rowan opened the door of her wardrobe. "Just see what she sent for me to wear to the masque, Mignon, ignoring my every refusal." She fingered the light gauze of the blue over-dress dolefully.

"I was to be Titania, the Faerie Queen. Sir Hector is to be Theseus, and Diana will be Hippolyta, and Oberon . . . no, Lord Wodesby . . ." Rowan closed her eyes, remembering the golden glow against the rippling muscle of his arm. "Of course, the mage figures as the Faerie King in Diana's plan. A pity that my absence will spoil things by removing one from her assemblage of Shakespeare's characters. But I am certain that Lord Wodesby will be able to find himself another Tita-nia in short order, even though he claims that he loves me."

Mignon cooed in sympathy.

"I vow, I can almost hear destiny laughing. I am so in-competent a witch that he must truly believe me an Out-sider." She remembered the sound of his heart, the touch of his lips on her throat. Even with *The Black Grimoire* goad-ing his mind, there had been traces of tenderness, restraint. Much as she wanted to, she could not bring herself to hate him. Yet if he knew the truth, he would surely despise her.

"It matters not," Rowan said, her expression hardening. "So long as he remains ignorant of who I truly am. We must make certain that he does not find me out until I have taken the contents of those last dispatches from Sir Hector's mind."

Chapter 11

The sun was barely up when Damien slipped into his wagon. He eyed his pallet for a moment before going to the corner and prying loose the board that lay directly behind the wagon seat. Against the darkness the small black velvet-covered box was near to invisible, but Damien found it with ease, as if his fingers possessed sight.

Minutes passed; he simply stared, scarcely daring to open it. It had been a long time since the day that he had finally acknowledged that his magic might be gone forever. Damien pressed the release, and the lid flew open. Faceted blue lights cast their brilliance into the dim shadows of the wagon. The Heir's Star stone glittered against the black fabric, the simply wrought rune band a mere frame for the fragment of heaven that it contained. But Damien's eyes were drawn to the empty space beside it, where the Mage's Star stone had once nestled. It had been taken from his father's body by his assailant and never recovered.

The family had tried all avenues, every fence and dolly shop between Coventry and the Continent was well aware of the exorbitant reward that was offered, no questions asked. Bow Street had found no leads. Astral quests had yielded nothing, and Old Gabrielle, a witch of venerable years, had lost her life during a séance while trying to contact Damien's father in the Realms of Light.

At the center of Damien's ring, a blue sapphire twinkled, symbol of the bliss, the sacred color of Woad from which the house of Wodesby drew its name, but the Heir's stone was but a shard when compared with the Mage's Star. Both had been handed down from Wodesby fathers to sons since the Merlin's time.

"Lord Damien?" Tante Reina's voice called anxiously from beyond the curtain.

Damien stepped from the wagon carrying the box in his hand.

"You caused great worry when you did not return," the old woman began to chide, but she ceased her scolding when she saw the young mage's haggard countenance. "Walked the whole night through, Angel said. You must be hungry. Tired."

Damien shook his head. "No, I have no desire for food, and I dare not sleep. If I sleep, I shall dream and I do not want to dream, Tante Reina, not after last night."

"*The Black Grimoire?*" she murmured, deeply disturbed by the haunted look in his eyes.

"Aye," he said hoarsely. "*The Black Grimoire.* Tomorrow night, I mean to destroy it. Such evil must not be allowed to exist." He groaned and bowed his head. "Hecate knows, you tried to stop me, but as always, I thought that I knew better. How she must hate me!"

"You make no sense, boy," the elderly Romany said sharply. "What has happened?"

"I have been an idiot," Damien murmured, rubbing his weary eyes. "A beef-witted animal."

"Progress, I see, if you admit this," Tante Reina said.

"This is no joking matter!" Damien exploded, his expression frenzied and bewildered. He shut the ring case with a snap. "All night long I walked, thinking, trying to decide . . . to decide . . ."

Damien fingered the latch once again, and stared down at the winking jewel without a word.

"I have word of Miranda," Tante Reina said, uneasily breaking the lengthening silence. "A healthy boy with a strong Gift, your mother says she feels his magic already. Your sister's Blood is strong. She is well."

"And the Blood continues," Damien said, intoning the ritual phrase automatically, a faint hint of a smile touching his lips. "Perhaps the chief magehood will continue through the Wodesby line after all."

"What is it you say, Lord Damien?" Tante Reina asked.

"I made a decision last night," Damien said, his smile fading. "Miranda has just eased my burden somewhat, but nonetheless, it will be difficult. Miranda's son can have my ring, and the band of Albion if he is worthy, someday. The farce is over."

Tante Reina gave a cry of distress, reaching out to grasp the mage's hand. "What have you done, Lord Damien, that you would give up your place?" She looked up into his face, her brows furrowing with fear.

His stark expression caused her heart to contract. "What have you done, boy?" she whispered. "Your eyes betray your heart. Evil has touched you, held you in its grasp. Tell! Tell!"

"I love her," he said, as if that in itself was a heinous crime. "You knew it, Dominick knew it, but I did not dare admit it, not even to myself. I tried to convince myself that what I felt was passion, a fit of fancy, but *The Black Grimoire* knew. It knew my heart even when I did not. When I thought that Sir Hector . . ." He shuddered.

"Jealousy and anger. Meat and drink are they to the dark book," Tante Reina stated, her look thunderous. "What did you do, Wodesby? The book, what did it urge upon you?"

"Rape," he whispered.

She spat on his boots. "In your face that would be!" she shouted. "If I did not know that you were driven! Poor child, I go to Missus Penham now, and do not be in my camp when I return, Lord Wodesby."

"I deserved that," Damien said, his shoulders sagging as the old woman turned and walked away. "But I did not ravish her, Tante Reina."

Tante Reina halted in her tracks and whirled to face him.

"You stood against *The Black Grimoire*?" she asked incredulously. "Liquor and anger in your belly, in your heart jealous envy and my charm the only magic to shield you? Great must be your strength, Lord Damien, greater than I believed."

"Not my strength," Damien said quietly, "hers; and the magic that saved me was hers as well. It was only by her grace that I stand here this morning a whole man instead of a slave to that cursed book." His head bowed in shame. "Mrs. Penham offered herself to me, when I would have taken her by force. She loved me, Tante Reina, and because of that magic she saved me from the worst in myself."

"Great is your debt," the Gypsy murmured. "You owe her your very soul. Her love called you from destruction. But dearly must you love her, if your heart made answer against the dark force of the book."

"I know it!" Damien agreed, opening the box once more and closing it with a sigh.

"A decision, you have made?" Tante Reina asked.

Damien nodded. "Aye. Miranda has salved my conscience somewhat. Perhaps, the covens will allow my sister's son to take Albion's band as chief mage someday. I have been forced to choose between a forbidden love and duty. The covens will never keep me if I am married to an Outsider. In order to avoid strife, I will resign."

A huge smile seemed to turn every one of Tante Reina's wrinkles upward. "Is good!" she exclaimed.

"I had thought that you would be angry," Damien said, rubbing his head in confusion. "This will place an incredible charge upon Mama until a new chief mage is chosen for the interim."

"A new mistress of witches will there be, to ease her lot," the Gypsy said, chortling.

"I suppose," Damien allowed, "if the mage that the covens choose is married."

"Aye," the Gypsy agreed cheerfully. "Married, he will likely be."

"Most likely, since there will be a craving for stability once I abdicate," Damien said, yawning. "The question may be moot, though, Tante Reina. What if Mrs. Penham will not have me after last night? The accusations that I made cannot be unsaid, even though I now know they were false. As it happens, Sir Hector is in love with Diana." He looked at her curiously; she did not seem the least bit surprised at the news. "But you knew that, it would seem."

"Many things, does a reader know, things that I can say to no one, though help I might or hinder." Tante Reina frowned. "Fate chooses its own course, always. You must sleep, Lord Damien, whether you dream or no. All will end as it should, in the fullness of time."

"Scant comfort," Damien mumbled, stumbling back up the stair. "Tell Dominick that I will help him set up the stage in the square this evening."

"Sent him to London, you did," Tante Reina reminded him, "to Lord Brand. Dominick left with first light."

"Serves me right," Damien said. "I suppose that I will have to set up myself."

"Would that everything else be so easily mended," Tante Reina said softly.

Fair day dawned bright and clear. By dawn the village square was already crowded with dozens of stalls. Meat pies and sausages, baskets and quilts, confections and delights seldom seen in the small village of Westfield were being offered for barter or coin.

Rowan kept a sharp eye on Lucy and Davy. From her vantage point on a small knoll at the very edge of the grounds, she could easily follow their progress, yet avoid the effort of keeping her mind continually shielded against the casual jostlings of the crowd.

With so many strangers about and the great variety of pleasures to be sampled, she had wished that she could put the two of them in leading strings. Instead, she had settled for one of her newly acquired spells that would keep the children from straying too far from her side. To her joy, the charm worked beautifully. As soon as Davy and Lucy reached the invisible boundary that she had set, they would come running back to her to point out some bit of food that they craved or sight that had to be seen.

"Mrs. Penham," Rowan stiffened as she heard the voice calling from behind. Though she knew that there had been scant chance of avoiding him entirely, she had hoped that he would have the decency to stay away.

"Oberon!" the children called gleefully, tugging her around to face him.

His Gypsy garb was just on the verge of garish, too brightly colored and obviously designed to catch an audience's attention. As he greeted them, Rowan could see that his smile was tense and the corners of his eyes bloodshot with weariness. It was scant comfort to know that he seemed to have had as much trouble sleeping as she.

"Your first fair, Mrs. Penham," he said, encompassing the crowded square with a wave as if he was presenting the whole spectacle to her as a gift.

"You have never been to a fair before, Penny?" Lucy asked incredulously.

"No, never," she admitted, directing a look at Oberon that was barely short of an outright glare. "I was rather enjoying it, until now. But the children and I would not dream of keeping you, sir. I understand that you will be giving a performance this afternoon."

"Indeed, I am," he said. "And it is kind of you to be concerned, Mrs. Penham, but I am well prepared. I would be honored to show you the fair, if you would let me."

There was an outright plea in his eyes, but Rowan reminded herself that she could not afford to bend. The dispatches had arrived early this morning and even now, Mignon was winging her way to France. Once the fair was done, Rowan would follow her familiar.

"I once promised to escort you on fair day," he said sotto voce, reminding her of the night on the beach.

"I had thought that there were no more obligations between us, Oberon," Rowan replied, trying to ignore the treachery of her body. Once again, her pulse was racing at his nearness. She put a hand on Lucy's shoulder, holding the child before her like a protective shield.

"No, Mrs. Penham, not an obligation, but a gift outright," he said pulling forth a single rose blossom and presenting it to her with a bow. "Real, this time, neither paper nor silk. No more illusions between us, and by the by, my name is Damien, Damien Nostradamus Wilton."

Any uncertainty that Rowan might have had was wiped away by that introduction. Damien Nostradamus Wilton, the man to whom she had been promised from the cradle. Lord Wodesby.

She wanted to refuse, to throw the blossom to the ground, but the children were watching, and she told herself that she did not want to spoil their pleasure or cause questions. A drop of dew trembled on the outermost petal, gleaming like a tear in the morning sun. He had told her his true name. Why?

"Damien Nostradamus Wilton," she repeated softly, her lilting syllables making it seem almost like the refrain of a sad song. "I almost think that I preferred the Faerie King, sir. Now, if you will excuse us, I am sure that you have a great many matters to see to."

"Oberon is far less of a mouthful, I agree," Damien said quickly, reaching into a concealed pocket. There was so much to say, but not with Lucy and Davy hearkening to every word. He would have to make the children disappear.

"In fact, I do have some very important business, but I need help." He bent at the knees and lowered his voice confidentially. "Davy, Lucy, I have misplaced at least twenty pennies somewhere. Ah! I see one, Lucy, in your ribbon." He picked a bright coin from the green band. "And, Davy, let us see what you have behind your ears today . . . hmmm . . . two, three, five pennies. You truly ought to be more careful about washing, lad, and ah, dear girl, I see another two under your chin." He tickled her lightly, and she giggled. "I was wrong, there are four here." Damien produced the coppers and pressed them in her palm. "And yes, I do believe if I shake Davy here a bit . . ." He lifted the child and jiggled him gently. A shower of coins spilled to the ground.

Lucy counted eagerly as she picked them up. "Seventeen, eighteen, nineteen. One is still missing Ober . . . I mean Mr. Wilton."

"Let me be Oberon for today, Lucy, since Mrs. Penham seems to prefer it," Damien said, striving to keep his tones light. "Ah, I think I have found the lost penny . . ." He reached toward Mrs. Penham, but she stepped back.

"No, I have nothing that belongs to you, Oberon," she said, her expression conveying her true meaning above the children's heads.

"I know," he acknowledged, brushing back his hair and producing the missing coin. He dropped it in Davy's hand. "Ten pennies apiece, I believe. Let us see if you can find something to spend them on. The tarts in Mrs. Brown's booth are the best in my opinion; however, you may wish to try the toffee at that stall near the stage."

The children looked anxiously toward their governess. She waved them away. "Go on with you," she said, grudgingly acknowledging the inevitable. "But do not wander too far, and try not to eat yourselves sick." With a sigh she watched them run off into the crowd. At least her spell would keep them close by.

"Shameless of me, to bribe away your chaperones," he said, coming to stand beside her.

"A resourceful trick," she said icily. After last night, she had hoped that he would no longer have the power to hurt her. Why was it that his proximity could make her ache still? "But then, clever deception is your forte, is it not?"

"I deserve that," Damien said quietly, hearing pain flowing beneath her words. "I said many unforgivable things last night, and I would retract them all if I could, except for one thing. I love you."

"Ah, ever the illusionist, paper and silk and now Spanish coin," she said, tossing the rose at his face, but he caught it deftly. "Poor Mrs. Penham, so starved for affection! Do you think a pretty flower and a few pretty words will turn me up sweet? You love me!"

Damien touched the disheveled petals. "I do," he said. "I think I did even before I ever met you, though you might not credit it. You see, Mrs. Penham, there are a few important things about me that you don't know, that you ought to know. Do you recall that I once asked if you placed credence in magic?"

Rowan remembered that afternoon on the beach, the day that he had purchased *The Black Grimoire,* barely two weeks before it was. Yet it seemed so long ago. "My philosophies and beliefs do not signify."

"What if I told you that magic does exist?" he asked earnestly. "What if I could say absolutely that there is more in this world than what you can see and measure?"

"If you wish to apologize for your behavior, you have already done so," Rowan said with an exasperated shake of her head. He was a mage, a Wodesby; her shoulder still bore the mark of his violent anger, she reminded herself. This

was the man who had never bothered to see his affianced
bride, to ease a child's fears of the unknown. If only . . . no,
she would not dwell on it, but neither could she bring herself to hate him.

"I need to explain about my family, about who and what
I am," he said, peeling away the bruised petals. "It would be
unfair to conceal the truth from you."

"You speak in riddles, sir," Rowan said, trying to hold
fast to her anger. It was her sole defense against him. "I had
best be seeing where the children have gotten to."

"You know damn well where they are! Stuffing themselves sick and buying the useless rubbish that every child
craves," Damien said, stepping in front of her. "I suspect
that they are better than halfway through the money by now,
so we haven't much time."

"Riddles again," Rowan tried to turn aside.

"Dammit, Mrs. Penham, give me some latitude," he said,
throwing the remnants of his rose to the ground in exasperation. "I want you, I want you more than any woman I have
ever met."

"Ah, the answer begins to dawn," Rowan said, her lips
narrowing to a thin line. "I am unworthy of marriage, but
heretofore worthy of respect. Now that you believe me to be
Sir Hector's light skirt, you intend to make your own offer
of carte blanche. I suppose that I should be flattered." She
turned away.

Damien put a hand out to hold her back, but she shrugged
it away, whirling to face him.

"Do not touch me again, Damien Nostradamus Wilton!"
she warned him, her eyes hard as granite. "Do not dare."

"Please hear me out. This is only the second instance in
my life that I have asked for a female's hand in marriage,
after all, and I must confess, I am beginning to think that it
was better done the first time around."

"Marriage?" Rowan said, scornful disbelief in her voice.
"To a governess, a woman who you believe is her employer's mistress?"

"According to my father, who plighted my first troth, my
infant fiancée began to wail and weep," Damien said with a
wry smile. "You look as if you are about to plant me a facer,

and in truth, I would not blame you. Not after what I said and did the other night. I know now that my accusations were baseless."

"You speak to me of marriage?" she said, bewildered by the look of supplication in his eyes. "This must be some ridiculous jest."

"Marriage, Mrs. Penham, is no laughing matter, especially in a family such as mine," Damien said, wondering how to make her comprehend, to believe in a realm that most of humanity mocked or scorned. "Shall I tell you about my first betrothal? The prospect of the alliance was so fearsome that my bride wet all over her father-in-law to be. Hardly an auspicious beginning."

It was her pledging that he was speaking of. Lord Peregrine had delighted in the fact that she had given the Wodesby a thorough soaking. Her father had always been jealous of the chief mage. "You are in earnest," Rowan said in wonder, smiling despite herself.

"Never more so in my life," Damien said, delighted as her lips curved upward. "My family would be quite shocked to hear that I have been anything else but serious. Since becoming head of my family, I am known for my utter lack of frivolity, my devotion to weighty matters. In other words, Mrs. Penham, I am usually accounted a rather dull dog."

"Indeed, what could be more prosaic than traveling incognito with a band of Gypsies and performing about the countryside?" she asked sarcastically. "I shudder to think what your family must do for excitement."

"As well you should, Mrs. Penham," Damien said, his voice like the touch of velvet. "But you must be wondering what happened to my erstwhile bride. She absconded with another man, and in truth, I no longer blame her for it. I never met her. She could only know me by her father's opinion of me, which had never been high."

"She was a fool," Rowan murmured softly, "a fool."

"Kind of you to say so," Damien said with a half smile flavored by melancholy memories, "but I was equally the fool. I should have followed my father's advice and paid the girl some attention."

"Why did you not?" Rowan asked, aching as the possibilities flitted through her mind. If she had seen him just once, she would have fallen in love with him. How could she have failed to do so?

Damien's shoulders rose in a self-deprecating gesture. "Youth, I suppose. Not much of an excuse, but I was bound to a child."

" 'Tis a fearsome thing, the uncertainty," Rowan said quietly, remembering. "To be tied forever to someone who might well despise you."

"But we cannot avoid the inevitable," Damien said, grateful that she seemed to understand. He pulled another rose from his hidden pocket and absently began to shred its petals. "If I had followed my father's advice, he might well be alive today."

The scent of bruised buds drifted on the breeze. Even without physical contact, Rowan could feel the waves of his pain and guilt. She did not want to know why he blamed himself for the Wodesby's death, yet she had to. "What happened to your father?" Rowan asked.

"He had gotten word somehow that the betrothal would be broken; spent half of an evening searching London's hells for me before he went on to Wales, leaving word for me to follow. He went alone, with a thousand pounds in his pocket and the offer of nine thousand more if the Comte Du Le Fey would consent to break the engagement. According to my mother, Papa felt that his offer would be accepted. Du Le Fey would rather have the gold than the girl. But in the end, he got both."

Sounds of the fair floated across the knoll, the reedy whine of a hand organ and the rival calls of barkers hawking the novel attributes of the pinheaded lady and the dog-faced boy at "ha'penny a peek."

"I found my father near the docks, without a pound note in his pocket and his ring gone," Damien said bitterly. "Had I been with him, the comte would not have risked tangling with us both."

"And you are certain that this comte killed him?" Rowan asked.

"He denied it, of course," Damien said, his jaw clenching in frustration.

But Rowan knew that the comte had not killed the elder Wodesby. She would have seen it, felt it among all the many evils that she had experienced in that first hellish intimacy. Still, she could not tell Damien, not without revealing her identity. Even if she dared to speak the truth, would he believe her?

" 'Might have beens' only cause grief," Rowan said, wishing that she dared to touch him, to comfort him, but she could no longer trust her ability to shield her thoughts against him. "Those everlasting regrets hang about like vultures gnawing at the soul."

"Unless we learn," Damien reminded her. "Can you forgive me, Mrs. Penham? I have lived my years with far too many 'might have beens' upon my shoulders. I love you, and last night you said that you loved me."

"You remember," Rowan whispered.

"Every word, all that I said, and to my shame, all that you offered for my sake." Damien moved forward, wanting to gather her into his arms, but the fear in her eyes stayed him. She did not want his touch, and he could not blame her. "Marry me, Mrs. Penham, else I shall spend the rest of my life living with regret."

"You do not know me," Rowan said, trying to swallow the bitterness that welled up in her throat. She wanted to scream, to rail against the Fate that had played hazard with her life and heart. "What will your family say, Damien, if you bring home a wife from outside your circle?"

"They will love you, as I do," he said, as if he were defying them not to. "Both my mother and sister married beyond the usual sphere. And if you worry about your daughter, I will accept her as my own, Mrs. Penham."

Rowan closed her eyes against the earnest appeal on his countenance. He loved her, even though he thought her to be an Outsider. He would embrace her daughter, sight unseen. His offer was no less than everything, for she knew the covens would never accept one who lacked the Blood as their mistress. He would be forced to give up the chief mage's band or risk strife within the covens.

So much love was being offered, yet all of it would surely turn to hate once he learned the truth. She had prostituted her Gift, and even now was using her skills to set a monster loose upon the world once again. "It is too much," she whispered as the pain knifed through her. "I cannot bear it."

Her soft cry of distress chilled Damien, reminding him that there was still a great deal that she did not comprehend, things about him that he could not yet reveal. He recalled his first encounter with the skeptical man who was now his brother-by-marriage. Would she believe that it was a magical influence that had turned him to a ravening beast? And how would she feel when she found out that he was Wellington's spy?

Time—they both needed time.

"I will not press you for your answer, there is still a great deal that I must tell you," Damien said. "But not now, not when I have promised to escort you to the fair. Will you come with me, Mrs. Penham, to see the sights?" he asked, offering his arm.

Rowan knew that she ought to refuse his arm and his hand then and there. Far better to hurt him now, than to postpone the inevitable, but the child in her cried out at the injustice of it all. The sky was bright, and the world was filled with the sounds of joy and laughter.

There was a desperate entreaty in his eyes, and though Rowan knew that this moment of happiness would be nothing more than another brief illusion, she threw away her caution. Shielding herself carefully, Rowan laid her hand upon his sleeve. Once again, she felt that curious sense of rightness, and at last knew it for what it was—love.

Chapter 12

Behind the horse blankets that served as a temporary curtain, Damien cursed his ridiculous suspicions. He would still be out and about, enjoying the fair with Mrs. Penham had he not sent Dominick to London on a wild-goose chase.

It had been like seeing through a child's eyes. Never before had he so enjoyed the simple pleasures of a country fair day. Her wonder was contagious, whether it was her delight at Mrs. Brown's cherry tarts or her admiration when he had won her a ribbon at the coconut throw.

Damien grumbled as he gave his props a final check. "Justice, I suppose," he remarked quietly to Angel, who lounged at the edge of the temporary stage. "The wages of jealousy. I should be out there winning her ribbons, and Dominick should be seeing to these last-minute details."

Gently, Damien smoothed back the feathers of one of the doves, setting her in her secret compartment until the time came for her miraculous appearance. With exquisite care he wrapped the stems of his rosebuds. Though real flowers were more risky to use in his trick, he would never give Mrs. Penham an artificial bloom again. As he imagined her look of surprise, Damien smiled.

"Oberon!"

Damien looked up to see Tess, the barmaid, motioning to him from the edge of the platform.

"John, he sent me t' warn yer," she said softly. "Two Frenchies come in ter Th' Ram terday. Might be in fer th' fair, then again, I think no," she added.

"Why?" Damien asked.

"Quality," she said, as if that was all the explanation necessary. "Leastwise one of 'em is, tall an' handsome, hair like a new guinea what's been touched by frost. T'thers's fat an' dark, hands like leeches on him. 'Come fer th' fair,' says they, as if t' were some Lunnon fair, when t'is no more'n a Punch and Judy with a few sharps fleecin' the flats with penny pitches an' 'hide th' lady,' " she added contemptuously.

"Where are they?" Damien asked, pulling a gold piece from one of his hidden pockets and presenting it with a flourish.

"No need, luv," she grumbled, nonetheless she slipped the coin into her apron. "Th' golden man, sittin' in th' rearmost row, direct behind the Southwood folk, he is, in front o' th' stage. Th' fat one just brought two dominos from Miz Henley th' mercer, black ones both, but I lost sight o' him. Sorry I am, but I can't stay'n see th' show," Tess added with a saucy smile. "Needs me, does John wiv this crowd about." She blew him a kiss and hurried away.

Damien sealed the flowers in their place before slipping stealthily to the front of the makeshift stage. Mrs. Penham, the Southwoods, and the Stanhopes occupied the front row. From Diana's glowing look, Sir Hector's ecstatic smile, and the glum expression on Lady Stanhope's face, it was simple to deduce that the dragon had been vanquished. Damien tried to banish all guilty thoughts of the reckoning that was to come, concentrating instead on the man in the center of the forth row.

An aristocrat to his toes. Damien observed carefully from behind the curtain as the Frenchman flicked a speck of dust from his sleeve with a gloved hand. Certainly, the man was as out of place as Brummell's beaver hat on a drayman's head. The Frenchy all but cringed as Sam Chaney plunked himself down beside him and began to wolf down a meat pie, none too tidily. One after another, the yeomen of The Ram's Head unobtrusively formed a square to fence in the foreign threat.

The Frenchman's dismayed expression when he found himself sandwiched amid the herd of John Bulls was almost laughable. Perhaps the bait that Wellington had set had finally tempted the hands that held Sir Hector's strings. At last, the secret of the baronet's web of spies might be revealed.

Tante Reina's great-grandson beat a tattoo on his drum, and the last of the remaining seats were quickly filled. Damien felt his blood pound in rhythm with that peculiar combination of dread and anticipation that is the performer's bane.

Sir Hector rose from his seat. "People of Westfield and honored guests, I offer a rare treat, a man who has become one of my dearest friends. Oberon the Magnificent!"

My dearest friend . . . But there was no time for guilt as the blankets were pulled aside. The audience applauded as Damien flipped a half-dozen silver rings into the air one by one. Metal flashed as it flew into the summer sun. Hoop after hoop he added, until they seemed to become a solid stream of silver. Then one after the other, he linked them together into a contiguous chain, seemingly unbreakable.

Though Damien meant to keep his eyes upon the Frenchman, it was Mrs. Penham who held his attention. *I love you,* he told her with his every move, trying to make the sadness vanish from her eyes. *This is for you; my every illusion and all my reality, yours and yours alone.* In her hand she threaded the red ribbon that he had won for her, twisting it nervously between her fingers. *Love me and do not be afraid of what I am.*

Rowan watched as Damien wove his veil of illusions, trying to paint a picture in her mind, to preserve the memory of this day. He did not know of the power that coursed through her blood, yet he had offered marriage. She reveled in the knowledge that it was herself that he wanted, nothing more. Insofar as he knew, the price of marriage would be no less than his ruin, but he was willing to surrender all for her sake.

With the setting sun, the terms of her oath were ended. In between the fair and the ball tonight, she would cloak herself in shadow and disappear without a trace. By morning she would have Giselle and her freedom. If Napoleon was destined to be loosed on the world once more, she had only hastened the inevitable.

As for the man who was pulling roses from the air, Rowan convinced herself that he would soon be over his midsummer madness. What use would there be in telling him the truth, that he had pledged his future to a witch who was no better than a whore, a woman who had sullied her Gift and spent her soul. In time he would likely be grateful that his unworthy fancy had disappeared before she had destroyed his life. The only permanent harm done would be to herself, for she knew that she would never forget him, never cease to regret.

Etienne had fully expected to be bored by a paltry performance. However, Oberon achieved his chosen superlative of "Magnificent." The illusionist was surprisingly skilled, executing his array of deceits with flawless technique and precision. As he bent to present Rowan with a bouquet, Etienne was surprised to see his icy stepmother blush like a schoolgirl. With the finale of a flight of doves, the crowd began to disperse, and Etienne searched once more for an opportunity to speak to her privately.

"Etienne!"

Etienne turned in annoyance. "Claude, I told you to stay out of sight. If Rowan sees you, it will make her all the more suspicious that her scheme has gone amiss."

"Lord Wodesby!" Claude whimpered. "The one who calls himself 'Oberon' is Lord Wodesby, I am certain of it. He is the very image of his father."

"He wears no ring," Etienne commented.

"The Mage's Star is lost," Claude reminded him. "Your father was all but accused of the theft."

"And murder . . ." Etienne murmured, his blue eyes glittering coldly. No wonder the performance had been perfection. He recalled Rowan's blush. "I confess, Claude, I had not quite believed that Rowan was false until now. Lord Wodesby . . . I have not forgotten."

Damien pulled the curtain back hurriedly. "Keep an eye on Adam's toys," he told Angel. "Make sure that no one trifles with them until I return."

Just as he was about to jump from the rear of the platform, and circle back around the crowd, there was the sound of boots upon the stair.

"Dominick! Excellent timing," Damien said, clapping his

friend on the shoulder. "Could you get Brand's baubles under wraps?"

"Greetings I bring you from Adam and your sister, and sad news," the Gypsy said, his eyes filled with sympathy.

"Miranda? The child?"

"No, no, all is well with the family," Dominick shook his head. "About your woman, I speak, Lord Damien. Adam did as you asked. Mrs. Penham's references, forgeries they were. She is not who she claims to be."

"I see," Damien said softly, staring at the jumbled heap of tricks upon the table.

"But this you suspected when you sent me," the Gypsy said, watching his friend's face harden into an emotionless mask. "Nonetheless, it gives me sorrow to tell you that this is true, Lord Damien, for I know that you care for her."

"My feelings are of no consequence," Damien said tonelessly. "What matters now is England's good and making certain that Sir Hector, if he is innocent, does not hang."

"And Mrs. Penham?"

Damien ignored the Gypsy's question, and ruthlessly sealed away the part of him that was raging, weeping. "Fortunately, we may now have an opportunity to find out how the information has been reaching France so rapidly," he said coolly. "Two Frenchmen have chosen to put an appearance at our humble fair. I cannot think it a coincidence." He jumped lightly from the rear of the platform and began to search.

A gust of wind swept across the square, snatching the hat from Rowan's head . . . "My hat!" she exclaimed, giving immediate chase. Hands reached out to retrieve the wayward bonnet, but it seemed to have gained a wily life of its own. Just when she seemed about to reach it, it eluded her again, carrying her beyond the square toward the churchyard. Finally, it landed near an oak, quiescent at last. She bent down to retrieve it, but a gloved hand reached it first.

"Your chapeau, madame."

Rowan gasped at the familiar voice. "Etienne!"

"Midnight, tonight, the cove," he said in an undertone as he brushed off the crown. "It does not appear to be much

damaged, madame," he told her aloud. "One must be prepared for unexpected happenings."

"Indeed, unexpected," Rowan echoed, trying to read beyond her stepson's mask of politeness, but there was no clue
to be found. His wintry smile chilled her to the bone.

A wind that had come from nowhere. Little beyond thirty,
yet the Frenchman's hair was touched with hoar. Gloved
hands in the summer and the telltale bump beneath that was
obviously a ring. According to Sam Chaney, the blond
stranger had simply vanished from sight. By themselves,
those small pieces would mean nothing, but as Damien
watched Mrs. Penham fumble with her hat, the puzzle began
to come together.

Magic . . . the empty space beside *The Black Grimoire* on
that night in the library, *The Ars Magica* missing . . . a little
bedtime reading, perhaps? A merlin for a pet—a familiar, of
course, the wings that could easily have flown information
across the Channel. Mrs. Penham's extreme reaction to *The
Black Grimoire,* her rapid expertise with the skills of illusion that were familiar to any witchling; sorcery supplied all
the missing pieces except for one.

How had she managed to obtain the information from Sir
Hector? Damien would swear that the baronet was not brag-
ging over the pillow. It was obvious now that the man was
heels over head for his young neighbor. From what Damien
had seen, Sir Hector was extremely careful with His
Majesty's business, and his iron safe was proof against
magic. The lady was either a skilled lock pick . . . or a
Mindwalker.

She had never offered him her name.

Married at thirteen.

What tree are you, then? His long-ago question echoed in
his mind.

*"A middling sort of tree that bears fruit that no one in his
right mind would savor . . ."* she had replied in a riddle,
probably laughing at his naïveté. But now he had the answer. A rowan.

Rowan Rhiannon, Damien's former betrothed. The wife
of the Comte Du Le Fey, France's mistress of witches. The

puzzle was complete. And she had seen the band of Albion, Damien realized with a start. No doubt she had thought his proposal and stumbling explanations highly ironic.

Rowan put on the mantle of blue gauze that completed her outfit.

"You look like a princess!" Lucy breathed, her eyes shining.

Davy gave a nod. "Almost as good as a pirate," he complimented.

"Perhaps we shall meet in fairyland someday," Rowan said softly, tousling Davy's head and dropping a light kiss on Lucy's cheek. It was as much of a farewell as she could risk.

By now, Tante Reina had Rowan's letter in hand, to deliver at the next full moon. Perhaps Damien would come to understand, even though Rowan knew that he could never forgive. But most important, if matters went awry, England's mistress of witches would do her best to save Giselle. Though Lord Wodesby might loathe Rowan, his mother would not deny her duty to a young vulnerable witchling who was as much a part of England as of France.

"Wave to us in the minstrel's gallery," Davy demanded.

"I shall," Rowan promised. "Good night, my dears." And good-bye, she added silently.

Damien stood before the bonfire, staring into the flames. His costume was of black silk unrelieved by any touch of color, a dark Faerie King, brooding and grim.

Silently, he took the Heir's Star stone from its place and slipped it onto his finger. "At least I will look the part of a mage. Hopefully, my enemies will be unaware that I am nothing more than an illusion."

"She is not your enemy. Keep vengeance from your heart, Lord Damien." Tante Reina shook her head in dismay.

"Do you know what she is?" Damien asked, startled by the elderly Gypsy's vehemence.

The old woman nodded. "Aye."

"You knew!" Damien roared, advancing to confront her. "You knew who she was, and you did not tell me, old woman! She saw the mage's band on my arm! No wonder she offered herself so readily. She could have killed me if she chose."

"Or all her secrets would have been revealed," Tante Reina countered, standing steadfast before his rage. "Or let *The Black Grimoire* take you for its servant. Think upon that, mage of England!"

She stood silent, letting him ponder that alternative, before speaking again. "A reader, am I, bound by laws beyond yours; well do you know this. There is much you do not understand, boy."

Damien turned away without a word and started toward Southwood Manor. With a soft apologetic whine, Angel followed.

As she came downstairs, Damien's breath caught in his throat. Her ebony hair was caught up in a crown of silken flowers, the overdress of gauze shimmered as she walked, making her appear as if she were floating. Too late, he recognized that the woman walking toward him now was the Dark Lady who had inhabited his dreams through the years, his heart's desire, his enemy.

Her eyes skimmed the crowd, but Damien did not emerge from his sheltered corner. Caught up in a whirlwind of emotion, Damien doubted his ability to shield himself against her power. One touch, and she might see that he had discovered her game . . . that despite everything, some perverse part of him loved her still, had always loved her.

She made her way through the crowd, smiling and nodding regally as if she were truly Queen of all Faerie. Women watched in envied awe, men gazed at her hungrily. She spoke for a moment with Sir Hector and paused to pick up a glass of champagne from the refreshment table, her gaze still seeking, but Damien stayed out of view. Two men in black dominos followed her unobtrusively. Then, in the blink of an eye, she was out the terrace door, her duo of shadows following close behind her.

Damien slipped into the night, Angel's black figure joining his as they trailed the Queen of Faerie and her dark retinue. A wind blew in from the sea, causing the trees to rustle and bend. He could feel the gathering storm in his bones.

As they reached the cliff path and descended the stair, Damien gave a silent signal. Obediently, Angel remained on guard as her master became one with the shadows.

Rowan looked out toward the waves, remembering another night where she had foundered without any prospect of rescue. But tonight, there would be no unexpected salvation; she was entirely dependent on Etienne's integrity. She had kept her end of the bargain. She could only hope that he would keep his. Still, she had hoped for a last chance to see Damien, to make her secret farewells. Perhaps it was better this way.

"Rowan Rhiannon!"

Damien took up a position behind the rocks, and surveyed the scene before him. Unless he missed his guess, the blond man on the beach was the new Comte Du Le Fey, France's chief mage, and his companion was likely a mage as well. Although Damien had opposed France in sorcery upon many a battlefield, he had never met its mage face-to-face.

Rowan turned slowly to confront Etienne, but there were two figures standing upon the beach. "Claude, an unexpected pleasure," she said, her blood chilling at the second mage's presence.

Claude? Could it possibly be Claude Du Le Fey? Damien wondered. That mage's unsavory reputation had even crossed the Channel. Rumor had it that he had pledged himself to the Dark. If there was a need for magical force tonight, Damien would be as helpless as a bat in daylight.

"What business have you here?" Rowan demanded. "This oath was between myself and my stepson."

"Indeed, it was," Claude said, moving with surprising swiftness. His hand shot out to grasp Rowan, and in a twinkling, a manacle clicked shut around her wrist. The chain dangled from Claude's hand, leashing her like a dog. He tugged viciously, sending her sprawling to her knees.

"Enough, Claude," Etienne said, his tones clipped in annoyance. "There was no need for that."

"By Hecate! How do you dare?" Rowan said, trying to

keep herself from trembling. She looked toward Etienne in defiance. "Do you sanction this use of iron, mage of France?" His chill expression gave her no comfort.

"For now," Etienne said.

"I come to accuse!" Claude said, pointing a sausage-like finger. "A crime against your vows, witch, against France and its mage. I charge you with oath breaking."

"You lie!" Rowan cried, rising to her feet. "You filthy swine, you lie!"

"Calm yourself, Rowan," Etienne commanded. "An accusation has been made. Present your evidence, Claude."

"First, the information that we have received from you is false, subtly altered to be sure, but in a way that would be difficult to discern," Claude said, his expression like that of a cat in a cream pot. "Our sources in Whitehall have confirmed the discrepancy."

"I know only what Sir Hector has been told," Rowan said, drawing herself up ramrod straight. She would not let them see her fear. "I have relayed these things to Mignon word for word, and as you well know, an animal is incapable of fabrication."

"How do you explain the variances?" Etienne asked.

"I cannot!" Rowan said defiantly.

"And how do you explain your liaison with Lord Wodesby?" Claude asked, with a knowing leer.

"There is no liaison," Rowan said. "He has no idea who I am."

"Come, Rowan," Etienne said, the hard look on his face belying his avuncular tones. "Surely, you do not expect us to believe that England's mage just happens to be on the spot?"

"I do not know why he is here," Rowan said, trying to keep the desperation from creeping in to her voice. "Nor did I know who he was until just yesterday. I had never met him."

"I told you that she would try to lie her way out of it, Etienne." Claude snickered. "From the moment I saw him at the fair, I knew that he was Lord Wodesby. He is his father's image, even to his sire's voice."

"Do you think that I would risk my daughter, Etienne?"

Rowan pleaded. "It was for Giselle's sake that I did this, because you compelled me on pain of seeing her wed to this *cochon*! You accuse *me* of falsehood, Claude? The man who persuaded the Comte that his son might be too honorable to allow his wife to be used as a whore for France dares to accuse *me* of deception."

"Another lie!"

"Is it, Claude?" she asked mockingly. "Would you swear to it by your talisman that you did not convince the Comte Du Le Fey to steal me from his son?"

Etienne eyed the rotund mage significantly.

"She wishes to turn you against me, Cousin," Claude sputtered.

"Ship walls are woefully thin," Rowan continued, "but you and the comte did not care for that, for you had me under iron lock and key in my cabin. And with all the brandy you had consumed that cursed night, neither of you troubled to control your voices while my fate was determined. Your words, Claude, I will never forget them. 'Make sure of her!' you told him. 'A son cannot wed his father's woman!' 'Take her for yourself.' Innocent as I was, I knew what you meant. I remember quivering in my bed in the dark, dreading the moment when the door would open, waiting in terror. If I had been less the coward, I would have killed myself."

As Damien pictured that child cringing in her cabin, the knowledge that he might have prevented her agony gnawed at his soul. All his anger began to dissipate. Whatever she had done, the woman that she had become—the fault lay partly on his head.

"She lies, Etienne," Claude bellowed. "But then, what do you expect from your father's whore?"

"If I am a whore, Etienne, then you are as much a pimp as your father was," Rowan said defiantly. "You steal my child from me, threaten me, and then you take *his* word? Claude wants Giselle, and he will do anything to get her. Do you honestly believe that I would not rather die than risk my daughter repeating the hell that I endured?"

"I did not take Claude's word, Rowan," Etienne said, regret momentarily softening his mien. "I myself, checked with our sources at Whitehall. Claude is not on trial here. While I may deplore what he and my father did, the fact remains that you have broken your oath to me. You know the penalty."

"Death," Claude said, crowing in triumph.

"My vow was fulfilled to the letter," Rowan said, lifting her chin with a show of proud disdain. "If you would become a slayer of kin and forfeit your place in the Light, Etienne, I can obviously do naught to stop you. But before you render your verdict, I would ask but two boons."

Etienne inclined his head in consent. "Speak."

"If the information that you have received from me is false, then obviously Whitehall is aware that something is amiss. Sir Hector is a good and kind man. Whatever you choose to do to me, make certain that an innocent man does not hang for what I have done. I would not face the Light with his blood on my conscience."

Damien's sense of helplessness grew as the details of Rowan's story unfolded. Clearly she was prepared to sacrifice herself. But without so much as a spell in his pocket, Damien had little hope of stopping France's mage. Unless . . . illusion was a paltry weapon, but it was the only one that Damien had.

Claude laughed. "You should be begging for mercy, foolish one. Why do you concern yourself with an Outsider's fate?"

"I have seen precious little kindness in my life, Claude. I would not repay good with evil," Rowan said, the sea breeze whipping her hair into her face. "But you could not understand that, could you? For if you would urge an old man to rape a child, there is no mercy in you."

"Liar!" Claude lunged toward Rowan, but Etienne clamped a restraining hand on the older mage's shoulder. "You do not believe her, do you, Etienne?" Claude whined.

The mage regarded him silently before turning his attention back to Rowan. "The baronet shall not suffer," he agreed. "And your second boon?"

Rowan took a deep breath. "Swear to me that you will not force your sister to wed according to your will or advantage, Etienne. Let Giselle find love; do not let her become the toy of this swine's lust and ambition. For if you do, I will abjure the Light and haunt you to your dying day, Comte Du Le Fey, and though I am the worst of witches, I swear that I shall be the most competent of ghosts."

Etienne smiled sadly. "I have no doubt of it, *belle-mère.*" He walked toward her and touched her cheek gently. "Ah, Rowan, my father has much to answer for; we could have dealt well together, you and I. You need have no fear for your cub, lioness. I will care well for my sister."

"You swear this?" Rowan whispered, feeling the regret in his thoughts, comforted by the softening of his expression when he spoke of Giselle.

Etienne raised his fist and clasped his mage's band. "I so swear."

"You cannot!" Claude bellowed. "The little one will have great power. She was to be mine!"

"You forget yourself, monsieur!" Etienne snapped. "You have no claim upon my sister, so do not whine like a thwarted child. I am the Comte Du Le Fey. I do as I please."

"Not always, Du Le Fey!" Damien said, stepping from the shadows.

"Lord Wodesby!" Claude gasped.

"This is a matter for France, Wodesby," Etienne warned, standing between England's mage and Rowan. "By the Laws of the Blood, you cannot interfere."

"Has the outcome already been decided, then?" Damien asked. "Would you shed the Blood without just cause, Du Le Fey?"

Thunder rolled in the distance as the two men assessed each other, taking measure. "Speak, Wodesby," Etienne said at last, "if you believe that you have anything to say that might make a difference. For though my name is Du Le Fey, I am not entirely without honor."

"Wellington has known about the seepage of information for months now," Damien said, making certain that his eyes met Du Le Fey's fully, willing him to believe the truth. "As you say, the documents from Whitehall that Sir Hector receives have been subtly altered, but Rowan did not know it, that I swear. Nor did she know who I was."

"Is this true, Rowan?" Etienne asked.

Rowan nodded. "So I have already said, but you would not take my pledge. I am sorry, Lord Wodesby, that it was necessary to deceive you."

"You expect us to believe such utter rubbish!" Claude sputtered.

Damien raised his arm in a reflection of Etienne's gesture. "By England's band, I swear it. If you recall, Du Le Fey, I asked for a similar oath from the comte upon the band that you now wear. I believed that he had killed my father, stolen the Mage's Star. Yet I accepted his word."

The mage of France's countenance was an emotionless mask.

"She did not break her vow, even though that bond was forged by coercion," Damien said, rebuke implicit in his words. "I was sent to weave my way into Sir Hector's household because the man is fascinated by illusion."

"And that is all that you have to say, mage of England?"

"All but one thing, mage of France," Damien said, his heart sinking at the Du Le Fey's brusque tones. "If you feel that you may justly demand Blood forfeit tonight, let it be mine."

"No, Damien!" Rowan cried. "This is none of your doing."

"I think it is, Rowan," Damien said, coming to stand beside her and taking her manacled hand into his. He squeezed her fingers lightly, trying to convey all his remorse, all his love in that gentle touch. "I should have made certain that you were willing to keep the vow that was made for us so long ago. If not for my selfishness, you would not be here tonight. You would have been with me, Rowan Rhiannon. I should have claimed you long ago."

"This is absurd!" Claude sputtered.

"He has the right," Etienne said calmly. "It is time to decide." The mage turned toward the ocean and stared silently. Lightning flashed upon the horizon, illuminating the spray that crashed against the cove's rocky mouth. He raised his hand as he faced Rowan once again. "You have kept your oath, Rowan, Comtesse Du Le Fey. You and your daughter are free. Release her, Claude."

"You were always a fool, Etienne," Claude said. The stock of his pistol glinted in the moonlight.

"Shot of lead, cast and molded." Etienne began a quick spell.

"Iron, Cousin! Cold iron, gun and bullets both, invulnerable to your magic." Claude laughed and took aim.

Etienne's eyes widened in surprise as the sound of a shot reverberated against the cliff walls. Rowan ran to her stepson's side as he fell to the ground, pressing the cloth of her mantle against the bleeding wound. Damien started for Claude, but the mage already had a second pistol leveled at Rowan.

"One word of sorcery, Wodesby, and she dies," Claude threatened. "Now, go stand beside the others."

Damien went to Rowan and the fallen mage.

"A pity that I had not planned for this," Claude said, his fleshy lips pursed in a pout. "I had expected that Etienne would take care of Rowan's demise, and then two iron bullets would be more than adequate to finish my dear cousin. But for three?"

"You had planned from the beginning to kill us both," Rowan said, smoothing Etienne's brow.

"He is not like my uncle," Claude said, his voice rife with contempt. "My cousin has always been weak. It was as I said to his father; Etienne would never have allowed you to be used in service of the family, Comtesse. But now that I am quite nearly mage of France, I can see that your death would have been a waste. Get up, Rowan, you are coming with me."

"No," Rowan said defiantly. "I will not become your slave, Claude. Better to kill me, so that I may haunt you." The chain on her hand rattled as she shook her fist.

Claude leered. "How kind of you to show me an answer to my predicament. Bullets, I have few," Claude said. "But locks and chains, I have aplenty." He kept his gun trained upon them as he bent to pick up a black bag and poured out its clanking contents. "We had planned to leave you chained, madame, to be taken by the sea when the tide turned. I suppose that I shall have to make do with the materials at hand. Chain Lord Wodesby, Comtesse," Claude commanded. "Bind him tightly, just as I tell you, or else I will kill him right now."

"Do as he says, Rowan," Damien told her, meeting her agonized gaze levelly.

Slowly, Rowan followed Claude's instructions, trussing Damien in iron ankles and wrists behind him. Every time she tried to leave the least bit of slack, Claude stopped her, forcing her to redo it until he was tied like an offering upon an altar.

"Now, chain Etienne to him," Claude demanded.

"He is half dead," Rowan said hoarsely. "Can't you just leave him be?"

"Not when he might wake and utter a spell. He must be ironbound. Do it!"

"At the legs," Damien murmured in an undertone, as Rowan bent to obey Claude.

"Get his wrists," Claude called.

"It does not reach," Rowan said, pulling at the length in demonstration. "And I cannot move him. Do you think that he will climb these cliffs in shackles to follow you, Claude?"

Claude's mocking laughter echoed against the cliffs. "You are correct, of course. Lock it, and go over there where I can keep my eye upon you. I shall inspect your work."

Keeping her in sight, he walked over to the prone men, pulling at the lengths of chain to make certain that both were well bound. "Excellent," he murmured, raising Etienne's sleeve to remove the mage's band. "It would be a shame if this would be swept out to sea. However, Wodesby's band will be no loss," he said, with a mocking chuckle, "since it has power only for England. But this"—his finger covetously brushed the Heir's Star stone on Damien's finger— "I have the match for this, Wodesby, taken off your father's body along with the thousand pounds that he had brought to bribe Du Le Fey. My uncle would doubtless have surrendered the girl for the money. The old fool did not recognize how valuable the services of a Mindwalker could be until I enlightened him."

Damien stiffened as the rune band was slipped from his finger.

"Honor among mages," Claude laughed, pulling a gold chain from beneath his shirt. A larger duplicate of Damien's ring glowed with blue fire in the moonlight. "Your father was guarded against magic, but not poison in his ale. It would seem that you are no less the fool than he, to come here with no weapon save magic. Oh, so noble! Oh, so stupid!"

"Perhaps we can make a bargain, Du Le Fey?" Damien said.

"What do you have that I want, Wodesby?" Claude asked mockingly. "I have your woman and your talisman and the band of France as well. And now"—he picked up the length of chain at the end of Rowan's manacles and tugged—"I have a boat to meet."

"A *Black Grimoire,* perhaps," Damien said. "The grimoire in Sir Hector's library in return for Rowan's freedom."

"No, Damien," Rowan groaned.

Claude chuckled. "Ah, you are even more of a fool than your *cher* papa, Wodesby. When you are dead, I will be *The Black Grimoire*'s rightful master. All I need to do is locate it." He looked at Rowan. "You will show me, *ma belle, n'est-ce pas?* Lest I do your dear friend Sir Hector or your lovely little Giselle some terrible harm." Claude pulled once more at her shackles. "Give my greetings to Neptune, Wodesby."

"No!" Rowan said defiantly. "Better to die cleanly here."

"My bullet goes through *his* head," Claude told her, waving the pistol in Damien's direction.

"Go with him, Rowan," Damien told her, "before the tide comes in. My Angel is watching over me."

"How very touching!" Claude snickered. "Walk ahead of me, Rowan, and no tricks or else I shall make certain that Giselle suffers the consequences."

As they made their way slowly up the stair, Damien began to twist himself.

"You should never have mentioned *The Black Grimoire,*" Etienne said, with a groan. "Without it, she might have been able to use her powers against him, but once that book is in his hands . . ."

"I was buying us time; he will head for Southwood now. Glad that you are among the quick, Du Le Fey, it will make this infinitely easier." Damien said, flexing his wrists. "Make yourself useful."

"How?" Etienne asked with an aching breath. "These are iron chains, Wodesby, iron locks!"

"And deuced poor quality, thanks be to providence," Damien said, flipping on his side. "In my back pocket are some small rods of metal on a ring; pull them out."

"What are you doing?" Etienne asked, searching for the pocket.

"Getting us free. As soon as my familiar, Angel, sees Claude bear-leading Rowan, she will seek help. In the meanwhile the tide is coming in fast."

"Ah, the 'guardian angel' you spoke of." Etienne gave a pained smile. "Luckily, I left my familiar behind; Suzette hates water." He pulled the ring from its hiding place. "What are these?"

"Picklocks," Damien said, contorting himself with a grunt and bringing his wrists forward. "A gift from my brother-in-law."

"An odd present, to be sure," Etienne said weakly.

"But quite useful, when magic is not," Damien said, as he grasped the ring and sorted through the various sizes. "Here we are. Try this.

An agony of minutes passed as Etienne and Damien painstakingly fumbled with pick after pick. Finally, the lock clicked open. Within seconds Damien had them both free. The tide was rolling in, the storm-driven waves lapping hungrily at their knees. Damien draped the Frenchman's arm over his shoulder, but Etienne slumped, his face pallid. "Leave me here, Wodesby," he said. "You must get to Claude . . . quickly, before he finds . . . *The Black Grimoire* and returns to France." He gave a mocking grin. "No doubt there has been many . . . a time that you have . . . wished me with . . . Hades, anyway. You were a . . . worthy opponent."

"No, Du Le Fey, I shall not allow you to stick your spoon in the wall just yet," Damien said gruffly, as he pulled the mage farther up the flooding beach. "Your meeting with

Hades must be postponed. Claude cannot call upon the powers of France's band, not while you live," Damien said.

"If I live . . . Wodesby . . ." he panted with effort, "it will be for . . . Rowan's sake, not . . . for yours. You will . . . have to use a spell . . . diminish my weight."

"I cannot," Damien said, tormented by his helplessness.

"I . . . understand," Etienne said. "Must not weaken . . . yourself . . . if you would . . . confront Claude . . . with magic."

"No, you do not understand. I have no power," Damien said, gazing up at the spray-slick stones of the stair in despair.

Etienne's eyes flew open and assessed the stark look in Damien's eyes. A resigned smile touched his lips. "Then you . . . must leave me . . . *mon ami.*"

"No!" Damien roared. "There must be a way, there has to be." For the first time in months, Damien reached down into his soul, seeking, fearing to find emptiness. Instead, he found a mote, small, but glowing bright. He was about to reach for that tiny spot of magic when he heard a bark at the top of the stair. Angel clambered down, followed by Dominick and some others of the tribe. "Bring him to Tante Reina," Damien commanded as they reached the bottom. "And tell her to keep Du Le Fey alive, if not for myself, then for Rowan."

The sound of music covered the tinkling of shattering glass as Claude broke through the terrace door. "Show me where *The Black Grimoire* is, Rowan," Claude demanded. "Show me. The sooner we are gone, the less likely it is that one of your friends will come to grief."

"I cannot see," Rowan said, hoping against hope that Angel would bring help to the beach in time. "The clouds have covered the moon."

Claude flicked his finger, and a beam of light radiated from his hand. Slowly, she walked toward the section of magical books, but Claude had moved ahead of her, pulling her behind him like a recalcitrant pup.

The scarlet binding had the sickening sheen of fresh blood. Like a man touching his lover, the mage caressed the vellum jacket, pulling it to him in anticipation. "By now, the tide will have entirely covered the strand. Etienne and Wodesby," he said softly. "And I am chief mage of France and master of one of *The Black Grimoires*." His tongue traveled slowly across his lips, "I shall make you my slave, Rowan, and you will be wild to serve my every whim. I have heard there is a spell . . ." He opened the pages and gasped. "This cannot be, the pages are blank . . ."

"Perhaps because its owner still lives," came a voice from the door.

"Damien!" Rowan cried.

"Wodesby? How?" Claude fumbled for his pistol. Rowan yanked at her chain, and the gun went tumbling, discharging and wounding Claude in the shoulder. The mage clutched his shoulder in disbelief and rage. But as Damien came toward him Claude's bloody fingers quickly sought Etienne's band. "As master of France's mages, I command . . ." he cried. A blue light shone from his eyes like a beacon. "I . . . I . . . mage of . . . F . . . f . . . fran . . ." His countenance turned crimson as he slumped to the ground.

"Fool!" Damien said, bending by the fallen mage to feel for a pulse. There was none. He lifted the limp head and slipped the chain from Claude's neck. The Mage's Star cast its blue glow into the dimness. Reverently, Damien placed the band on his finger and fished the Heir's Star ring from the Frenchman's pocket.

"I do not understand," Rowan said in confusion. "He is dead, Damien, and it was only a flesh wound."

"He called upon the band's power while Etienne still lives," he said, gently taking her fingers and leading her outside. By moonlight he worked the lock of her manacles. The chain clinked to the ground as he smoothed the skin that the metal had rubbed raw. "Surely, you know the dire consequences of using a talisman that belongs to another living mage or witch."

"No, I did not," Rowan said, trying to look away from him. "You might as well know now that I have less magical learning in me than the most backward of witchlings. Why, I have yet to complete *The Grimoire for Novices*. Would that were my only failing."

"You have others?" Damien asked, rubbing softly at the pulse of her wrist.

"No doubt you heard what Claude said on the beach," Rowan murmured, forcing herself to look into those enigmatic green eyes. "It was true. I have walked through unwilling minds, Damien, and taken thoughts from them like a thief." She shuddered. "I have trespassed upon the deepest secrets at their center, the guarded places of their essence. Who would want to touch a spirit like mine, a soul diminished, besmirched? Who would want to be touched, and have the truths of their heart revealed to someone like me?"

"I would, Rowan Rhiannon," Damien said, clasping her to him. "But do you want me? My sorcery is gone, perhaps never to return. The only magic I have now is you."

He bent, his lips finding hers as the walls between them came tumbling down.

In the corner of his mind lurked the secret fears that are at the core of every man. Rowan saw his pride, his fear of failure. She saw a boy with the weight of his heritage upon his shoulders. There was pain for his Giftless sister, Miranda, and distress when she chose an Outsider for her mate. Memories passed before her of agonizing choices, the lives of men, the fate of a nation in his hands. Love there was aplenty, for his family, his country, but for all the affection given and received, there was a barren place within him that nothing could fill. His loneliness matched her own.

Lust, selfishness, dark imaginings warred with honor and restraint. Good and bad mingled, fought for the domination of his soul. The evils of war, the stark solitude of a man doubly set apart, feared by Outsider, dreading the scorn of the covens. A mage without magic. In the corner of his mind Rowan felt a dark presence, *The Black Grimoire*'s creeping intrusion. *Power*, it whispered seductively, *I can give you back your power.*

So can I, Rowan told him wordlessly. *So can I. You gave me my life again, Damien Nostradamus, let me heal you in return.* Rowan reached into the depths of his soul, grasping his pain, taking it into herself and transforming it. Stone by stone, she battered at the walls in his mind, his horror became hers, his guilt weighed upon her soul. Death, so much death and destruction, and she wondered how he had borne the pain of it.

All the while *The Black Grimoire* taunted her.

He will be mine, it jeered. *In the end they all turn to me.*

No! Rowan screamed silently. *By the Merlin, you shall not! I love him!* Suddenly, Light burst from the darkest core of his being, sweeping the insinuating demon aside, casting it out and away.

And I love you, Rowan, the Light told her. *I have loved you always, I will love you, with all of me good and bad, I will love you. I would give my life for you.* And behind that burst of love something followed, something wondrous. As the last walls of his mind crumbled, magic began to flow.

Rowan sagged into his arms, spent. He cradled her gently, stroking her hair, pouring all of his newfound strength into her. Wearily, she opened her eyes, feeling the healing balm of the bliss.

"Do you realize what you have given me, Rowan?" Damien asked in exultation. He felt his Gift flooding through him, making his Blood sing with magic. "I am whole again!"

"It was not I, Damien. Your Gifts never left you," she said quietly, feeling the trickle of moisture down her cheek. "You would have found them yourself in time."

"Tears, Rowan?" he asked, looking down at her tenderly as he brushed the glimmering drops away. "Surely, you see how I feel? Marry me, Rowan Rhiannon."

"You could have any witch you chose now, Damien, as an equal partner," Rowan said, trying to turn away. "There is no need to ally yourself with a tainted woman."

Damien cupped her chin with his hands, forcing her to look directly into his eyes. "It is you. I will have you, Rowan Rhiannon, no other but you."

Rowan saw the look in those green depths, but she was afraid to believe. He could not want her, not if he became fully aware of the truth. There was no way he could understand unless she showed him. "You may believe that you know me, Damien, but you do not. You could not love me if you saw what I truly am. See me, Damien Nostradamus," she whispered. "See me, and decide if this is what you want." One by one, she tore away the barriers to her mind until her very being stood naked before him.

Damien was pulled into her core, passing through the open doors of her soul's dwelling place. He met the forsaken girl that she had been, hungry for knowledge, starving for affection, rejected by her father, used as his pawn. Through her memories, Damien felt the terror that only a woman can know, the helplessness as the Comte Du Le Fey tore at her mind and body. With her he experienced the wracking pangs of birthing a child. His spirit cringed as he walked with her through the minds of men and women, the dregs of human turpitude.

Sssoiled. She . . . is ssstained. Damien heard the faint hiss of *The Black Grimoire,* but he knew the magic to banish its insinuations, a magic that he could have used long ago had he but known. *"I love her,"* he told it. *"I love her."* The whispering voice ceased, and he continued on unhindered in his exploration of the woman that was Rowan.

Amid the horror and degradation of her marriage, he saw her strength, the courage that even Du Le Fey could not stifle: the hopes, the fears, the dreams, the nightmares . . . Damien saw himself through her eyes and felt the love . . . so much love. Damien stepped back, overwhelmed by the generosity of her spirit.

"I thought not," she whispered, her lip trembling. "How could you love me?"

"How could you forgive me, Rowan, for all the pain that I have caused you?" Damien asked, his voice deepening in self blame. "If only I had . . ."

She put a finger to his mouth. "No, 'if onlys,' no 'might have beens,' they would drive us mad. Best to part now—"

"Never, Rowan," Damien said, pulling her close. "If you can bear to see my darkness, if you can abide the secrets of my soul, then I would have you, but only if you share the joy that I feel when I am with you, only if you let me help you bear the burdens of your Gift, then I would love you always, Rowan Rhiannon, always. Belong to me, and I shall belong to you."

"So be it," Rowan said, smiling in delight. "I will belong to you, Damien Nostradamus."

Gently, Damien lifted the spectacles from her nose and tossed them into the hedges. "No more illusions, Rowan. No more illusions between us."

As their lips met once more, they knew each other in truth, joined in love that could allow deception or lies, a devotion that would endure and sacrifice, a dedication that would understand and forgive imperfection. Gift met Gift, and Damien felt the touch of a Vision. He saw Rowan at his side. In the distance he heard the laughter of children and knew that they were the fruit of his love and hers. Joyfully, he joined his thoughts with hers, sharing that image of the future.

"You cannot deny me now, Rowan." Damien laughed. " 'Tis not often that a seer has a Vision of his own future."

"Who am I to contest fate?" Rowan asked, nestling contentedly in his arms.

The Black Grimoire screamed in frustration.

"Stay here, Rowan," Damien said, glaring through the open library door.

"No," Rowan said, "I want to see it done, Damien. That cursed book has harmed us both."

Damien nodded grim agreement. He led her back into the room, easing her into a chair. Luckily, there was a fire already laid in the hearth. With two words and a snap of his fingers, Damien set it ablaze.

"Noooooo!" the book cried, as Damien grasped the iron fire tongs. *"You could rule . . ."*

As the tongs caught *The Black Grimoire*'s binding, the book gave an unholy shriek. *"Noooooooooo!"* The flames licked at the covers, sending off a noisome choking scent. Damien took Rowan by the shoulders and led her out into the night, gathering her into his arms until the last of the demonic cries faded.

Epilogue

In the gardens of the Wodesby ancestral home, the last roses of summer were blossoming in a final blaze of glory. The morning mizzle had begun to clear just in time for the end of the wedding breakfast. As the clouds began to drift slowly away, a breeze played gently with the stream of ribbons that had been hastily tied to Lord Wodesby's carriage.

"I vow, I have never seen the like of it. How did Wodesby manage to have all those doves fly in a pentagram and then chirp in chorus? And not a lady with a speck on her bonnet to boot," Sir Hector asked Adam, Lord Brand, as the guests filtered into the courtyard to see the couple off on their wedding journey.

"Magic, of course, Sir Hector," Adam said, laughing as he looked at the merry twinkle in his wife's eye. "Magic. Surely, you of all people should know that lovers share their own special sorcery?"

The baronet smiled fondly toward his fiancée. Diana was speaking to the Duke of Wellington as Davy and Lucy chased each other around the courtyard. "True enough," he said. "True enough."

His arm still in a sling, Etienne stood with Damien, waiting at the foot of the stair while Rowan was changing into her journey clothes. "I would not have this debt hanging over my head, Wodesby. That you chose to blame all upon Claude and tell Wellington nothing of my involvement, this I can bear. But I owe you my very life, and that I cannot tolerate. Name your boon, and I will pay."

"Let me name the price, Damien," Rowan said, as she descended in a soft rustle of green silk to stand beside Damien, her hand slipping in to his.

For once the stolid Du Le Fey's countenance was easy to read, and Damien understood the sadness in those steely blue eyes. It did not take a Mindwalker's Gift to know what Etienne was thinking. This woman could have been his. No punishment that Wellington could have dealt would have equaled that pain, the balance of a lifetime spent in barren longing.

"I yield to my wife, Du Le Fey," Damien said, his heart lightening as he savored that word on his tongue. *Wife,* this woman was his, forever.

"As well you should, if you are wise, Wodesby," Etienne said with a sardonic twist of his lips.

"You have had a vision of Napoleon, Etienne," Rowan said softly. "If that is fated, then there is naught that can be done to change it, but if England and France fight once more, stay out of the fray, for the sake of the covens, and the new friendship between our families."

"You drive a hard bargain, *belle-mère,*" he said with a frown. "But the boon shall be paid as you ask."

Rowan reached into her reticule and pulled out the gold talisman of the mistress of France. She held it out to Etienne. "This is for your wife when you find her, Etienne. I cannot serve France and England both."

Etienne took the finely wrought necklace, letting it dangle limply from his hand. "Farewell, Rowan," he said. "May you be blessed, *belle-mère.*"

Giselle came running excitedly. "Maman! Etienne! *Grandmère* Adrienne says that I may have my own pony if I finish *The Grimoire for Novices* by Samhain!"

"You will spoil the child, Adrienne," Etienne said, watching fondly as the girl went off after the other children.

"What else is the purpose of a grandmother, then?" Damien's mother said with a pout as she entered the hall, her husband Lawrence trailing her. "And as for you, young Du Le Fey, is it not time that you think of doing your duty to family and Blood. My sister's daughter is of an age," she said, putting her hand on his shoulder and guiding him toward the courtyard. "You may have heard some tittle-tattle about our Cassandra, but by Hecate, not a one of those things is true."

"Poor Etienne," Lawrence said with a grin. "The man had best mind his step, or Adrienne will have him wed to that nodcock niece of hers before he knows what has hit him."

"Lucy says that she and Giselle are going to turn me into a toad," Davy screamed in the hallway.

"You already are a toad, looby!" came Lucy's reply.

"Children, children, please," Damien said. "Go on outside and find something to throw at our departing backs, preferably something soft and clean." He turned to his new wife and offered his arm, feeling the warmth and security that radiated from her touch. "I must say that I admire your serenity in the face of chaos, my love," he said, kissing her lightly on the forehead.

"I find myself wondering, if this is all real," Rowan said, looking up into his eyes.

Damien looked at the clouded misty heavens and raised his hand. Slowly, the clouds began to rearrange themselves, scudding across the sky to let the light pass. A rainbow arched its way above the trees. "My pledge, Rowan, it is real, as real as the magic between us."

Heedless of the watchers, Damien pulled her into his arms and proceeded to give his wife a more tangible token of love's reality.